THE
KABRINI MESSAGE

An Alien Race. A Shocking Message . . .

J. R. Egles

BALBOA.
PRESS
A DIVISION OF HAY HOUSE

Balboa Press books may be ordered through booksellers or by contacting:

Balboa Press
A Division of Hay House
1663 Liberty Drive
Bloomington, IN 47403
www.balboapress.com
1 (877) 407-4847

Because of the dynamic nature of the Internet, any web addresses or links contained in this book may have changed since publication and may no longer be valid. The views expressed in this work are solely those of the author and do not necessarily reflect the views of the publisher, and the publisher hereby disclaims any responsibility for them.

The author of this book does not dispense medical advice or prescribe the use of any technique as a form of treatment for physical, emotional, or medical problems without the advice of a physician, either directly or indirectly. The intent of the author is only to offer information of a general nature to help you in your quest for emotional and spiritual well-being. In the event you use any of the information in this book for yourself, which is your constitutional right, the author and the publisher assume no responsibility for your actions.

Any people depicted in stock imagery provided by Getty Images are models, and such images are being used for illustrative purposes only.
Certain stock imagery © Getty Images.

Print information available on the last page.

ISBN: 978-1-9822-0983-4 (sc)
ISBN: 978-1-9822-0985-8 (hc)
ISBN: 978-1-9822-0984-1 (e)

Library of Congress Control Number: 2018909197

Balboa Press rev. date: 09/06/2018

Contents

Part Three

The Crystal City

~ Acclaim for J.R. Egles ~

Praise for *The Kabrini Message*

"[A]n articulate and intriguing journey… Driscoll, the main character, is believable and passionate in his search for the Kabrini's message to humans. The dialogue is witty and fast-paced, and the storyline is reminiscent of a big-budget alien movie (but with a kinder ending!). All in all, great story, great message."

—Author Erin Moore, *Kissed by Moonlight*

"Mystery, adventure, an alien race with a message to the world—all the right ingredients, served up by the late author into a highly satisfying dish. I literally couldn't put this novel down until I had finished it, and the ending did it full justice."

—Author Catherine Cavendish, *Nemesis of the Gods Trilogy*

"The Kabrini Message is first and foremost an adventure story. The plot moves quickly, taking the reader around the world and into deep space. The characters are likable and main theme and the sub plots keep one briskly turning the pages. I enjoyed it."

—Author Megan Sebastian, *Meet Me in Atlantis*

~ ACKNOWLEDGMENTS ~

A very special thank you to Amy Bell of WritePunch Inc. (www.writepunch. com) for her hard work, friendship, and the immediate connection and bond that we formed, and for really "getting it". I knew Amy could fill in the pieces of *The Kabrini Message* that Joe was not here to do himself. Ultimately, not only did Amy do just that, but she was so enthusiastic and emotionally connected that we often read each other's thoughts and came up with the same ideas at the same time, though we live a thousand miles apart. We have been on the same wavelength, with a lot of help from above, throughout this entire process. There is no doubt in my mind that Amy Bell and this book are, quite literally, a match made in heaven!

I also wish to thank:

Matt Powals for always being there to bounce ideas off of, for always being there in general, for his advice, for encouraging me and for always being as excited as I was about the project!

My good friend Pennye Scullin (www.pennyestarinsight.com). Important advice: When attempting to publish a science fiction novel regarding planets, the solar system, star systems, etc., it's extremely helpful to have a good friend who is a professional psychic and astrologer.

To my family, especially my son, Steven Carhart, for his enthusiasm and encouragement all throughout the process and for his assistance in marketing.

Gwen Jones, Joe's wife…and yes, Joe named the news reporter character in Chapter Sixteen after her! Thank you for all of the invaluable insight you were able to provide. Gwen was there the entire time Joe wrote *The Kabrini Message* and privy to his thoughts and feelings while he wrote each chapter during that period, over 25 years ago.

To my brother, Joseph Robert Egles (aka, J.R. Egles) for writing this incredible book.

And most especially to our mother, Marie Egles, for encouraging Joe in writing the book, for painstakingly typing the book and leading me to its discovery a quarter of a century after it was written, and for watching over and guiding this entire process from beginning to completion.

~ DEDICATION ~

This novel is dedicated to its author, my late husband Joe. After all his hard work and devotion to this book, he would be thrilled to know it finally will be read by so many others.

To his late mother Marie, who was always there to lend a helping hand and loving support while Joe was writing this manuscript.

To his sister Marie, who made the publication of this book possible, thanks to her love for her brother Joe, her tireless determination, and her vision to make it happen.

To each and every reader who will be touched by Joe's imaginative mind.

Please enjoy!

~Gwen Jones, Wife of Late Author J.R. Egles

In Loving Memory of Gwen Jones.
We love you and miss you very much.

PROLOGUE

Hovering in a small shuttle against the endless backdrop of black and stars, Mark Ranier wiped the faceplate of his suit to get a better look at the destruction. He squinted as he took in the scene, attempting to wrap his brain around what had happened. From what he could tell, a support stanchion had caught the arm of the torch, breaking it at a joint. The broken segment had pushed backwards into the torch, smashing its hastily rigged control panel. The torch must have ignited as it rammed into the coupling, and it had already cut halfway through the massive metal link holding the two ships together.

"Mark," Lou said. His face was strained. So was his voice. "We can't shut it down!"

A shudder raced through Mark's body as his mind suddenly made the terrifying leap to the only logical conclusion of their situation. If they wanted to save the Network—mankind's only form of contact with the Kabrini—there was no turning back. Not to the City. Not to Earth. Not to anywhere other than the Barge's pre-programmed course to oblivion in the darkest depths of space.

PART ONE

The Secret of the Oracle

Fifteen Years Earlier

Chapter One

The Big Safari

Bradley Prescott never saw it coming. He certainly never heard it. He didn't cry out or do any of the things people do in the movies when they get shot. He just fell. He was dead. It was that simple. He was alive before, and now he was dead.

Jennifer Prescott, on the other hand, did all of the things people do in the movies when they see someone get shot. She stared, she pointed, she screamed, she ran, she fell down, she got up and, mercifully, she fainted. If she had continued running, she probably would have been hit too. But now collapsed in a heap in the tall grass, Jennifer was hidden from view and safe for the moment.

Jeffrey Driscoll watched from the edge of the woods where he had dropped like a ton of bricks as soon as he heard the shot. He wondered what he should do. If he tried to crawl to Mrs. Prescott, the movement of the grass would give him away.

He considered running, but he felt a nagging responsibility for having forgotten his very own personal first rule of guidesmanship: the richer people get, the stupider they get. He knew they couldn't really be that stupid or they wouldn't stay rich; but these wealthy folks sure took a lot for granted. The Prescotts, a loaded couple in their early 60s, were as easily confused and naïve as two little children. He had told them repeatedly never to go anywhere without him…but as he was breaking camp, the filthy rich idiots had run ahead.

Driscoll silently cursed them now as he lay motionless in the grass. He was positive that Bradley Prescott III's last living thought was, "How dare you kill me! I'll sue!" And he probably would—or at least his estate would. The trouble was they would probably sue Driscoll. This guide business really sucked. Driscoll despised escorting these senseless affluent assholes through the jungles of Africa, and he'd been threatening to quit for some time. And this looked like a real good time.

But Driscoll's sense of duty won out. So he concentrated his gaze on the thicket across the river, where he was fairly certain the shooter was hiding. Driscoll then proceeded to fire an entire box of twelve gauge shotgun shells into the thick underbrush, the gunshots exploding in earsplitting echoes throughout the jungle. He had to stop once to reload and let the gun cool off for a minute. Seeing absolutely no movement in the thicket, he dove across the grass and landed a few feet from where Mrs. Jenny Prescott lay. He dragged her back, half-conscious, to the camp, thinking all the way that he should have just left her there and got the hell out. Now there was one, possibly two, people dead. And if this woman didn't recover, guess who'd be left holding the old bag? He snickered at his clever pun.

By the time Driscoll reached the camp, Jennifer Prescott was awake, sputtering and gasping something about dear old Brad. Driscoll threw her into the back of the Land Rover and proceeded to beat what he was certain must be the all-time speed record between Khartanga and Moombato Bay. He never entertained the slightest notion of going back for Bradley, as Mrs. Prescott seemed to think was so important. "There's no point going back for your husband…he's dead!" Driscoll shouted toward the backseat. Mrs. Prescott continued her pleas until he reminded her, in graphic detail, of that instant before Brad fell, when a rather large part of his head started off for town ahead of them. Only then did she shut her trap. Actually, Driscoll's cram course in Creative Anatomy did more than shut her up. Now she was in shock, Driscoll realized with a twinge of guilt. But at least she was quiet…and alive.

Later that night, Driscoll sat alone in a dark corner of a small, dingy bar in Moombato Bay, where he got very drunk as he tried to figure out what had happened. What had he missed about that spot? Why would that place be so damned important to somebody? There's nothing of any value there. Nothing. He took another swig from his beer. Well, that wasn't quite true. The place was a study in natural beauty, and the Prescotts weren't the first to visit that lush area of pristine jungle. He had taken other tourists through there himself, and he knew other guides had as well.

As he continued to wrestle with his thoughts, Driscoll ran his fingers through his ruffled brown hair and turned his sky blue eyes up to the ceiling. Out of habit, he rubbed his face stubble with calloused fingers before he grabbed his beer, downed it in one big gulp, and slammed the mug on the table. He motioned at the bartender for another. Driscoll was only twenty-five years old, but he felt like he'd lived a lifetime since he'd left the States just five years before.

Though most of his friends in Africa would never guess, Jeff Driscoll was a dropout from Princeton's prestigious Astronomy program. In fact, he had been fascinated with the stars since the age of ten. Not coincidentally, that was the same year his dear old alcoholic dad hit rock bottom. Tom Driscoll got off work at the auto parts factory at four o'clock every evening and headed straight to the local pub, where he bellied up to the bar and drank for four hours straight. Each night like clockwork, at eight fifteen on the dot, Tom would stumble into the house reeking of cheap gin just as Jeffrey and his mother were washing the last dishes from dinner. Seeing the crazy look in his father's glazed over eyes, Jeffrey would race upstairs and hide out in his room for the rest of the night. He'd spend countless hours building his own telescopes from scratch, studying constellations and poring over books about the universe…anything to escape from the grim reality that festered downstairs. As he tinkered with his telescope parts, he'd slip on his headphones and turn up The Ramones full blast to drown out the sounds of his wasted father yelling, sobbing, and breaking dishes. Jeffrey would gaze out his bedroom window at the endless vista of stars and daydream about visiting space—where he imagined it must be peaceful, silent, and completely safe from raving alcoholic lunatics.

One October night, a few weeks after Jeffrey turned eleven, he and his mother stood side-by-side at the kitchen sink washing dishes. As she rinsed the last plate and handed it to her son to dry, a cool breeze gusted through the kitchen window, rustling the curtains and sending a chill down Jeffrey's spine. And then something strange happened: The clock clicked over to eight sixteen. Jeffrey and his mother stood by the sink staring at each other in silent expectation. They both held their breath, listening for the familiar sounds of tires screeching on the driveway followed by the front door slamming. A dog barked in the distance. And then…nothing. Jeffrey's father never stumbled through the door that night or any night after that. The drunken bastard had disappeared into thin air.

For the next seven years, Jeffrey's mother showered him with love and attention, constantly struggling to fill the gaping hole Jeffrey's father had left behind. She worked two full-time jobs just so she could buy every telescope part and constellations book her son's heart desired. Although Jeffrey was a precocious child who excelled in math and science, his teachers often referred to him as a "lazy genius."

Things just came too easily for him—and in reality, he wasn't so much lazy as he was distracted.

By the time he turned twelve, his passion for the great beyond was often overshadowed by his obsession with beautiful girls. Jeffrey was a charmer, an athletic kid with rugged good looks and rippling muscles. He played baseball and racked up a record number of homeruns during his high school career. "It's all physics," he once told his mom when she asked how he always hit those balls out of the park. "It's like I can see the trajectory in my head when the ball is coming at me."

Although he was clearly a brainiac, Jeffrey kept this bit of information under wraps for the sake of his reputation. Every few weeks, he could be seen walking arm in arm with yet another cheerleader or homecoming queen, each more gorgeous than the last. The nerds Jeffrey quietly beat out at the Science Fair year after year absolutely despised him: Jeffrey Driscoll, the magnetic, handsome genius who seemed to have it all.

Driscoll's mother was absolutely delighted when her only son scored an Astronomy scholarship to Princeton—though she suspected it might have had something to do with the attractive, young biology professor on the interview panel who spent more time fluttering her eyelashes at Jeffrey than asking him questions.

As a Princeton freshman, Driscoll treasured the many hours he spent in the observatory—but he quickly grew bored of his Intro to Astronomy courses, which focused on fundamentals he'd been secretly studying in his bedroom since he was ten years old. So once again, he turned his attention to beautiful women…both on and off the Princeton campus. For nearly a year, he wined and dined the loveliest ladies throughout the Tri-State area until his bank account— and his scholarship funds—ran completely dry.

In the wee hours of a brisk April morning, Driscoll staggered toward campus after an interesting evening with a gorgeous Psychology TA. So TA stood for Teacher's Assistant? He could think of something else T and A stood for. He wore a smear of crimson lipstick on his neck and reeked of Scotch. Then he spotted it: a bright yellow flyer tacked to a telephone pole, flapping in the wind as if trying to get his attention. Driscoll snatched the paper off the pole and read:

Need Extra Cash?

"Hell yeah, I do!" he slurred loudly in response as he swayed on the empty sidewalk.

Crave excitement?

"You bet your ass!"

Become a Tour Guide in Africa!

"*Africa?*" He stared at the flyer for a few moments before folding it up and jamming it in his pocket. "Okay, then. Why the hell not?"

Less than two months later, Driscoll found himself in Moombato Bay, where he quickly learned the art of African guidesmanship. And now, with five years of experience under his belt, he was like a cynical old veteran guzzling beer in a grimy local bar.

Leaning back in his chair, Driscoll propped his crocodile boots on the edge of the table and considered how lucky he was after today's shooting incident. Not only was he alive, but he wasn't even behind bars! Lord knows he had been an overnight guest of the Moombato Bay jail quite a few times before, and for offenses much more minor than this. The local Police rated men like himself on a scale that ranged between Adventurer and Cutthroat. But the Moombato cops tolerated Driscoll and the other guides because the same rich tourists that hired them also spent a lot of money in the town, doling out cash for unnecessary permits before and after their big safari. Funny, Driscoll thought as the bartender set yet another mug of beer on his table. They didn't have a word for bribe in the native language.

But things were different this time. He had set off with two of their best high-spending American big shots, and now one was a basket case and the other was Jungle Pizza. This was definitely not travel brochure material. When Driscoll had taken Mrs. Prescott to the station earlier that day, he assumed they would lock him up at least until the old lady could coherently confirm his story. But after questioning Driscoll, the Police told him he was free to leave the station as long as he did not leave town, which he couldn't do even if he wanted to. The cops had impounded the Prescotts' Land Rover, Driscoll's only means of transportation, and poor old Bradley never had a chance to pay him his fee—which meant Driscoll couldn't really afford to do anything but stay put.

He took another long, slow drink of beer. Now that he had time to think about it, the Police really hadn't seemed that put off or surprised at all by the whole jungle fiasco. In fact, they almost seemed prepared for it—which was a little fishy because, around here, no extension of the government was ever prepared for anything.

It suddenly occurred to Driscoll that there was only one thing about that spot in the jungle today that was different from any other day: Bradley Prescott had been in it.

Driscoll dropped his boots to the floor with a loud thump and sat up in his chair straight as an arrow. He had been set up. He began to wonder if he had killed the man in the thicket. He hoped now that he hadn't. It wouldn't do his reputation any good around here, and somebody, somewhere, might be slightly annoyed with him for eliminating their hit man and almost fouling up an otherwise successful assassination.

When he was leaving the Police barracks earlier that day, he had noticed a Jeep and a truck heading off in the direction he had just driven in from…to recover the bodies, he knew. He also knew that in this place you could buy anything if you knew the right people. And he just happened to know all the right people—and tomorrow he intended to buy a look at the death certificate of Bradley Prescott.

CHAPTER TWO

Bon Voyage

About a thousand miles away from where Jeff Driscoll was planning his bargain for information, Roger Coridif was floating in the crystal blue Caribbean Sea and making arrangements of his own. It was the cruise ship's third night out from port, and the weather was absolutely beautiful—a warm, gentle sea breeze and not a wisp of cloud in the star-filled sky.

Roger, who had spent most of his fifty-seven years accumulating great wealth, was now determined to offset his failing health by putting a large portion of his fortune back into circulation. He had spent the evening wooing an exotic young lady with long raven locks and striking brown eyes, finally convincing her to leave the ballroom for a moonlight stroll on the deck. After their short walk, he planned to invite her back to his suite for a drink—where he was certain if he couldn't seduce her, his money could.

On deck, Roger and the stunning girl leaned against the rail to admire the breathtaking view as anewly hired steward approached from behind with a tray and two glasses of champagne. This was perfect. He couldn't have created a more romantic setting. The moon, the sea, the ever so gently swaying deck beneath their feet. And she was so beautiful. Her olive skin, her long dark hair, her gorgeous eyes, her soft hands clenching around his neck…

As Roger crashed into the water and struggled in the waves, he sputtered and gasped, trying to scream out at the ship gliding away from him. Then his thoughts switched to wondering how far he could swim. Not far enough, he reckoned. He was right.

When the ship docked, some of the Coridif family were already there, all wailing and sobbing in appropriate shock and mourning. The Police had been unable to recover the body, and they did not suspect foul play. After all, the poor, dark-haired girl was visibly shaken, and a steward had witnessed the unfortunate "accident." According to their story, Roger Coridif simply had too much to drink and lost his balance, tumbling over the railing.

The girl went along her way, and the steward never showed up for the next sailing—or anything else, for that matter.

Chapter Three

The Friendly Skies

Flight 702 from Dallas arrived right on time into JFK. "This is a first," the Texan muttered to himself. He hadn't had a good flight, but then he never did. Even the amenities of first class did little to dampen the annoyance he always felt when he traveled. As far as Roy Piterman was concerned, nothing was ever where it should be, when it should be.

He knew that since his flight was on time, odds were that his luggage would be delayed—if it was in fact even in the same airport.

Roy Piterman did not travel for pleasure. He traveled for business and only when he absolutely had to, which lately, seemed to be all the time.

He grumbled his way through baggage claim and yelled at a hotel reservations rep on his cell phone before heading out the main doors to the rent-a-car lot across from the airport entrance.

As he crossed the road he hoped his secretary had gotten it straight this time. Full-size, dammit, full-size. What was so hard about that? Not compact, not subcompact, and not intermediate, whatever the hell that was, but *full-size*.

He figured he would be lucky if there was any car waiting for him at all. But there was.

Unknown to Roy, someone besides his secretary had arranged for a car to meet him. It was indeed a full-size, and it met him head-on at about fifty miles per hour without stopping, killing the grumpy old Texan on impact.

To make matters worse, Roy Piterman was charged a no-show penalty for not calling to cancel his rent-a-car.

CHAPTER FOUR

Driscoll's Marauders

Driscoll was sitting at the same table as the night before, but tonight he hadn't been alone. Mondo, his friend and informant, had left just moments before with a pocketful of Driscoll's money after handing over a copy of Bradley Prescott's death certificate. Now, Driscoll sipped a beer as he tried to make sense of what he had just purchased. The official cause of death listed on Prescott's death certificate was a gunshot wound to the head, which the corresponding police report listed as a "hunting accident."

An accident? That shooting was an accident only in the sense that the guy who fired the shot was trying to blow Prescott's *whole* head off, not just *part* of it. This information alone was worth the price he had paid Mondo, but there was more. According to Mondo, Jennifer Prescott never recovered from her traumatic experience in the jungle, and she had succumbed to her injuries during the night.

"Injuries? What injuries?" Driscoll had asked Mondo, who had just shrugged.

"That is all they said, my man," he answered in his thick African accent. "She died from her injuries."

Mrs. Prescott was scuffed up a little and pretty well dazed, Driscoll remembered. But the last time he had seen her, she was sitting at the Sergeant's desk fumbling with her American Express Platinum Card. Although she was clearly shaken, she certainly didn't appear to be on death's doorstep.

If that intel wasn't enough to make Driscoll's purchase well worth the expense, the last piece of info made it a real package deal. Mondo said after the soldiers removed Bradley Prescott's body, he watched them take a second body out of the truck. It appeared to be a khaki-dressed native riddled with bullet wounds. The goddamned sniper. He must have killed the poor bastard after all. But then Mondo mentioned something else he saw that pointed to the contrary: Just before dumping the body from the truck, a soldier had removed a knife from the back of the native's neck.

But now Mondo was gone, and Driscoll was left to sort out the details on his own. Why would someone stab a dead man? But then he quickly realized the answer. Because he wasn't dead. So Driscoll hadn't killed the sniper after all. He'd shot him up pretty good, but the fellow must have still been alive when the Feds got there. These African law enforcement officers were known for their swift, albeit blind, justice—but their retribution always took place in town so they could set a clear example for other criminals. This time, things were obviously different, because he had heard no mention of this other body until now.

Driscoll shifted uneasily in his chair and unconsciously glanced from side to side. He was beginning to feel like an endangered species, and he decided to do something about it before somebody did something about him.

But he needed help, and not from just anyone. It had to be someone of strong moral convictions, somebody he could trust. But since there weren't any people like that in this country, he decided to go back to Mondo.

A tall young African born and raised in Moombato Bay, Mondo knew the area much better than Driscoll did. In fact, Mondo knew the area well enough to realize he wanted to get out, if he could ever save up enough money. He always talked of moving to Khartanga, where he could enjoy "the city life."

"Oh yeah, Khartanga's a real metropolis," Driscoll would respond drily with a roll of his blue eyes.

It was obvious that Mondo had not been many places outside of Moombato Bay. After all, he was only about eighteen, maybe nineteen years old (although even Mondo himself didn't know his precise age). But he had a sense of humor and a craving for American dollars—two qualities Driscoll appreciated.

As quietly as possible, Driscoll pushed his chair back from the table, leaving behind a half-empty beer. He quickly sidestepped out of the bar, his eyes darting from side to side as he raced into the street.

Within minutes after leaving the bar, Driscoll tracked down Mondo. At over six feet tall, he was easy to spot, and Driscoll found him kicking a dusty soccer ball around with a gaggle of African kids. Gangly and stick-thin with skin as black as midnight, Mondo had a lean, chiseled face that usually displayed a huge, childlike grin. He beamed at Driscoll as he walked away from the hollering throng of boys. "Back so soon, my friend?"

"Yeah," Driscoll muttered, nervously rubbing the back of his neck as he looked around. "Could we talk in private for a few minutes?"

In a trash-filled alleyway between two dilapidated buildings, Driscoll told Mondo he needed his help with a bigger job. "For twenty dollars, you have my faithful services and unswerving loyalty," Mondo answered. When Driscoll pulled his wallet out of his back pocket and handed the young African a wrinkled twenty dollar bill, Mondo's face broke into a huge smile, revealing his crooked, yellowing teeth. He quickly pocketed the cash, and his grin faded as he took on a more serious tone. "For another twenty, you get my rifle *or* my sister."

Driscoll had seen Mondo's sister. She looked more like Mondo's brother. "I'll take the rifle," he answered without hesitation, pulling another bill from his beat-up leather wallet. When he looked back up, Mondo was glaring at him with bloodshot eyes. Driscoll stood frozen in place, eye to eye with the suddenly malicious-looking African, until Mondo suddenly let out a thunderous boom of laughter. "Good choice, my man!" he shouted as he grabbed the second bill from Driscoll's hand and patted him on the back. "Good choice!"

Driscoll let out a relieved laugh, once again admiring Mondo's rare sense of humor among this country full of solemn natives. "Okay, first things first, Mondo," Driscoll said as he pulled a ratty bandana from his back pocket and wiped the sweat from his brow. "We're going to need more support...we need at least a couple more men."

"No worries, my friend," Mondo answered with a wink, still grinning ear to ear. "I know just the guys for the job."

He referred Driscoll to the infamous local smuggling team of Goldstein and Mohammed. A few years back, Goldstein and Mohammed had stolen a truckload of guns. Goldstein smuggled the guns, which he got from Mohammed, to the Jews. Mohammed smuggled the guns, which he got from Goldstein, to the Arabs. It took the Jews and the Arabs almost a year to realize they kept buying the same damned batch of guns, which were just being passed back and forth by Goldstein and Mohammed. Needless to say, the pair was now unemployed.

So Driscoll had his commandos. Now he needed a plan. The next night, the four men met at what Driscoll called Mondo Manor, Mondo's hovel-on-the-bay that brought new depth to the word "squalor." But it did insure privacy. No one would suspect that anything of importance was going down in this fleapit.

Goldstein was short, fat, and balding on top, and, according to him, used to be able to outrun any black man or cop in Brooklyn, which he referred to as "The Old Country." In the end, it was a black cop who finally caught up with him. "I'm tellin' ya, it just wasn't fair!" he insisted. "That guy was some kind of robot or a, a…whaddya call it? A clone…yeah he was a goddamned clone. They must've bred him special from parts of Carl Lewis and Sherlock Holmes just to nail me!"

Not surprisingly, Goldstein immediately proved to be the financial brains of the outfit. He came up with a plan, based of course, on money.

"An equal split, four ways," he said in his curt New York accent.

"Split what?" asked Driscoll, hoping Goldstein was on to something, since he didn't really have the money he'd promised to pay for their services anyway.

"The reward, of course," barked Goldstein. "There's got to be a reward. I mean, goddammit, these whaddya call 'em…the Prescotts? Those old fogies were stinkin' rich. There must be somebody out there who'll pay big bucks to find out what really happened to them."

"Relatives," grunted Mohammed, who had been completely silent up to this point. The bearded Arab sat in a lump, dressed traditionally, looking much like a laundry pile. He claimed to be in his 20s, but his dark brown, deeply lined face resembled wrinkled old luggage. He was a dangerous-looking man who had clearly spent too much time riding a camel in the desert sun without a lick of sunscreen.

Mohammed sat fondling his knife, running his thumb along the edge of the curved blade. "Always go to relatives first. They will pay. They always pay," he grumbled in his heavy, almost incomprehensible accent. "Tell them if they do not pay, they never see them alive again," he shouted vehemently, and stabbed his dagger into the wooden table. "Then, we cut off something and mail it to them," he added matter-of-factly.

Driscoll looked at Mohammed and squinted, not sure if he had heard him correctly. Then he glanced over at Mondo, who shrugged.

Goldstein grabbed Mohammed by a dangling piece of turban, pulling the Arab's wrinkled, bearded face close to his. "Look, you sun-fried camel jockey. I told you on the way over, they're already dead, goddammit, and we *ain't* kidnapping nobody this time. Now pound the sand out of your ears and listen!"

Goldstein let go of Mohammed, who suddenly took on the sulky appearance of a scolded child. He crumpled back into his lump and grunted, and Goldstein turned to Driscoll. "You'll have to excuse my brown brother from another mother," he explained. "He just hasn't been himself lately. Not since Desireé was killed." Goldstein looked down at the dirt floor respectfully. "She was murdered by police in Morocco. It was her sacrifice that allowed us to escape."

"Oh, shit. I'm sorry for the loss of your…your, uh, wife?" asked Driscoll.

"His snake," said Goldstein. "A guard sat on it, and it bit him in the ass. Killed the snake. The guard, too."

Driscoll peeked over at Mondo, who was clearly trying to stifle a laugh.

Mondo quickly cleared his throat. "So what about the relatives, how do we reach them?" he asked. A few ashes from his homemade cigarette fell in each of their glasses as he reached around the table to refill them with some kind of red-tinged alcohol.

"Maybe we don't want to reach them," said Driscoll, poking at the debris in his wine, or whatever the stuff was. It sort of tasted like wine. "What if some relatives *paid* for the Prescotts' accident?"

"No, no, no….who *really* paid?" Goldstein said, thinking out loud. "Whoever paid to have those filthy rich bastards killed must have stood to make a bundle from insurance, or something." Goldstein got a faraway look as he scratched the few remaining dark brown wisps on his sweaty balding head. "That's it! Travel Insurance…of course! We've got to get to their insurance company."

"They had that Platinum Card thing," said Driscoll. "Don't they get free travel insurance with that or something?"

"Nah, that's free burial, I think," said Goldstein.

"I'm not sure. But anyway, snooty assholes like the Prescotts don't use anything if it's free. We'll call all of the big international-type insurance companies and explain the situation. I'll betcha we find them."

"It makes sense," said Driscoll. "The people with the most to lose are the ones who will take the quickest action."

"And hand out the biggest reward," added Goldstein with a twinkle in his beady black eyes. "Personally, I'd rather have all the gangbangers in New York City after me than Insurance Fraud Investigators." He shuddered. "Those insurance guys are even more ruthless than the Credit Card Cops."

"So what now?" Mondo asked.

"I'll tell you what," said Driscoll, leaning forward in his chair. "Mondo, you get your sneaky ass back into town and keep your eyes peeled for the payoff. The Prescotts' bodies should be back in the States by now."

"Yeah, you're right," agreed Goldstein. "Nobody in his right mind would pay these local boneheads in advance for a weather report, let alone an assassination. I bet someone will be showing up with a wad of cash soon."

"I'll start making some phone calls to insurance companies," said Driscoll. "You two scrounge up some guns," he added, pointing at Goldstein and Mohammed.

Mohammed brightened visibly at that. Stealing guns, after all, was his first love.

"Guns!" he grunted with a smile, exposing his rotten teeth—or at least the few he had left.

"How many we need?" asked Goldstein.

"I've got this," chimed Mondo, holding up in the lamplight what Driscoll was sure to be Dirty Harry's .44 Magnum. The vintage gun appeared to have a never-ending barrel that stretched into the darkness surrounding the table before it disappeared.

"What the hell is that?" asked Goldstein, eyeing the antique.

"It is a gun…what do you think?" said Mondo, visibly insulted.

"Who has to hold up the other end when you shoot it?" prodded Goldstein.

Driscoll tried to mask his smile at Goldstein's joke as he added, "I've got my shotgun and Mondo's rifle. And I've still got a set of keys to the Prescotts' impounded Land Rover."

"Wait now, back up a damn minute," said Goldstein. "You've got Mondo's rifle?" He turned to the young African. "Mondo! Are you crazy? You sold your rifle? Where's your sister?"

Mondo attempted to scowl at Goldstein, but he couldn't hold it. His black face melted into a huge grin, and he shook the table with a booming laugh.

CHAPTER FIVE

Armed and Dangerous

Late the next morning, all four vigilantes met back at Mondo Manor. While snooping around town, Mondo had learned the Commandant was expecting a visitor named Demura that afternoon.

"No shit," Driscoll shouted, flashing a pearly white smile. "Are you sure the name's Demura?"

"Yes, they said Demura," Mondo answered, mirroring Driscoll's grin. "The Commandant himself will be driving out to the airport to meet the man's plane at four o'clock today."

But the big news was Driscoll's: Five million dollars. Even split four ways, it was a lot of money.

"And we're talking real dollars," said Driscoll. "Not this monopoly shit they use around here. The insurance company is itching to get their hands on whoever has been bumping off their clients. It's costing them a fortune, so five million bucks is a drop in the bucket for these guys. Turns out the Prescotts weren't the only targets…it's all part of an elaborate insurance scam led by a man named Vito Demura."

"Demura?" Mondo asked, smiling again. "The same Demura that's flying in today?"

"You bet your ass," Driscoll said. He stood up so fast he knocked over his chair.

"Where the hell are ya goin'?" Goldstein yelled at Driscoll's back as he raced out Mondo's door.

"I gotta make another call to the insurance guys!"

Driscoll shouted over his shoulder. "I can't get any damn reception out here in the boondocks!"

Half an hour later, Driscoll returned from town. He had called the insurance company, who were extremely interested in what Driscoll had to tell them. "They promised they'll have their investigators here in a few hours," Driscoll gasped, out of breath from his jog back to Mondo's shanty. "They're bringing soldiers from the capital…and the reward cash. We've just gotta stall Demura somehow until they get here."

"Praise Allah, we're billionaires!" Mohammed shouted as he leapt from his seat and danced a strange little jig with his arms held out from his sides like airplane wings.

"Not so fast, you sand-blasted towel head," Goldstein yapped. "First of all, before we see a single red cent, we gotta figure out how to hold up this guy, Demura. And second of all, if we do get the reward, we'll be *millionaires*, not billionaires. Jesus Christ, do you people not learn math in your country?"

"Okay, Goldstein," Driscoll interrupted, "Let's take stock of our weapons. What did you guys score?"

"Oh yeah, I got this," Goldstein said as he handed Driscoll a small, purse-size .22 automatic.

"What the hell am I gonna do with this?" asked Driscoll as he stared at the miniature gun in his palm. It made his hand look giant.

"Well, it's nice and small," explained Goldstein, "so you can shove it in your pocket."

"You can shove it up your ass," Driscoll said as he tossed it back.

"Come on, Driscoll, it's a concealed weapon," insisted Goldstein. "You can't walk in the airport carryin' your double barrel shotgun!"

"It is cute," said Mondo, picking it up. "And if you shoot someone in the head five or six times, you might really hurt them. My sister may have a small purse you could borrow…"

"Very funny, Mondo," Driscoll said, only slightly annoyed. He grabbed the tiny .22 back from Mondo and slipped it in his pocket. "What else have you got?"

"That's it," Goldstein said.

"That's it?" repeated Driscoll, dumbfounded. "Well, where the hell do you think you are,

Driscoll?" retorted Goldstein." There ain't no National Guard Armory around here. Their idea of a weapon around here is a sharp, pointed stick!"

Driscoll looked at Mohammed. "What about you?" Mohammed produced three small devices that looked like grenades with foreign writing on them— probably Russian, Driscoll guessed.

"Where'd you get those?" asked Goldstein, surprised.

"I found them," said Mohammed. "I think they call concussion grenades, but I like to call 'gas bombs.' They make bright flash and loud bang. First, we throw gas bombs in to knock them out," he said, fingering his knife. "Then we go in and cut off…"

"Wait a minute," interrupted Driscoll. "What the hell is a concussion grenade…or gas bomb as you like to call it? Are you absolutely sure that's what those things are?"

"I think so," said Mohammed, scratching his long beard as he inspected the unfamiliar writing on the side of one of the grenades.

"You think so!" snapped Goldstein. "You *think* so? The only gas bomb around here is you, you goddamned lizard brain! If those things are real grenades, we'll blow ourselves right out of that reward money, and I'm not taking any chances." He reached for the devices, but Driscoll grabbed them first.

"No, no. I'm sure, I'm sure," protested Mohammed. "They are concussion grenades. I know. I'm sure. I bet my life on it."

"You're betting all our lives on it," reminded Mondo, not smiling for once.

"Well, if he's really sure," said Driscoll, it sounds like these are exactly what we need."

"I'm sure, I'm sure," insisted Mohammed again. "And I have a rifle. And this." He flashed a long, curved sword, which had been hidden under his billowy clothes.

"Humpf!" Goldstein snorted. "Thank God the samurai is here to save us."

CHAPTER SIX

The Assault

The police station was an old wooden two-story building that looked more like a rickety shanty. Mondo surveyed the station from across the street until he saw the Commandant leave with his driver—on their way to meet Demura at the airport, he figured. A few minutes after Mondo confirmed that the Commandant had departed the building, Driscoll walked briskly into the station, where the Sergeant was manning the front desk.

"Where the hell is the Commandant?" Driscoll shouted at him as he pushed past two guards. "He's held onto my wallet long enough, and I want it back now!" Driscoll knew the Commandant's office was upstairs, where the jail cells were located. After causing this commotion, Driscoll raced up the stairs with the Sergeant and two guards right on his heels.

As he and the three angry Africans made it to the second floor, Driscoll thought, "Good, we're all in place." He felt for the minuscule .22 in his jacket pocket, and he couldn't help but feel the three concussion grenades pushing up against the inside of his shirt—he hoped the Sergeant didn't notice them. Driscoll knew Mohammed was in the rafters by now after climbing in from the tree overhanging the roof in the rear.

"What is all this about?" the Sergeant fumed as the two guards stood behind him dutifully. "The Commandant is not here right now."

"Fine, then I'll wait for him here," Driscoll responded drily as he casually checked his watch. In ten seconds if all was clear outside, Mondo, who was watching from across the street at a pay phone, would call the police station. That was the signal. The station's only telephone was located downstairs, which was currently unoccupied. When Mohammed heard it ring, he would drop through the ceiling, surprising the Sergeant and two guards, allowing Driscoll to pull the .22 from his pocket and get the drop on them while Mohammed took their guns. Then he and Mohammed would shove them into the cell, lock it and toss in the three concussion grenades ("One for each African," Driscoll thought with a smile). Driscoll and Mohammed would then race downstairs before the grenades went off. At the same time, Goldstein, who was waiting outside with the bigger guns, would run into the police station to meet Driscoll and Mohammed. Then, all they had to do was wait downstairs, armed to the teeth, until the Commandant and Demura arrived. With everyone upstairs knocked out cold from the concussion grenades, there would be no one to warn them—and Demura would walk neatly into Driscoll's trap.

But things didn't go quite as planned.

With five seconds to go before Mondo's phone call, Driscoll heard a toilet flush downstairs.

"What the hell was that," asked Driscoll, caught completely by surprise at the sound.

"A toilet, you fool," said the Sergeant, wondering just how long Driscoll had been out in the jungle.

"Dammit!" thought Driscoll in a panic as beads of sweat suddenly appeared on his forehead. He had completely forgotten about the bathroom downstairs. A goddamned guard had been in the crapper this whole time! There had to be nobody downstairs when Goldstein ran in with the guns. Driscoll heard the bathroom door creak open and slam shut, followed by footsteps thumping across the first floor. It was too late…there was no way to call it off.

At that moment Mondo called the station from across the street. The guard picked up the phone and said, "Hello?"

Hello? Suddenly frozen in fear, Mondo pressed his ear into the pay phone receiver. There wasn't supposed to be a damn hello. He looked across the street at Goldstein to see what was going on.

Goldstein, who appeared to be leaning against a pile of garbage, took Mondo's glance as his cue and leapt into action. He pushed aside the garbage, grabbed up the guns, and ran through the downstairs door of the police station, carrying a shotgun, a long rifle, Mondo's extra-long .44 Magnum straddled across his arms and a variety of bullets in belts and boxes trailing behind him. As he made it inside the building, Goldstein stopped dead in his tracks—just a few feet from the front desk, where the guard was sitting with the phone held to his ear. For a few seconds, Goldstein and the wide-eyed guard stood face-to-face, just staring at each other. Finally, Goldstein managed a sheepish grin as he asked, "Wanna buy a gun?"

Upstairs, Driscoll heard an ear-piercing shriek as Mohammed, crisscrossed with bandoleers of bullets and brandishing a rifle in one hand and a scimitar in the other, dropped through the ceiling right on cue.

The Sergeant and two guards were startled, alright. Their eyes bugged out as they caught sight of Mohammed in midair at full screech.

But as a result of gravity and the combined weight of the Arab's armaments, Mohammed hardly even slowed down as he crashed right through the second floor and onto the guard who was still standing behind the front desk downstairs. Once the dust cleared, the guard, who had barely moved a muscle throughout the ordeal, found himself standing between the desk with Mohammed on top and Goldstein, who was still frozen in place with his armful of guns.

Mohammed, who hadn't quite yet grasped the scope of his surprise entrance, looked at Goldstein with annoyance and asked, "What the hell you doing with those up here?"

At that precise moment, Driscoll, who was still upstairs, yelled, "Oh, shit!" He tossed all three grenades into the cell, intending to push the Sergeant and two guards in after them. As he reached for the purse-size .22 in his pocket, Driscoll silently prayed that Mohammed was right about them being concussion grenades. He wasn't. They were just grenades. The resulting explosion took out the entire upstairs back wall. The roof of the unstable building slid off, hit the tree, crashed into the floor, and pushed the rest of the building forward. As it fell, Driscoll dove under the roof and out the back wall, landing on the impounded Land Rover.

Goldstein dropped the guns and jumped back out the front door, pulling Mohammed with him. The front wall and sides of the wobbly police station collapsed around them but, miraculously, never touched them. They could hear the Sergeant and three guards moving and coughing in the huge pile of rubble...somewhere.

Mondo, who had left his post at the pay phone, was now sitting on the edge of the police station gutter with his elbows on his knees and his face in his hands, shaking his head as he looked at Goldstein and Mohammed. He was the only one who had witnessed the whole disaster, and he couldn't believe what had just happened.

Less than fifty yards from the station, a Jeep had stopped in the middle of the dirt road. A man with black glasses and a wide brimmed hat was sitting in the backseat. "What the hell is this?" he yelled to the Commandant, who was sitting next to him. "Get me out of here!"

The Commandant whacked the driver across the head with his hat and ordered, "Turn around! Quickly!" The Jeep sped away from town.

Driscoll, who had seen the Jeep and its passengers, jumped down from the roof of the Land Rover and scrambled in his pocket for the keys. The .22 was still wedged in his pocket, and he grabbed it to push it out of the way. It went off and shot him in the foot.

"Goddammit!" he yelled as he doubled over in pain. "I don't believe this shit! Mondo! Mondo, get over here and drive this damn thing!" As Mondo climbed in, he grabbed the keys from Driscoll's hand, shoved them into the ignition, and cranked up the Land Rover. "Follow them!" Driscoll grunted with a grimace as he pointed to the Jeep racing off in the distance. "No, wait…pick them up first." He gestured toward Goldstein and Mohammed.

Goldstein was pulling the guns from the wreckage as the Land Rover scooped them up.

All four men, mostly in one piece, spun off in pursuit of the Jeep, Demura and the reward money, just as the first police guard was pulling himself from the dust and debris.

CHAPTER SEVEN

Going for Broke

As they cleared the town, they could see the dust trail spinning out from the Jeep far ahead. Vito had quite a lead on them, and Mondo was searching all over the place for third gear.

"How the hell did this happen, Driscoll?" shouted Goldstein from the rear. "How come I found myself standing in front of that guard with an armload of rifles like a goddamn door-to-door salesman hawkin' vacuum cleaners? You forgot to tell me that part of the plan, Driscoll."

Driscoll was trying to prop up his injured foot to protect it from the rough ride. "Shut up, Goldstein," he yelled to the backseat of the Land Rover. "I don't want to hear your whining…I've been shot, dammit!"

"Yeah, you're a regular hero, ain't ya Driscoll?" Goldstein continued to shout over the roar of the engine. "When the going gets tough, the tough shoot themselves in the foot."

Driscoll whirled around and grabbed Goldstein by the collar with both hands and shook him. "It was that goddamned, piss-ass, piece-of-shit toy gun of yours, Goldstein! It went off in my pocket! I'm lucky I wasn't killed!"

"Relax," said Mondo, flashing his enormous yellow smile. "That tiny thing couldn't kill you Driscoll, even if it blew up in your pocket." He had finally found third gear and was now searching for fourth.

Driscoll released Goldstein's collar and turned to Mondo. "What I want to know, Mondo, is how the *hell* did the Commandant and Vito get all the way back from Khartanga so fast!"

"Khartanga?" repeated Mondo. He looked dumbfounded.

"Yeah, *Khartanga*!" said Driscoll. "You said they were meeting the airplane there at four o'clock!"

"Yes, yes. Four o'clock. But not Khartanga. I never said Khartanga," protested Mondo.

"Well, that's where the damn airport is," yelled Driscoll. "What did Vito do, parachute out from his plane?"

"No, no. Not that airport," said Mondo. "Not the real airport. I meant the little field up the way here. Demura flew in a small private plane. Much simpler and closer to use this one. Other people use this field too, for… ah…well, different things." He looked at Driscoll and gave him a knowing wink as he flashed his toothy smile again. "I thought you knew that."

"Well, I do now," said Driscoll as the Land Rover jolted over a large pothole in the dirt road. "Ow!" he yelled, scowling in pain as he reached for his wounded foot. "Keep your damn eyes on the road, Mondo!"

"Wait a minute," shouted Goldstein from the back. "If Vito flew into this little podunk field, then which airfield are the Feds flying into?"

"Probably this one," said Mondo, pointing ahead. "Well, if their plane is small enough."

"Probably?" shouted Driscoll, still holding his damaged foot. "Goddammit, Mondo!"

The road that led out of town was lined on either side by lush green jungle growth and towering trees. Because the trees were so thick, it was easy to see the narrow dirt road that cut through the trees to the right. They still hadn't caught sight of the Commandant's actual Jeep, but the dust cloud spewing out behind it was now traveling down that tiny side road.

"Looks like Vito is headed back to his plane!" Driscoll yelled above the clatters and thuds of the car lurching across bumpy road as Mondo tried to downshift.

"How far down that road to the clearing?" Goldstein bellowed from the backseat.

"Not far," shouted Mondo as he swung a wide right down the winding side road in third gear—he had never found second. "The runway starts where this road enters the clearing in the trees. It's just big enough for a small plane to get in and get out…well, usually."

Driscoll noticed a sprinkling of airplane parts dangling from the treetops around them as they approached the clearing.

Throughout the ride, Mohammed sat quietly, picking wood fragments from his beard and loading guns. Goldstein suddenly seemed to remember that his Arab friend was there.

"And you…you overcooked Haji!" he screamed at Mohammed, who casually glanced up at Goldstein with an expressionless face. "You and your goddamned gas bomb! We could have all been killed! I should have my head examined for ever…"

"Shit!" shouted Driscoll. "Look!"

As the Land Rover approached the edge of the clearing, Driscoll pointed to the Jeep, which had pulled off to the left side of the road. In it sat the Commandant and his driver…but no Demura. He apparently had already boarded his small private plane, which quickly taxied to the far end of the runway and then turned into the wind for take-off.

Just as Mondo sailed the Land Rover past the Jeep, the plane started its take-off run. It was heading full speed ahead right for the Rover.

"We're too late!" cried Driscoll. "He'll get off the ground before we reach him!"

"Good!" yelled Mondo. "What did you plan to do, just crash head-on into his plane?"

"Oh, didn't Driscoll tell you about that part of his plan?" shouted Goldstein over the hum of the approaching plane propellers.

"We shoot son-of-bitch down!" grunted Mohammed as he stood up in the backseat with Driscoll's shotgun in his hands.

"Here!" yelled Goldstein, grabbing the shotgun from Mohammed and tossing it to Driscoll in the front seat. "See if you can hit him in the foot!"

Driscoll ignored the remark. The wheels of Vito's plane were just leaving the runway as the Land Rover continued to hurtle towards it. Goldstein and Driscoll stood up in the bouncing vehicle (Driscoll precariously balanced on his one good foot) and leveled their guns at the plane's windshield, straight ahead.

Driscoll looked up from his aim and off into the distance. "Wait, what's that?" he shouted.

"It's a goddamned plane!" Goldstein yelled in response.

"The Feds," shouted Mondo, "from the Capital!"

Mohammed looked up at the sky and abruptly leapt from the fast-moving vehicle.

Skimming the treetops, coming in low, very low, directly behind Vito's plane, was a plane nearly twice its size. It was flying low because it was overloaded with soldiers, weapons and insurance men—the maximum amount of people and weight that could be crammed into a plane small enough to land in this tiny airfield. The insurance people were not worried about taking off again; they could leave at their leisure from the bigger airport at Khartanga. All that was important now was getting into Moombato Bay as quickly as possible with some government troops who would quickly grab Demura in the act of conducting his illegal business. This little non-scheduled flight had been engineered to do just that. If they came in low enough they would have one shot, and one shot only, at a quick landing into the wind. So as the government plane cleared the trees at the edge of the clearing behind Vito, they were already past the point of no return. They *were* landing.

As the bigger plane was coming down, it was traveling much faster than Vito's smaller plane taking off. It quickly caught up with Vito's plane just in front of the Land Rover.

As Mondo made a sharp right, steering the Land Rover off the runway, Driscoll could see Vito laughing behind the plane's windshield. Vito had interpreted Mohammed's bailout and Mondo's quick turn off the runway as surrender—and his victory. He was completely oblivious to the larger plane directly behind him.

Just as Vito's plane was about to clear the Land Rover, the government plane made a perfect three-point landing directly on the smaller plane's back. The impact caused Vito's plane to dip, and the left wheel caught the rear corner of the Rover. The Land Rover spun around in four or five dizzying circles before it finally came to a stop on the right side of the runway.

Both planes, now locked together, spun off in the opposite direction, crumpling into the Commandant's Jeep, and the entire twisted mass of metal rolled into the soft jungle.

"Oh God, don't let it burn!" Goldstein screamed as he stood up in the backseat of the Land Rover. "Sweet Jesus, Jehovah, Buddha, Allah, Anybody who's listenin'…just don't let it burn 'til we get the goddamned money out!"

With that, he jumped from the Rover and raced toward the wreckage on the opposite side of the runway. Mohammed, who had survived his earlier leap from the Rover with only a few scratches, was already on his way.

About a hundred yards into the jungle, Vito Demura toppled out of his plane and into the Jeep below him. He landed directly on top of the Commandant, who was trying to climb out of the vehicle.

Suddenly, a door opened in the plane above Vito's, and soldiers began tumbling out, falling on top of Vito and the Commandant. Mixed in with the unorganized crowd were three men in civilian clothes. One of them was a very pale, nervous looking fellow grasping a large duffel bag firmly in both hands. Sweat trickled down his forehead as he searched for a way to get to the ground.

"That's the guy!" yelled Goldstein as he and Mohammed approached the rubble. "The one in the Kmart khakis with the leather bag!"

Mohammed gave Goldstein a hoist up onto Vito's plane.

"I'll take that, thanks," said Goldstein as he grabbed the bag from the speechless insurance man, who just stood staring into the distance with a dazed look. Only the pilot had seen Vito's plane before they hit it. The rest of the passengers didn't quite understand what had just happened. While some of the soldiers gathered their wits and took charge of Demura and the Commandant, others wandered around the jungle, stumbling through the thick brush as they gazed up at the pile of twisted vehicles. Sitting in the midst of the jungle like that, the wreckage looked like some strange artwork left by an ancient civilization.

Goldstein and Mohammed raced back to the Land Rover, climbed into the backseat, and opened the briefcase.

Driscoll had never seen so much money in one place before. None of them had. They all looked around at each other until Mondo broke the silence with his thunderous laugh. Then Mohammed slowly started to chuckle, followed by Goldstein and then Driscoll.

They laughed uncontrollably and pounded the sides of the Land Rover with their fists.

Driscoll accidentally rammed his tender foot into the dashboard. He screamed out in pain, which momentarily silenced the three other men. Then Goldstein pointed at Driscoll's bloody foot, and they all started laughing hysterically all over again.

Chapter Eight

An American in London

The fire in Professor Gregory's study burned low. Outside, it was just getting dark and the first drops of a cold London rain splattered against the windows.

Gregory poured brandy into two huge snifters and handed one to Driscoll.

"So why did you call me here?" asked Driscoll. He didn't much care for brandy, and he thought the glasses were stupid.

"Because I need help, dear chap," Gregory replied in his haughty upper-class British accent. He took a sip of his amber brandy before casually adding, "Oh yes, and I need money; and I happen to know you've recently run into some."

"Actually, it nearly ran into me," Driscoll said with a smirk. "And that's putting it a little mildly, Gregory. I nearly died for that money, you know."

"Ah, yes, how is the gammy foot?" Gregory said, trying to sound serious as he glanced down at Driscoll's scuffed boots. "On the mend, it appears."

Driscoll chugged his brandy. It had been six months since their exploits in Moombato Bay, but everyone seemed to know about Driscoll's unfortunate accident. Damn that Goldstein! Was there anyone he hadn't told? Driscoll knew it wasn't Mondo. Mondo was far too loyal to leak that kind of information. Of course, Mohammed never said a word about anything to anybody—and when he did speak, it usually didn't make any sense anyway. So it had to be Goldstein. Hell, you shoot yourself in the foot once, just once, and they never let you forget it. Driscoll poured himself another brandy. "Anyway, I've got plans for that reward money," he said aloud to Gregory.

"Oh, have you now, mate? What's her name?" Gregory inquired as innocently as possible.

"I don't know yet," Driscoll replied. "So why don't you just go to the school? They sponsor some of these archeological digs, don't they?"

"Oh, sure," said Gregory. "I'll just waltz into the Dean's office first thing tomorrow morning and say, 'Hope I haven't caught you short this month, old chap, but I could use a couple hundred thousand quid to go dig up some old junk in Greece.' And he'll say, 'No problem, Gregory. Just take what you need from that great pile of cash over there, and if you need any more, shoot me an email.'" Throughout his sarcastic diatribe, Gregory gestured with his large, pale hands and wobbled his head back and forth. Yet his perfectly coiffed brown waves, just starting to gray at the temples, never moved an inch.

The professor, now in his early 40s, was insanely intelligent and incredibly impatient with anyone of inferior intellect. Driscoll had first met Gregory in Africa a few years earlier when the professor hired him as a guide. Gregory claimed to be searching for some unnamed artifact in the jungles outside of Moombato Bay, but Driscoll suspected the professor was really in need of a paid vacation. During his month-long trip, Gregory spent more time sightseeing and drinking in local bars than combing the jungles for this mysterious "relic." Yet it seemed that the professor had grown much more focused since his little African holiday.

"Well, I know it's not that easy to get cash from the school," admitted Driscoll, "but…"

"Not that easy, bollocks. Nowadays it's damn near impossible," Gregory said, as he buttoned up his scholarly-looking wool coat sporting leather patches at the elbows. He grabbed an iron poker and proceeded to jab it violently at the fire. "Bloody hell, it's cold in here. Anyhow, the college doesn't hand out money unless you're from a third-world, undernourished, over-populated, minority desert country that happens to have large oil deposits—and you're the son of the bloomin' King," he added bitterly.

"That tough, huh?" Driscoll sympathized as he took another swallow of the brandy. It tasted a little better with every drink. "Hey, I could get

Mondo to apply. He qualifies." Driscoll paused, then added, "Well, no… not quite…Mondo's not the son of a king, he's just a son-of-a-b—"

"Is it impossible for you to be serious, Driscoll?" Gregory complained. "Perhaps, just this once you could refrain from acting like a daft cow?"

"Sorry," said Driscoll, taking on a more solemn tone as he straightened his posture in his chair.

"Anyhow, they don't care *what* rubbish we dig up," Gregory said sourly. "They don't really expect anyone to dig up anything worthwhile at any of those sites. It's just a bloody status symbol for the school, sponsoring a dig. But they don't just hand them out— they're favors."

"Oh," Driscoll said. Of course, Driscoll was much smarter than most people realized, so he already knew all of this. He was just testing the professor to see just how serious he really was about this little project. And Gregory was practically starting to beg. Driscoll was impressed.

"And besides," Gregory was saying, "I need a bloke with your experience and, ah…sense of adventure."

"Sense of humor, you mean," replied Driscoll. "So far, it sounds like I'd have to be nuts to get involved in this."

Gregory looked put off, scowling like a sulky schoolboy.

"Now don't pout, professor," Driscoll said with a chuckle. "I mean, I'm as much for the advancement of science and technology and the enlightenment of civilization as the next guy; but, as my good friend Goldstein would say, 'What's in it for me?'"

Driscoll took a pull from his drink and looked steadily at Gregory. "I mean, besides my name on a small brass plate in a museum somewhere?" Driscoll added.

"Is that all you care about, Driscoll? Bloody money?" Gregory asked as he leaned back in his desk chair.

"Of course not!" said Driscoll. "I care about lots of other things, like a big house, a fancy car, a beautiful—no make that a *gorgeous*—woman. You know, things like that. But don't kid me, Gregory. You know better than to invite me over here and just ask me to do a good deed."

"Of course, mate," replied Gregory, who seemed to have cheered a bit. "I know you better than that. I'll make it worth your while, I promise. Just bear with me a little longer, and I think you'll find your niche in all this."

"Okay, I'll try," said Driscoll. He poured another drink, plopped down on the couch opposite from Gregory, and propped his cowboy boots up on the coffee table.

"Alrighty, then," Gregory started as he sat down behind his desk. "As you may know, the Romans had umpteen gods. So did the Greeks. So what's one more soothsayer? With a god for every occasion, they were only being religious by convenience anyway. That's why I never took this damn thing so seriously in the first place."

"Took what seriously?" asked Driscoll. "The Romans…or the Greeks?"

"Neither," said Gregory sounding exasperated already. "I'm talking about the Oracle, the Oracle, you numpty."

Gregory was clearly annoyed. He was used to dealing with his razor-sharp archeology students, and they were used to paying attention to details. Driscoll was not…at least, not to the point required for Gregory's complex explanation. Driscoll practiced what he liked to call a holistic approach to life situations. In other words, he took in the big picture and then did whatever was necessary to keep from getting chucked out of it.

"The Oracle, right, at Delphi," said Driscoll. "You mentioned that on the phone. But what's the fuss? It's not news. That's where rich folks went for advice about the future, right? The place where people went for prophecies…from priests or something."

"But the Oracle wasn't just a place, like a fountain or a shrine," corrected Gregory. "It was supposed to be a person, or a deity, who only spoke through priests. The priests in turn doled out the information to the faithful."

"And by faithful you mean those who could afford to pay," said Driscoll.

"Well, yes," agreed Gregory. "But my point is, it couldn't have been all rubbish or they wouldn't have kept coming back for advice. And they did…important people, like Caesars and such. There must have been something to the Oracle's prophecies."

"Unless it was just fashionable," said Driscoll.

"Ah…wait, what?" stammered Gregory. Driscoll had broken his train of thought, which stunned the professor into silence. That was why it was so difficult to talk to Driscoll. He never knew when to expect an intelligent comment. This one had caught him by surprise.

Driscoll kept talking as Gregory struggled to regain his composure. "I mean, in those days, you couldn't impress your wealthy friends by buying a flat screen TV or a Ferrari—so you blew a load on the Oracle to show off."

Gregory was mildly shocked. Had money made Driscoll wise? No, no, surely not. It never worked that way. But trust Driscoll to do everything ass-backwards, including getting smart.

"Precisely!" Gregory finally answered. "And what do you suppose the priests did with all that wealth, mate?"

"I don't know," Driscoll responded as he thoughtfully scratched the stubble on his cheek. "Neither did anyone else," Gregory said with a slight leer in his eye. "Until now."

Driscoll dropped his boots to the floor and leaned forward on the leather couch. This had definitely piqued his interest.

"Listen to this," said Gregory, producing a notebook from his jacket pocket. "This is an exact translation from a scroll my colleague Jessup unearthed near Delphi."

The professor flipped through the tattered pages of his composition book and read aloud:

I am an apprentice to a scribe. But by the time this is read, I will not only have been a scribe, but will have been dead for some two thousand years.

However, due to my experience as apprentice to Piros—scribe, scholar and personal acquaintance of the Great Emperor Claudius—I have access to certain knowledge, which if I do not set down, may be lost forever; unless the High Priests forsake their vows, which is not likely.

But to share this knowledge in my own time would certainly be the cause of my death. Therefore, I share it with yours.

Gregory paused and glanced at Driscoll, who seemed to be mulling over the words.

"So this guy has something important to say, is that it?" Driscoll said sarcastically.

Gregory rolled his eyes. "Yes, yes…brilliant.

Now, listen to this part, mate," he said. He continued reading:

In my time, I have no understanding of what I have seen. Yet I hope the passage of many centuries may bring wisdom to my words so that you, in your distant world, though you are standing exactly where I am now, may read and understand.

For I have seen the Oracle at Delphi. And It is not Human.

"Not human," Driscoll repeated. He was leaning so far forward now, Gregory thought he might tumble off the couch.

"That's what the bloody man says," said Gregory, "and he should know. He claims to have been there several times and seen this Oracle thing twice. Once while it was reclining and going about business as usual with the High Priests, and once when it was being carried out. During this second viewing, the scribe said the Oracle didn't look at all well. It might have been dying or perhaps already dead, and the priests were taking the body to some secret burial place. Anyhow, It was never brought back. Apparently, interest in Delphi seemed to wane after that, at least among the big shots. For the Caesars and the like, the Delphi prophesies seemed to have lost most of its punch. The priests continued to sell prophesies, but more so to the public—at a cut rate, I presume."

"Discount prophecies," Driscoll said with a pensive grin. "Talk about bargain shopping." He paused briefly to take another sip of brandy. "Did he write anything else about the Oracle, Itself?" he asked anxiously. He was already getting involved. "I mean, did he say what it looked like?"

"Oh yes," said Gregory with a smug smile. He knew he had Driscoll now. "In fact, he was quite descriptive. The scroll was very long. I only copied the first part, but I read Jessup's entire translated version. He said the Oracle's appearance was that of a boy with longish hair—except it had pale blue skin and dark blue hair."

"Holy shit...sounds like some kind of freakish Smurf!" Driscoll said.

Gregory restrained from rolling his eyes this time. "Also, its eyes were clear, or maybe white. The translation is not precise on that point."

"Pretty strange, either way," Driscoll said, genuinely interested.

"Yes, and it gets even stranger," continued Gregory. "The scribe's description was from that first occasion, when the Oracle was reclining on a couch and being attended by the priests. He said it appeared to be nude except for a thin, light blue veil and—are you ready for this Driscoll?—It had the sexual organs of both male and female!"

Driscoll said nothing. He just sat on the edge of the couch, his elbows resting on his knees, his empty glass dangling from one hand.

Gregory stood up, stretched, and walked out from behind his desk. He leaned against the front of the desk and said slowly, "Driscoll, I think that Oracle was an alien. Those High Priests had found, and were keeping, a bloody alien!"

The rain tapped on the windows. The darkness from outside seemed to crowd into the study, despite the blazing fire.

Driscoll slowly set his glass on the coffee table and stared into it for a few moments. His mind raced back to his boyhood bedroom. He recalled all those sleepless nights he'd gazed at the stars through his homemade telescope as his drunken father raged downstairs. Fast-forwarding to college, he remembered the countless hours he spent in the Princeton observatory studying the infinite depths of space, examining each pinprick of light. Every time he'd ever looked up at that endless vista, he'd always had a feeling there was something—or someone— looking back at him.

"Gregory…" Driscoll began stiffly. For once, he was truly at a loss for words. "Gregory, are you…that is, well…don't you think you might be jumping to conclusions? I mean, isn't it more likely that that poor thing was the sad result of generations of inbreeding or something? We know it went on all the time, back then. Maybe that or some terrible disease or something…"

"Goddammit, I'm a scientist, Driscoll!" Gregory interrupted. "I don't jump to bloody conclusions. It's true, I don't have any real proof, but that's where you come in. And anyway, there's more. About the crash site."

"What?" said Driscoll, looking a shade paler by the minute. "What crash site?"

"Well, at least that's what I think it was," Gregory said as he sat back down behind his desk. "Listen, according to the scroll, the priests supposedly brought the Oracle to Delphi from somewhere on the island of Delos. They referred to this place as the Old Temple. The priests who brought the Oracle from that original site died soon after they reached Delphi. Consequently, the generations of priests that followed held a belief that the Old Temple spelled certain death for anyone who went there. Apparently, some plucky bloke would try to visit the Old Temple from time to time, but each one always met the same fate: death. After a while they stopped trying to go there. The Old Temple just became known as a sacred, forbidden place, and the location was kept a secret. That is, until our friend the scribe showed up."

Gregory folded his hands on his desk and took a deep breath before continuing.

"So here's my theory, Driscoll. An alien ship crashed on Delos. The crash site was lousy with radiation, for quite a few years anyway. So anyone who traveled there was exposed to deadly amounts of radiation—which is precisely why they always died shortly after their visit. Anyway, my guess is that some people witnessed the crash or just stumbled onto the site, and they removed the alien and brought it back to Delphi. Who knows what kind of deal they may have made with it? It probably wasn't in the best of health here in our atmosphere or maybe it was injured in the crash—either way, it needed constant nursing from the priests. But still, it lived much longer than humans. Wherever it came from, it probably had a natural lifespan that made us look like a flash in the pan."

"Wait a second." Driscoll snapped out of his shocked stupor for a moment. "The scribe never mentioned anything about a crashed space ship on Delos. Wouldn't folks be talking about that kind of, uh…sighting?"

"The remains of the ship may well have looked like the remains of some mostly buried ancient temple," Gregory responded. "Anyhow, these priests would have no way of describing a crashed spaceship. Unless they saw it come down, it never would have occurred to them that what they saw sticking up out of the ground had come from outer space. In fact, they likely assumed that it had never been anywhere other than where they had found it. So with absolutely no understanding of the greater universe, the best they could come up with was that the alien was some kind of god. And come to think of it, even if the priests *did* see the ship come down, the ignorant boobs would have reached the same conclusion—that a god had simply 'fallen from the sky.'" Gregory finally paused for a breath and reached for the bottle of brandy.

Driscoll's head was reeling. "That's a very impressive theory. A little weird, but impressive. Did this scribe say anything else about the last time he saw the Oracle?"

"Yes," Gregory answered before taking a small, gentlemanly sip of brandy. "Well, not too much, really, but enough for us to make some pretty good educated guesses. As I mentioned earlier, after the priests removed the Oracle from Delphi, our scribe was never brought back as part of Claudius Caesar's entourage because of the lack of interest. However, he wrote that he believed the Oracle was taken back to the Old Temple on Delos and buried there."

"How did he know that?" asked Driscoll.

"Because there was a bit of a flap about it at the time. According to the scribe, it was all the gossip at high-powered private parties. It seems a suicide team of novice priests was sent out with the sacred task of returning the Oracle's body to the forbidden Old Temple, along with most of the offerings the Oracle had accumulated from Caesars and such. I guess they convinced these poor bastards that, though they would never return, they were lucky to be picked for such a holy mission." Gregory took another sip of his brandy and flipped through the pages of his notebook. "But by then, the radiation at the crash site had dissipated.

"Of course, these folks didn't know a bloody thing about the radiation, so no one ever expected to hear from these poor blokes again. After they left, the High Priests went about the sacred task of deifying this suicide team…you know, making them out to be real heroes to keep interest alive in their temple. They were really making progress and attracting all kinds of business to the temple, when the sons of bitches stroll back into town! The bloody suicide team actually returned to Delphi!

"The locals went nuts. They thought these guys must really be something special to survive, and they treated them like saints. The suicide team of priests ate it up, but the High Priests were bloody brassed off. These new guys were a big threat to their authority, so the High Priests discredited them. They said the suicide team chickened out and never went to the Old Temple. They told the people the novices just dumped the Oracle and pocketed the wealth, and they had every last one of them put to death…off with their heads. But our scribe friend believed that the suicide team *did* go to the Old Temple and did what they were supposed to do, because he knew for a fact that the High Priests had them followed.

"So as it turns out, the High Priests knew all along that the novices had taken the Oracle to the Old Temple, but they couldn't explain how the bloody hell they'd survived the trip…and it threatened to undermine their religion."

"So the High Priests just covered up the whole thing," Driscoll said.

"Yes…the High Priests and two thousand years of time," said Gregory.

"Then how do you expect to find the site now?" asked Driscoll.

Gregory reached for a pen and twirled it around his fingers. "Well, you see, that scribe was pretty damn bright. He suspected something was a bit dodgy before everything came to a head. You see, we have Claudius' manuscripts today because the Oracle told him to bury them and they would be found about two thousand years later—and he did, and they were. Quite interesting, don't you think, Driscoll? Anyway, while our scribe was assisting his master in copying manuscripts for Claudius, he got a chance to see a map. It was a map to the Old Temple! Apparently old Claudius had a curious interest in all this too, but I guess he never made much out of it all. So before his death, Claudius destroyed all the information he had accumulated over the years, including the map. The only documents he preserved were those detailing his family history— these were the ones he buried as the Oracle had advised him."

"Okay…so the scribe copied the map before Claudius destroyed it?" Driscoll asked hopefully. Now he was the one growing impatient.

"Well, not right away. Not 'til years later when he was writing the scroll that Jessup found," Gregory said. "It would have been too risky for him to have a copy of the map, so he memorized it. Then, years later, he drew it from memory at the end of the scroll."

"Shit, I hope he had a photographic memory," said Driscoll.

"Well, he seemed pretty sure of himself," Gregory said. "He was taking a big risk just writing it all down. If anyone had found it in his possession before he had a chance to bury it, he would have been lion bait in a bloody hurry. I think he knew about Claudius burying his manuscripts and did the same, but for different reasons of course."

Gregory let out a sigh and visibly relaxed. He looked like a man just unburdened from a great weight, Driscoll thought.

"Well, that's pretty much it," he said. "So…are you in, old boy?"

"I'll bet you've been just dying to tell me all this since you found out," Driscoll said as he got up and poured another glass of brandy before plopping back down on the couch.

"There's been little else on my mind," said Gregory. "And time is of the essence, of course. The first step is to see Jessup—he's got the map. Along with something else."

"What is it?" asked Driscoll.

"The scribe mentioned something about a message from the Oracle," Gregory said. "A message for all mankind, or something of the sort. It all seemed quite profound, but the High Priests never released it. They kept it a secret. My guess is that they didn't understand the message and were sitting on it until they could make some sense out of it. But they translated it…into Greek."

"And Jessup has this message?" Driscoll prodded. "Well, what the hell did it say? I and all of mankind have a right to know."

"No, Jessup doesn't have the message. No one except the High Priests have ever seen it. But Jessup has the key to the translation. With the key, we can translate the message from whatever language it's written in to Greek, letter by letter. The scribe did copy that.

"So we can only hope that the original message is buried out there on Delos with everything else. Personally, I think it is. Something so religiously significant, in their view anyway, would have been preserved by the priests. So I bloody well think it's there."

Gregory looked away from the fire, where he had been staring as he talked, and glared at Driscoll through brandy-glazed eyes. "Well?" he asked again, "What do you think, mate? Are you in?"

Other than the crackling fire, the study was absolutely silent. The rain had stopped outside and the night was eerily still.

"Let me think about it," said Driscoll as he got up from the couch. He drained his glass and started for the door.

Gregory looked disappointed. He had hoped for a more immediate response. That's one of the things he admired about Driscoll—he was usually impulsive. Gregory had been counting on that particular character trait tonight.

Fortunately it paid off. With the door open and his hand on the knob, Driscoll turned around and faced Gregory. Gregory assumed he was just going to say goodnight, but instead he said, "Okay."

"Okay, what?" said Gregory, brightening a little. "Okay, let's do it!" Driscoll said with a smile.

Gregory's grin broadened until it seemed to stretch completely around his head and meet in the back.

"Brilliant!" he said. "Goodnight, mate."

Driscoll silently strolled out the door and was quickly enveloped by the darkness.

CHAPTER NINE

Old Friends

Driscoll and Gregory sat at a chic bar on the rooftop of their swanky Athens hotel, taking in the spectacular scenery. The circular restaurant was surrounded in glass, offering a panoramic view of the Acropolis and the historic district in all directions. Complete with shiny black marble floors and a neon blue illuminated bar top, the contemporary restaurant was a strange contrast to the ancient ruins surrounding them, Driscoll thought.

"We need people we can trust," Gregory said as he suspiciously eyed the fruity cocktail a bartender had just set on the glowing bar in front of him.

"That's out," said Driscoll. "I don't trust people I can trust. How about Goldstein and Mohammed? And Mondo?" he suggested. "Well, if I can find them." He took a gulp of whiskey.

"Well, that's who I had in mind," said Gregory. "After hearing the stories of your last exploit, who else?"

"Exploit!" Driscoll said, slamming his empty glass on the bar. "I'll have you know that operation was a carefully planned strategic maneuver."

"Ah, I see. So when exactly did your 'carefully planned strategic maneuver' turn into the bloody fiasco I heard about?" Gregory asked mockingly.

"Fiasco?" Driscoll said, raising his eyebrows. "I think I like exploit better. Anyhow, it came out right in the end, didn't it?"

"Indeed it did," admitted Gregory, "and I suppose that's what counts. How soon can you reach your mates?"

"I'll start making calls right now," Driscoll said. "I know where Mondo is. And Goldstein too, I think. But God—or Allah, I should say—only knows about Mohammed."

"Well, I certainly hope not," Gregory said. "I don't think I want God or Allah watching us. Since we don't exactly have all the permits for digging up and removing treasures from these fine people's island." He gestured to the glass surrounding the bar. "I'd rather be unobserved."

Driscoll grinned, tossed a few bills on the bar, and headed for his hotel suite.

Mondo was easy to reach. He was where Driscoll had last heard from him, in Khartanga. He had moved there soon after the Demura debacle, abandoning his hovel-on-the-bay for the finer things the big city had to offer, now that he could afford them. And he had so enjoyed that insane drive from Moombato Bay to the airfield in their commandeered Land Rover that he had bought his very own Jeep. At least, it had started out as a Jeep. Where Mondo ever found all those outlandish accessories for it in Africa, Driscoll couldn't imagine. With all of its new customized add-ons, Mondo's Jeep could now handle everything from cruising and partying to all out warfare.

Unfortunately, by the time Driscoll called him from Athens, Mondo's driving privileges in Khartanga had been revoked—forever this time. Since he could no longer legally drive there, Khartanga was losing some of its thrill, and Mondo was ready for a change. He agreed to fly to Athens, where he would rent a car and meet them at the hotel. They would then drive the rental car to Jessup's place, located in a secure location outside of Athens.

As Driscoll had predicted, getting a hold of Mohammed was a bit trickier—partly because Mohammed didn't own a cell phone, and partly because he wasn't on the ground much anymore. After their exploit in Moombato Bay, Mohammed had gone one better than Mondo's Jeep. When he got his portion of the Demura reward money, he used a big chunk of it to buy a helicopter. And purely by the grace of Allah, Driscoll was certain, Mohammed had somehow learned how to fly it—well, sort of fly it— without killing himself, anyone else, or any of the local sheep that he regularly terrorized. He did once land it on a pig, though. He had to pay a fine for that one.

"A fine?" Driscoll snickered into his phone. Sitting in a white leather chair, he gazed out his massive hotel window at a sea of stars twinkling above the Acropolis, which was all lit up for the night.

"Yeah, he got fined for squashing a pig," Goldstein responded drily into his wireless headset. He was lying face down on a massage table on the terrace of his rented penthouse in Egypt. "Cost him fifty bucks for pig parking. And the judge made him pay for the pig, so Mohammed ate him—the pig, I mean, not the judge." Goldstein rolled over on his back, and a busty blonde in a red bikini handed him a drink before she proceeded to rub his shoulders. "But don't worry, I'll get him, I'll get him. It may just take me a day or so to hold him down long enough to explain everything to him. But trust me, he'll come. He's been in a real good mood lately, ever since he got a new snake. He named it Vito. But it'll be good to get him away from here for a while. The locals are getting pissed. You should see him and Vito buzz those damn sheep in their chopper!" Goldstein chuckled.

Goldstein promised to bring Mohammed and his helicopter to Athens by the end of the week. It would take a few hops to make the trip by chopper, but they could use it on Delos. Gregory had permits for digging on the island, but not for removing anything from the country. That was legally impossible. That's where Mohammed's helicopter would come in handy. It would eliminate those long, tiresome lines at Customs…and ensure they wouldn't get caught red-handed with a bag full of ancient scrolls.

"One other thing, Driscoll," Goldstein added. "We'll probably have to bring his damn snake, too. I can just see it now, cooped up in a helicopter all the way to Athens with the Arabian Red Baron and a goddamned snake named Vito. Friggin' fabulous!"

"We might need the snake," Driscoll said, "in case we need to have a guard bit in the ass again."

"Driscoll," Goldstein said seriously, "if you can convince Mohammed to leave the damn snake home, I promise I'll bite anybody you want in the ass with my very own teeth."

CHAPTER TEN

Jessup's Map

"Is Jessup coming with us?" Mondo asked as he caught the bottle of beer Driscoll tossed him. All five men—Driscoll, Gregory, Mondo, Mohammed and Goldstein—had convened at Driscoll's hotel suite in Athens. The extravagant suite was decorated completely in white, from the milky marble floors to the snowy satin comforter on the oversized King bed. The entire length of the outside wall was made from glass, offering a breathtaking view of the Acropolis and a cloudless cobalt sky.

"No, Jessup will not be joining us on this adventure," Gregory said. "The old chap has other plans—mainly moving to some other part of the world as soon as he gets our money...ah, well, *your* money, that is, gentlemen," the professor added as he unbuttoned the cuffs of his shirt. "You see, Jessup has one vice, and he pursues it to the fullest: Gambling. And it seems that recently, Lady Luck hasn't exactly smiled on him. In fact, if you ask him, dear Lady Luck shit all over him, and now there are some quite unpleasant people trying to catch up with him. So he's been lying low."

"Well, I hope nobody's done anything nasty to him yet," said Goldstein as he stretched in his chair with a yawn, puffing out his ever-growing gut. He certainly hadn't missed any meals since their last adventure. "Are you sure he's waiting for us?"

"No," answered Gregory, "but that doesn't matter. If he's not there, I know where he keeps the map. He wouldn't carry it with him anywhere."

"So what's it like at Jessup's place?" Driscoll asked as he stood staring out the hotel window. "Will anyone ask questions if they see us snooping around?" He turned around to face Gregory and took a swig of his beer.

"No. It's a rather remote area," Gregory answered. "Too bloody remote for me, no one around for miles. But Jessup likes it that way."

"Good," Driscoll said. "Then we can fly the helicopter right in to Jessup's tonight, grab the map, and leave for Delos while it's still dark. That should get us there by dawn." Driscoll turned to Mohammed. "Mohammed, why don't you head back to the air field and get your chopper. File a flight plan for anywhere—anywhere but Delos, that is. Gregory can you give Mohammed directions to Jessup's?"

Gregory nodded. Driscoll looked around at the other men. "The rest of us should pack up the car and leave immediately. By the time Mohammed gets there we'll have the map and be ready to go."

"What about the rental car?" asked Mondo.

"We'll leave it at Jessup's," answered Gregory. "He can drop it back in town for us."

Driscoll tossed his beer bottle in the trash and casually placed his hands on top of his head. "Well fellas, here we go again," he said as he looked around at the other men.

"Hey, if nothing else, it's something to do," yawned Goldstein.

The trip out of town to Jessup's took over an hour by car, even with Mondo driving like a madman. In the meantime, it took Mohammed almost that long to get himself launched and on his way. But a lot more went on under Mohammed's turban that he usually let on. Back at the airfield, he wisely filed a flight plan to Rhodes, a route that would take them directly over Delos. That way, no one would question their presence in Delos air space later that night.

"I must say, Mondo," Goldstein called from the backseat of the rental car, "your driving has certainly improved."

"I'm not sure improved is the word I'd use," said Driscoll who was clinging to the handgrip in the front passenger seat. "Maybe accelerated is a better term. Feels like we're in the goddamned Indy 500. Exactly how many times have you lost your license back in Khartanga, Mondo?"

"Oh, who's keeping count?" Mondo said, flashing his yellowing, crooked smile. "It's like a game—I go out on the road, and they try to catch me."

"And from what I've heard, they've caught you quite a few times," chided Goldstein.

"It's the odds," explained Mondo. "I'm the only one who can outrun them so I'm the only one they chase now. And they've got to win sometimes," Mondo grinned.

"Well, what do you expect in that one horse town you stuck yourself in, Mondo?" Goldstein asked, rubbing a chubby hand across his bald head. "You're the only game in town."

"Khartanga is not a one horse town!" Mondo shot back, insulted.

"Yeah, that's right," Goldstein said with a smirk. "I forgot. The horse died, so now all they've got is donkeys and camels; they've got these two places there, ya know, like used car lots. One's called Camels-R-Us and the other is Jack-Asses-2-Go. Come on, Mondo, why don't you pry yourself out of that jungle metropolis and move to the real world? I mean how much life in the fast lane can you take?" Goldstein snickered.

Looking rather ashen-faced, Gregory sat quietly next to Goldstein in the backseat and strained to look ahead, down the dark road. "Okay, up here," he said. "Turn here."

Mondo jerked the Jeep off the paved road they had taken south, out of Athens, and onto a rough dirt path.

"Jessup cut this road out himself," said Gregory. "With what, a goddamned fork?" Goldstein asked as they bumped and lurched down the uneven road.

"Where else does this road go, Gregory?" asked Driscoll as he turned around in his front seat and looked out the back windshield.

"Nowhere," answered Gregory, "just Jessup's place. There's nothing else out here in the sticks. There it is," he pointed with a freckled finger, "up ahead."

"Well, you'd better turn around and have a look," Driscoll said, still staring out the back windshield. "Because these folks behind us are either going to nowhere or coming to Jessup's with us."

Gregory and Goldstein both spun around and looked. Mondo glanced in the rear view mirror. There were two pairs of headlights behind them.

"What do you think, Gregory?" Driscoll asked. "Maybe it is Jessup?" suggested Mondo.

"I don't think so," Gregory said nervously. "It looks like there are two vehicles, and Jessup doesn't usually bring anyone out here with him."

"Maybe he got lucky," smirked Goldstein. "I mean, the guy must get pretty tired of sheep after a while, out here in this no man's land," he added, looking around at the dark, empty landscape. The dirt road was eerily illuminated by the bright moonlight.

"And he was expecting us," Gregory continued, ignoring Goldstein. "He most certainly wouldn't bring anyone here when he knows we're coming for the map."

"I don't like the looks of this," said Driscoll, still craning his neck to peer out the back window. "They're gaining on us."

Just then, a bullet flew between Gregory and Goldstein in the rear and then Mondo and Driscoll in the front. A matching pair of holes had appeared in the rear and front windshields.

"Holy shit!" yelled Goldstein. "They're shooting at us!"

"Everybody, get down!" shouted Driscoll.

"Except you, Mondo!" Goldstein yelled from the backseat floorboard.

Mondo slumped down as far as he could without losing sight of the road and pressed the gas pedal all the way to the floor. It didn't make much difference in their speed, but it made him feel better. They were almost to Jessup's house.

Gregory didn't care much for this excitement at all. He cowered in the backseat floorboard, a quivering, sweaty ball with wide, petrified eyes. The professor had never considered himself a courageous man, and his interest in this adventure was purely scientific and economic. The thought had never crossed his mind that they may encounter dangerous situations along the way. But he considered himself the brains of the outfit, and he fully intended to return with his intact.

Mondo's eyes widened as they approached Jessup's property. "I hate to be the bearer of bad news…but I do not think Mr. Jessup is home," he yelled.

"What do you mean?" Gregory practically shrieked from behind him. By now, the car's headlights lit up the place where Jessup's house was supposed to be.

"Jessup is definitely not here, Gregory," shouted Driscoll as he peeped over the dashboard and through the front windshield. "Neither is his house!"

Gregory and Goldstein both carefully sneaked a peek over the front seat. It appeared that Jessup's place had either been blown up or burned to the ground, maybe both. Either way, the place was a mess. Just then, another bullet whizzed through the car. Gregory dove back down on his belly in the backseat floorboard and cried, "Oh, bloody hell!"

"What do we do now?" Mondo shouted as he continued to drive, quickly approaching the scorched house.

"Whatever we do, we better do it fast!" yelled Goldstein, who was crouched down next to Gregory.

"We've got to stop at the house," said Gregory, attempting to muster up some courage. "I can get the map, I know where it is. Stop directly in front of the house, I'll run in." Gregory had shocked himself when he heard himself suggesting such a thing. What in the Queen's name was he saying? He hadn't even thought about it before hand; he just blurted it out. That wasn't like him at all. Gregory always thought through everything, analyzed issues from every angle, and considered every possible implication before making his answer known.

But Gregory was just now figuring out what everyone else in the car had already learned, and that was the First Rule of Adventures (which also happened to be Mondo's First Rule of Driving): When a man says go, it doesn't matter what is behind you— just keep going!

Mondo was just as surprised to hear such fearless words tumble out of Gregory's silver-spoon-fed mouth. But he followed the professor's orders and drove over the rubble of a ruined sidewall and right into the remains of Jessup's house.

Driscoll jumped out of the front seat and Gregory leapt out of the back and ran toward what was left of the fireplace hearth while Mondo turned the car around in the house.

Goldstein yelled, "Pop the trunk!" to Mondo. He then hopped out of the car, raced to the trunk and fumbled through their baggage for the gun. They only had one weapon this time, but it was a beauty. Mohammed and Goldstein had scored an Uzi, a small machine gun capable of filling the air between the shooter and the target with tons of metal in the blink of an eye. But since this was firepower far in excess of what Driscoll ever expected to need, he had insisted on packing it deep down in their luggage and supplies. That way, if they were stopped for something stupid like speeding—a highly likely event with Mondo driving—they wouldn't look like a band of terrorists on their way to blow something up.

"You mean like the Moombato Bay police station?" Goldstein had said with a smirk when they discussed the Uzi earlier that day.

This time, Goldstein threw stuff around the back of the car, cussing like a sailor, while the first of the two cars pursuing them reached the house. The second car drove around the side of the charred house, and bullets whizzed and twanged off the few walls that remained as Gregory ripped a box from under a stone in front of Jessup's fireplace.

"Goddammit, Driscoll!" yelled Goldstein, who by now had abruptly unpacked every item they had brought. Clothing and supplies were strewn all over the place, in, on, and around the car. "I told you we shouldn't have packed the friggin' Uzi!"

"Hurry up!" shouted Mondo as he yanked someone's pants off his head, where they had landed during Goldstein's desperate search for the Uzi.

Gregory dove back into the car, with the small box clutched tightly in his shaking hands. Driscoll jumped back into the front seat and yelled, "Let's go, Mondo!"

"I can't!" Mondo shouted back in his booming voice. "They're blocking our way!"

Driscoll looked up and saw that both cars had positioned themselves in front of the small opening Mondo had driven in through. There was no other way out.

"Where's the goddamned Uzi?" shouted Goldstein, still digging through the bags he'd pulled into the backseat with him. "Where the hell is it? I told you, Driscoll, I told you we would need it. If there is one thing I've learned about having a gun," Goldstein barked, "If you have one—you're gonna need it."

Driscoll decided he would wrestle with that little gem of logic later and said, "How was I supposed to know Jessup had sons of bitches like this waiting for him?"

The sons of bitches had gotten out of the cars and were beginning to approach the house.

"You should have known your plan would go to shit as soon as we started, Driscoll," Goldstein yelled. "I mean, for Chrissakes, the last one did! I just can't believe this went down the toilet so damn fast—even for you, Driscoll."

Driscoll was a little surprised himself. "These guys do look a little heavily armed for the welcome wagon," he admitted.

"This is positively depressing," Gregory added in an unsteady voice. He now had beads of sweat dripping down his prominent British forehead.

"What do we do?" asked Mondo.

That's when they heard the helicopter. Before they knew what was happening, out of nowhere came Mohammed. He and his glorious chopper suddenly materialized in the glow of the headlights, hovering just above the tree line next to Jessup's house.

"It's the goddamned Arabian Cavalry!" said Goldstein. Mohammed made a low pass over the two cars and sized up the situation. He swung out and around and came in for another run.

During Mohammed's first fly by, the assailants assumed it was the Police and decided not to shoot at cops if they could help it. They began scrambling back to their cars in a panic—but they didn't move fast enough. Mohammed came in slower and lower this time, with his right hand on the controls and the missing Uzi in his left. He was leaning out of the cockpit as he passed over and sprayed the cars with bullets. The remaining gunmen scattered, fleeing into the darkness.

Mohammed wasted no time. He landed just outside the house and beckoned to the other men. Mondo, Driscoll, Gregory, and Goldstein abandoned the rental car and piled into the helicopter.

"Watch out for my snake," said Mohammed as they all climbed in.

"You bet," said Driscoll, carefully checking his seat before he plopped down.

"You crazy, beautiful A-rab!" Goldstein hollered. "I could kiss your damn snake. But the gun, Mohammed, why didn't you tell me you had the gun, goddammit? I coulda' got killed lookin' for the friggin' gun, and you had it all along!"

Mohammed paid no attention to Goldstein's ravings. Driscoll shouted, "Get us the hell outta here!" and Mohammed was doing just that. Gregory looked a little dazed, but he still had a firm grip on the box that held the map and the translation key.

Mondo said, "What about our stuff?" All of their clothes and supplies were still scattered throughout the remains of Jessup's house. As Mondo looked down, he could see shirts, pants, and underwear swirling in the rush of wind from the helicopter.

"Forget it," said Driscoll. "We'll have to make do with what we can get on Delos."

"Well, at least we're off to a smooth start," Goldstein added as he punched Gregory in the arm.

The professor managed a nervous chuckle as they sped off into the night sky toward Delos.

CHAPTER ELEVEN

The Dig

When they first reached Delos, Gregory was in his glorious element. He supervised the dig while the rest of the men dug. And dug. And dug. After three days, Gregory decided to pitch in and start digging too. But still, they found nothing. Everyone but Gregory seemed to be getting pretty well fed up.

"There just ain't nothin' to do in this goddamned hole, Driscoll!" Goldstein repeatedly pointed out as he tossed a handful of dirt into the air.

In the meantime, Mohammed was starting to twitch a lot (which Goldstein warned was a very bad sign), Mondo constantly whined about how much he missed his Jeep, and they were quickly running out of food.

By the fifth day, Driscoll decided to have a talk with Gregory. He climbed out of the helicopter, where he had been examining the GPS device and attempting to plan out a route back to civilization.

Back in the hole, Goldstein made some crack about how Vito, Mohammed's snake, would fit neatly into a hoagie roll. Mohammed promptly threw a shovelful of dirt at Goldstein but missed and nailed Mondo right in the face. Mondo angrily returned fire but missed and hit Goldstein.

As Driscoll entered Gregory's tent, he found the professor studying the scribe's map that had brought them here in the first place.

Gregory looked up, furrowing his brow. Even after five days of digging in the sweltering sun, not a single brown wave was out of place on the professor's proper British head. "I've been expecting you, chap." He gestured toward the opening of his tent, where the shouting from the hole indicated an escalation in the dirt fight. "So what has that mob out there decided to do with me—bury me in the hole and watch the ants eat me alive or just lynch me right quick and get the hell off this God-forsaken island?"

Driscoll laughed, running his fingers through his own messy, dirt-coated hair. "Nobody wants to lynch you, Gregory, but we would like to get the hell out of here," he said. "We're pushing our luck staying here this long and, so far, all we've dug up is a goddamned hole. What do you think—do we still have a chance of finding anything?"

Gregory tossed the map on his small makeshift table. "You know, Driscoll, I've been thinking."

"I'm glad to hear it," Driscoll said. "I can't seem to do it anymore. My brain is fried after spending all these hours in the sun."

"I mean, I've been thinking about this map," Gregory continued. "If there is an inaccuracy, it would more likely have to do with the site of the Old Temple, rather than where the novice priests buried the Oracle."

"What do you mean?" asked Driscoll. He didn't usually follow Gregory's explanations the first time around.

"Well," Gregory continued, "this map is an accurate copy of the map used by the priests to return to the old Temple to bury the Oracle…but by the time they used it, it may already have been in error as to the exact location of the original crash site."

"Well now, that's just bloody brilliant!" said Driscoll, mocking the professor's haughty British accent. "You know if we're off by just a hundred feet, we could dig forever and never hit it." Driscoll looked out the tent opening. "So what do you suggest, Gregory? You're the damn expert."

"I suggest we keep digging just a little while longer," Gregory said. "We may not find the remains of whatever it was the old priests originally found the Oracle in, but I still think the map is accurate concerning the Oracle's burial place. And that's where the gold is—and the message," he reminded.

The message, thought Driscoll. It had been tormenting his mind over the past few days. He wasn't sure which he wanted most anymore: the gold or the message. This message must be something truly profound. After all, it was a communication to all of mankind from the Oracle—which was, according to Gregory, some sort of fortune-telling alien or superior being. Once again, Driscoll's mind raced back to the years he'd spent studying the universe, always feeling deep in his bones that there was something else out there.

"Alright, I'll talk to the fellas about it," Driscoll finally responded. He left the relative cool of the professor's shady tent and ventured back out into the suffocating heat.

That night, as they gathered around a fire near Driscoll's tent, Goldstein expressed his opinion the only way he knew how—bluntly, with plenty of New York attitude. "I wouldn't give you a sun-shriveled fig for all the secret messages buried between here and Brooklyn, Driscoll," he said. "But for the gold, well, what the hell—I mean we're already here and all. I say we stick with it. For a while."

Mondo and Mohammed seemed to share the same opinion, which delighted Gregory.

So on they dug, for two more days. Then, late one scorching afternoon, the orange sun blazing overhead, Mondo's shovel hit something hard and sturdy. A metallic clang echoed through the hole when he struck it. "My friends!" he called, wiping the sweat from his brow. "I've found something!"

Gregory leapt into the hole, nearly knocking Mondo to the ground, as Driscoll, Goldstein and Mohammed peered over the edge with hopeful faces. Gregory proceeded to gently brush away the dirt surrounding the massive item.

A few hours later, when the professor had finally finished his meticulous dusting, the men stood over a huge box with gold figures and elaborate markings on the outside, which indicated to Gregory that it was indeed some type of coffin. But this container was far too large and heavy to be just a coffin.

Within a matter of seconds, Driscoll was grunting with the effort of pushing one end of the box as Mondo and Mohammed pulled at the other. "The damn thing won't budge," Driscoll panted. "If we can't even get this heavy son of a bitch out of the ground, how the hell did the priests get it all the way out here, Gregory?" He stopped struggling and looked at the professor, who appeared to be lost in deep thought.

"Because they didn't bring it here," Gregory finally answered in a pensive whisper. "Bloody hell, that's it! They must have assembled the box in the ground here and then filled it up. That's what we're going to have to do, but in reverse. We'll never get it out in one piece—we'd just end up destroying it anyway."

"But what about the Oracle's body?" asked Driscoll. "With the box out of the ground, you'd be able to get at it better."

"I don't think there'll be any body, as such," Gregory responded as he stood over their newfound treasure. "Nothing but dust by now, I presume. Maybe some bones if I'm lucky. But the artifacts…those should be something!" Gregory was beaming. "Relics never before seen outside of the Temple of the Oracle, and very few people ever saw them there."

"And the message?" Driscoll inquired casually even though his heart was pounding in his throat. "Where do we look for the message in this huge thing?" He pointed to the box, still sealed shut but mostly unearthed, lying in the excavation.

"We'll start by looking around whatever is left of the body—if anything *is* left," Gregory began. "That's probably where the priests would have put something that had been the personal property of the Oracle. If we find nothing there, we'll search through the religious artifacts that are doubtlessly contained in the vault." Gregory turned his gaze to the top of the hole, which was growing darker by the minute. "We're quickly losing daylight, so we won't be able to dismantle this beast until first thing in the morning." He and the other four men started to climb back up the cliff they had worked so hard to dig. "By this time tomorrow, Driscoll, we'll know what we've got," Gregory added as he scrambled out of the hole. "We'll either be deliriously drunk or dismally disappointed."

"I vote for drunk either way," said Goldstein. "Count me in," Mondo said with a hearty laugh. "Alright then, mates, let's get pissed!" Gregory said cheerfully. "I brought a nice bottle of brandy just for the occasion."

Later that night, the men crowded around the fire, sipped brandy and swapped war stories while Mohammed quietly fed his snake. But all the brandy in the world couldn't drown Driscoll's apprehension about the Oracle's message. He tossed and turned all night long in his sleeping bag, anxious to get his hands on it.

When the first rays of sunlight peeked over the horizon, the men were horribly hung-over…but no one was disappointed. As they carefully removed the cover and two sides from the vault, it was like Christmas morning. It was packed to the brim with jewels, gold coins, and priceless artifacts.

Gregory was practically in shock. Driscoll overheard him mumbling something about "buying the whole bloody university" and turning it into a museum for his private collection. Then the professor scurried around inside the hole, muttering things none of them understood, about dynasties and eras and not since this and not since that. They all assumed he was pleased.

Goldstein was in a daze. He just sat next to the opened vault, holding handfuls of gold coins up in the air and letting them slip through his fingers, enjoying how they blinded him as they sparkled in the brilliant sunlight when they fell.

Mohammed, as always, didn't seem all that impressed. His cut of the reward money from their last adventure had pretty well pushed him to the limits of his comprehension of wealth. With this latest windfall, all he was really sure of was this: If he crashed his helicopter, he could afford to buy a new one now. And that made him happy.

"That does it!" announced Mondo, as he fondled a glittering diamond and emerald necklace. "There just aren't enough things for sale in Khartanga for me to buy with all of my new money—I am moving to California!" He shook with a great boom of laughter, and Goldstein slapped him on the back.

"It's about time you escaped that goddamned bush city!" he said with a chuckle.

Amid all the chaos, Driscoll continued to hunt for the message. He and Gregory searched the vault for some type of scroll or parchment... but there was nothing. Driscoll was about to give up hope when Gregory shouted, "Wait a bloody minute, mate!" He wiped away an inch of dust from the top of the vault. "By God, I think I've found it!"

Gregory pointed to what they had assumed were just decorative panels in-laid on top of the vault. Now that it was dusted off, Driscoll could clearly see there was some sort of message etched into the four crystal panes, which were about eight inches square and tinted in light blue.

Driscoll and Gregory carefully removed the crystal panes and carried them off to the professor's tent. Gregory opened the small box that held the map and removed a second yellowing piece of paper: Jessup's translation key. Using the key, Gregory slowly translated the message into Greek and then into English.

Two hours later, the sun had set and Gregory and Driscoll finally emerged from the tent. Mondo, Mohammed, and Goldstein were lounging by the fire, all sparkling with jewels from head to toe. "That's a good look for you, Mohammed," Goldstein chuckled as he pointed to the ruby rings glistening on the Arab's leathery hands. Between their peals of laughter, Mondo overheard the professor saying, "I promise, Driscoll. After all, it was part of our original bargain. I won't go back on my word, mate."

Gripping the crystal panes in his hands, Driscoll walked deliberately over to the fire and abruptly tossed all four of them into the smoldering rocks at the center of the blaze. The fragile items smashed and disintegrated into dust-size particles that glimmered in the firelight.

Driscoll walked away from the fire and tucked a tiny piece of paper into his pocket. He could feel some sort of mysterious change taking place inside of him. He felt renewed. He felt enlightened. And he felt special, as if he had somehow been chosen, handpicked for this mission. But most of all, he felt anxious. However, he knew he would have to wait some time. He was close; a hell of a lot closer than the Oracle had been, but still not close enough…not yet. He'd have to wait at least another five or ten years, maybe more.

Driscoll smiled. He could wait. He looked up at the canopy of constellations overhead. Anyway, he could use the time to prepare himself. He had plenty of things to do—big things. And with the information in his head, and the celestial coordinates in his pocket, he could afford to wait.

He gazed at the brilliant stars gleaming in the jet-black Mediterranean sky, and for the very first time found himself thinking about a future far more distant than next week. That night, as he sat in his dimly lit tent, Jeffrey Driscoll made some significant long-range plans.

PART TWO

The Message

Seven Years Later

Chapter Twelve

California Dreaming

Driscoll sat back in a plush leather chair, swiveled slightly toward the window, and took a long sip from his glass of whiskey. It was just getting dark, and he watched as the points of light appeared in the azure sky. He remembered watching the same stars glittering in a cloudless Mediterranean sky, far away from here. He couldn't believe seven years had passed since that exhilarating night on Delos.

He thought briefly about Mondo, Mohammed, and Goldstein and wondered what they were up to these days. Driscoll spoke with Gregory occasionally. While the professor still worked part-time at the University, he had started his own archeological institute after their fruitful dig in Delos. However, Driscoll had lost track of Mondo, Mohammed and Goldstein somewhere along the way…it must have been after he met Carol in Jamaica six years ago.

A stunning redhead with creamy porcelain skin, Carol had caught Driscoll's eye immediately. It was a sweltering day, and Driscoll, who was nursing a rum hangover, stumbled down the beach searching for a quiet spot where he could take an afternoon nap. That's when he saw her. Wearing a miniscule, emerald green bikini, she was lounging in the protective shade of a huge red umbrella, sipping a Piña Colada and giggling with her friend. Driscoll strolled past the two ladies, attempting to act nonchalant even though the scorching sand was searing the soles of his feet. He approached the umbrella next to Carol and her friend, and tossed his beach towel on the lounge chair beneath it.

"Oh, excuse me, ladies…" he said, flashing his most charismatic smile at Carol. As she turned to face him, she tossed her ginger hair over her shoulder and it glistened when it caught the sun's rays. "Is this seat taken?" he added, running his hand through his own disheveled hair. Carol casually took a sip from the tiny straw in her frozen drink. As she slowly lowered her oversized sunglasses and peeked over the rim, Driscoll caught a glimpse of her aquamarine eyes, a perfect reflection of the Caribbean Sea behind him. She looked Driscoll up and down, taking in his muscular build and his handsome face. "It is now!" she said with a playful grin.

Driscoll spent the rest of the afternoon wooing her with his irresistible wit and boyish charm as they chatted on the beach and splashed in the surf. That night, he took her out to the fanciest restaurant in Negril. He quickly discovered that Carol, a Director for a prominent event planning agency in Los Angeles, was not just a gorgeous redhead—she was also smart as a whip. With every clever remark he launched at her, she fired back with her own sarcastic wit. Driscoll found himself laughing until his sides ached every time they were together. He had met his match. The two of them were married within a year.

Driscoll snapped back to the present, and quickly gulped down the remainder of this drink. He only vaguely remembered General Hodge leaving his office a minute ago, offering some kind of half wave half salute from the hallway. Probably something generals reserved for petty civilians.

Driscoll was still in shock about the conversation they'd had before the general had made his awkward exit. Because he had played his hand well, Driscoll Mining had just won the contract for the largest mining operation the world had ever seen. He was still stunned. But why the hell not? The Washington people had nothing to lose. Driscoll would have to hand over the celestial coordinates for the big Lunar dish long before he would become personally involved with any of the preparations. Shit, if anyone was risking anything, it was him. But he was confident that this was a sure thing. When the time finally arrived, his mining company would have the job. They would work in coordination with a contractor called National Dynamics, which would provide the mechanization to convert the ore to metal and deploy it.

And of course, the Army would handle the operation of the Polarizer and provide transportation to Titan, Saturn's largest moon, and maintain life support systems there. In the end, Driscoll Mining would be elevated to giant status in the mining business. The enormity of the project would insure extreme prosperity for himself and his corporation for many, many years.

As well it should. He had waited on pins and needles for seven long years for this very moment. Actually, he had done a great deal more than just wait. He had wheedled his way into one of the world's major mining companies and eventually taken over as the head of the entire corporation.

And it all came back to Carol, the fiery redhead who had changed his life in so many ways. Soon after their romantic rendezvous in Jamaica, Driscoll had packed up his Manhattan apartment and joined her in California. He had done a little research on mining companies in Southern California—and he figured if he could somehow land a job with on one of those companies, he would be one step closer to solving the mystery that had haunted him since that last night on Delos.

As always, things fell perfectly into place for Driscoll. During his first week in LA, Carol invited him to attend a fancy charity dinner she was organizing. She was well aware that Driscoll had plenty of money left over in his reward stash, and she knew a generous donation from her handsome boyfriend would score huge points with her client *and* her boss.

"Of course, I'll go," Driscoll said as he ran his finger down her silky arm. She had her head propped up on one elbow in the bed next to him, her crimson waves cascading over her pillow. "Shoot, I'll even donate $10,000 to the cause...*if* you can do me a huge favor..."

"What's that?" she said, batting her long eyelashes at him.

"Well, there's this very wealthy man named Walter Blake. He's the owner of Blake Mining...and I've heard he's quite the philanthropist."

"Oh yeah, he comes to all of these charity events. In fact, I'm pretty sure he'll be at this dinner."

"You're *pretty* sure he'll be there?" Driscoll said, suddenly sitting up in the bed. "Could you make *absolutely* sure he comes? And score us a seat at his table?"

"Well, well...aren't you just full of requests today?" Carol said with a smirk. She tousled his chestnut hair and looked into his pleading eyes. "How could I say no to those beautiful baby blues?"

Carol kept her promise. The night of the charity dinner arrived, and sure enough Driscoll found himself sitting right next to good ol' Walter Blake. He glanced over at Carol who gave him a quick wink and a kiss on the cheek before she ran off to check on the food and entertainment. Driscoll, who easily struck up a conversation with Walter, proceeded to charm the pants off of the old man. After a few too many glasses of champagne, Mr. Blake slapped Driscoll on the back and shouted a little too loudly in his Texan twang, "Now you are one smart, down-to-earth fella! I tell ya, you gotta dang good head on your shoulders."

Driscoll responded with a laugh and a humble, "Why, thank you, Mr. Blake."

"Mr. Blake was my father's name! You can call me Walt." Then Walt lowered his voice and pointed a wrinkly finger at Driscoll's face. "You see, my two younguns, they ain't nothin' like you...I'd like to retire, but I don't trust either of those spoiled rotten trust fund babies to take over the business. I need someone smart—somebody with charisma and drive. A fella like you, Driscoll!"

Driscoll grinned hopefully as Walt shouted to the server for another glass of champagne. "I know we just met, but what the hell? Driscoll, you wanna come work for me? I'd love to teach you my business. You can be like my apprentice...but I promise not to be as ornery as that dang ol' Donald Trump."

Of course, Driscoll promptly accepted the offer. After working side by side with Walt for two years, Driscoll knew everything there was to know about the mining industry. Walt finally had a chance to retire, and he turned every day operations of Blake Mining over to Driscoll. Less than a year later, Walter Blake passed away...and his will ruffled quite a few feathers. Much to his son and daughter's chagrin, Walt left Blake Mining and all of its future profits to Jeffrey Driscoll. To top it off, he specified that upon his death, the name of the company would officially be changed to Driscoll Mining. He wrote, "My ungrateful kids and cheating ex-wife don't deserve to have a damn company named after them." Of course, Walt's ex-wife and children tried, unsuccessfully, to overturn the will. But within six months after Walt's death, Jeffrey Driscoll was officially the owner and CEO of Driscoll Mining.

Still Driscoll waited patiently, with the coordinates locked safely away. He waited for technology to catch up to him. He waited for the sensitive Lunar dish to be installed on the moon, to escape the bothersome terrestrial noise level of Earth so they could finally detect faint signals that had been buried in static before.

The last few years had seemed to drag on the longest. But at this moment, he couldn't have been more pleased with himself.

Once again, he gazed out of his office window and watched the stars glisten in the night sky. He tried to predict where the Pipeline Project would be one year from now, two years from now. How much longer would he have to wait? He was elated that he'd gotten this close, but the anticipation of what was yet to come was killing him.

But he had no other choice…he would have to keep waiting. Just a little bit longer, and it will all be worth it. He rolled his chair over to the telescope pointing out his office window and fixed his eye on the eyepiece. As he scrutinized the constellations, Driscoll was overcome with that all-too familiar feeling that something or someone was looking back.

CHAPTER THIRTEEN

The White House, Three Years Later

Two men in dress uniforms walked down the short corridor to the new president's office. General Hodge from the Defense Department had been here before. Dr. Cottman, the Surgeon General, had not. The general carried his hat. The doctor carried a DVD. Both men were visibly nervous.

This hallway was always so damned quiet. He was a tough yet distinguished man in his early sixties with silver hair and icy blue eyes. A war-hardened veteran, Hodge had seen his fair share of combat, both on the battlefield and from behind the commander's desk. It took a lot to rattle him, but he had absolutely no patience for politicians.

Hodge casually glanced down at his gold wristwatch. They were on time. He hoped the fifteen minutes they had been allotted would give them enough time to make their point to the president. Once they presented the critical details and communicated the urgency of the matter, the general felt quite certain the president would give them all the time they needed.

One of the first duties of a new president was to be briefed by experts about on-going projects left over from the previous administration. Most of these projects didn't directly involve the president, but it was his job to know about them. It was also his job to pretend to be interested. And the newly inaugurated president did this very well.

So as the general and the doctor entered his freshly redecorated office, the president greeted them with a genuine smile and feigned interest. However, the general was fairly certain that once they showed the president their DVD, his fake smile would quickly be replaced by profound interest.

After shaking hands and exchanging all the appropriate pleasantries, the president sat down behind his massive desk and motioned for General Hodge and Dr. Cottman to take a seat across from him.

The general started, "So Mr. President, you've heard of the Pipeline Project, haven't you?" "Only as much as everyone else. From what I understand, it's a way to beat the time delay of long distance space communication, and involves mining a lot of, uh, some kind of metal on one of Saturn's moons." The president was quite pleased with himself. Most of these briefings were complete news to him, and he stumbled into them completely ignorant about the subject matter. He couldn't stand to come across as uninformed. Luckily, he'd been properly informed for this particular briefing.

Dr. Cottman and General Hodge were also pleased. At least they wouldn't have to start from scratch.

Hodge continued, "That is essentially correct, sir." The general displayed his most charming smile as he folded his hands on the desk in front of him. "To give you more detail, the Pipeline Project involves the placement of an incredibly long, thin solid rod in space between two communications stations to eliminate the delay inherent with speed-of-light modes of communication, such as radio. The operation of our defense technology would be greatly enhanced if that time delay were eliminated. The basic idea of the solid rod is that any actual mechanical movement of the rod at one end causes instantaneous movement at the other end. These are slight movements, of course, but they are still perceptible to sensitive instruments. Variations of the movements are converted into a computer language. As a result, our military members could carry on an entire conversation across a vast distance while the enemy waits for a single signal reply sent by conventional methods."

The general briefly eyed the president. Noticing that he still looked interested, Hodge continued. "The rod will be strung through space by an ore-processing barge that will actually form the rod and draw it out behind it as it travels through space."

"Like a spider stringing a web," said the president, who was finding this briefing more interesting than he had thought he would.

"Exactly!" beamed the general. This was going even better than he had hoped. "Naturally, creating this rod will take an enormous amount of allidium ore, hence the mining operation on Titan, Saturn's largest moon."

"What kind of ore?" queried the president, wrinkling his brow.

"Allidium, sir," Hodge responded. "It's a metallic ore that's almost a natural alloy in itself. It has been discovered in incredible abundance on Titan, yet it exists practically nowhere else. Its properties are particularly suited for the Pipeline Project, as it is almost impervious to the Polarizer rays."

The president was beginning to look slightly confused. And he was. He had always believed that a little knowledge was a dangerous thing. Apparently he knew just enough about the Pipeline Project to ask intelligent questions that required answers he didn't understand. Perhaps this would have gone smoother if he'd just played dumb at the outset. He fiddled with a pen on his desk.

"So if it's impervious to the Polarizer rays, then what good is the Polarizer in mining it?" the president finally asked.

"The Polarizer doesn't really mine the ore," General Hodge answered. "It changes the molecular structure of the rock surrounding it by reversing its atomic polarity, then back again, and back and forth. When the frequency of alternation is matched to the density of the rock, the rock molecules lose their ability to adhere to one another and the rock crumbles around the allidium ore, which is left lying in a pile of dust, ready to be collected."

"Impressive," said the president. That seemed like a safe comment. At least it didn't invite any more lengthy technical descriptions. He thought he would try a simpler question. "So how's it going?" he asked.

Unfortunately, this was the most difficult question he had asked yet. General Hodge stared at the president. The doctor stared at the disc in his hands. To the general, the sudden silence in the room seemed even quieter than the corridor outside. Not that the general was ever one to duck a tough job, but he couldn't help wishing that he were back out in that corridor already. This next bit would be sticky. No time to pussyfoot around the issue. He smoothed the front of his highly decorated coat. Time to fire all guns. Once the smoke cleared, he'd know where he stood.

He finally responded stiffly but sternly, "Well, it's not going at all, Mr. President."

The president's smile began to fade. "What do you mean, *not at all*? Has there been some kind of trouble?"

"Well, sir, there's good news and bad news," Hodge began.

"What do you mean?" repeated the president, but more emphatically this time. His smile had completely disappeared.

"It means, sir," the General said gruffly, attempting to regain his command of the situation, "that the project is no longer active. It's somewhat of a cover-up."

"Shit!" thought the general, *"Wrong word."* He knew the politicians in D.C. hated the word "cover-up." It was different in the military, where public deception was a way of life.

Hoping the president wouldn't notice his poor choice of words, he quickly continued, "In fact, sir, except for the preliminary preparations and transportation, there has been no Project Pipeline for more than a year now."

"What?" snapped the president, all traces of his smile long-gone. "Well, just what the hell are all those people doing out there? Or aren't they out there? And more importantly, where the hell has all the money been going?"

"Yes sir, they're out there, and there was, and still is a Project Pipeline," the general added hastily. "It's just been sort of put 'on hold' for a while."

"On hold?" the president responded, more calmly this time. He didn't like losing his composure, but he liked being duped even less. "But I thought this thing was so damned important?"

"It is, Mr. President, but something has come up…ah…concerning the use of the Polarizer."

"You mean, the gadget that digs the ore," said the president, trying to keep track of all the details in his mind.

"Well, it doesn't exactly dig it, if you recall our earlier conversation, Mr. President," Hodge responded with a courteous smile. He knew he didn't understand all that. "So that brings us to the Methuselah incident," Hodge said.

"The what?" the president asked, sounding somewhat intrigued as he rubbed his chin. "And let me guess. This doesn't exist either, right?"

General Hodge ignored the smart-ass remark and continued. "Code name: Methuselah, sir, that's the official title. There are very few people in the world who know about it. Very few."

The general looked intently at the president, his piercing blue eyes practically nailing the Commander in Chief to the wall. "What you are about to hear and see," he gestured toward the disc in the Surgeon General's hands, "is strictly classified. Do you understand, sir?"

"Of course," said the president, who had taken on a serious tone. The general knew his fifteen minutes were up, but the president wasn't paying any attention to the clock. He seemed completely absorbed in what Hodge was telling him.

The general continued, "Since the Polarizer involves electro-magnetic radiation of an almost nuclear nature, standard medical tests were conducted to see if its use had any harmful effects on its operators. But I believe this is Dr. Cottman's domain." He looked to the Surgeon General. "Could you take it from here, doctor?"

The doctor had been silent so long that both he and the president, who had almost forgotten anyone else was there, seemed to be caught by surprise.

"Ah, yes..." The Surgeon General, a reserved, balding black man, adjusted his silver framed glasses, cleared his throat, and picked up where Hodge had left off. "These tests were conducted on laboratory animals, mice mainly, in various states of health. The team tested young, healthy mice; old, feeble mice; middle-aged mice; mice with minor health issues such as the common cold; and mice with more severe diseases. Even mice with cancer were exposed to the rays of the Polarizer to see if it worsened their condition. It did not. All tests were negative. The rays had no detrimental effect whatsoever on living tissue, as expected. So they gave the Pipeline Project the go-ahead...and Driscoll Mining was permitted to begin the Polarizer mining operation on Titan."

Noting that the president seemed to understand Dr. Cottman's explanation, General Hodge continued. "So the Driscoll Mining folks set everything up and began to run the operation. I'm afraid we've left them in a bit of a hole, so to speak, but it couldn't be helped."

"Don't worry about them," the president said, "the taxpayers will make it up to them somehow. They always do."

Hodge hesitated momentarily before he continued. "Well...we'll get to that. Anyway, it took them nearly two years to get all the people and equipment sent out and set up on Titan," General Hodge explained. "The original test mice, as well as some new mice, were sent along with the medical team's lab so they could continue tests and observation during the mining operation. It's standard procedure, I believe." The general looked to Dr. Cottman for confirmation. The doctor nodded, and Hodge resumed. "During that time, Dr. Cottman's people on Titan began to notice a few, ah, interesting developments."

The doctor abruptly stood up and turned on the president's flat screen TV. He gently removed the disc from its cover before sliding it into the DVD player.

"What sort of 'developments'?" the president asked, looking up at the Surgeon General, who was pointing a remote at the TV. "Did the mice get sick?"

"Not at all, sir," replied Dr. Cottman, turning to face the president. "In fact, they got better."

"What do you mean, better?" asked the president. "Well, sir, the cancerous mice…with or without exposure to the Polarizer rays, they should have gotten worse over time as the disease progressed. But they all recovered! They're in complete remission."

A genuine look of shock spread across the president's face, and he stared open-mouthed at the doctor for a few moments. "Just what are you trying to tell me, gentlemen—that we've found a cure for cancer?"

The Surgeon General gestured toward a small cage that materialized on the president's TV screen. "Mr. President, the footage on this disc was recorded one week ago. Take a look at these mice."

The president watched the screen intently. He saw three active, healthy-looking mice scurrying around a cage.

"Notice anything wrong with them, sir?" Hodge asked.

"No…should I?"

"Yes, sir," replied Dr. Cottman in his soft voice. "Okay…can you give me a hint?" the president asked, taking on a somewhat impatient tone. "They're five years old, sir," said the doctor. "Are they full grown?" asked the president. General Hodge could no longer contain himself.

"Full grown!" he blurted out. "They should be halfway back to dust by now! These are the doctor's 'old and feeble' mice, sir," he said as he pointed toward the TV screen. "These rodents were at death's door when the tests were first conducted—over three years ago! The normal lifespan for a mouse is about one to two years!"

The president pulled his eyes away from the screen and looked at the general. He then glanced towards the doctor for confirmation.

"That's correct, sir," the doctor said. "Mice generally live about one to two years. On rare occasions, maybe three."

The president, his gaze still fixed on the Surgeon General, said very slowly as the implications set in, "Then these mice are almost twice as old as any mouse has ever been?"

"That's correct, sir," the doctor said flatly as he sat back down next to the general. The footage of the mice was still playing on the TV in the background.

The president stared at the TV screen and tapped his fingers on his wooden desk. His mind was spinning. When he finally regained his composure, he said, "Well, gentlemen, since this could be the greatest discovery of our time, or anybody's time for that matter, the mice must be the good news. Now…what's the bad news?"

The General didn't beat around the bush. "We've lost all contact with the operation."

"That's it?" the president asked rotating in his chair to face the general. "Nothing else?"

"That's it, sir," General Hodge said. "Nothing else."

There was another long pause. The president let out a long sigh. "Any ideas?" he asked.

"Ideas, Mr. President?" the general said. "Well, sure. Besides the obvious possibility of sabotage, it could be that they're not responding to our radio transmissions because something in their life support system failed and they're all dead; or they had a loss of basic power, in which case, by this time, they're all dead; or something in their food supply poisoned them, and they're all dead; or…" Hodge shot a sideways glance at the doctor before he continued. "Or something in that damn machine backfired…"

"And they're all dead," finished the president. "That is the key phrase, sir," the general said with a frown.

"You don't seem to hold out any hope that they might have survived," said the president. "Is this your opinion too, Dr. Cottman?"

"Well, sir…my prognosis would not be good, but the general really has the expertise in these matters," he added quietly. He had a stronger natural abhorrence to death than General Hodge.

"I'm not just trying to be morbid, Mr. President," Hodge said. "But in space, you either have everything you need…or you're dead. There's no in-between. No wiggle room. When you lose all contact with a distant space outpost for a prolonged period of time, it's time to face reality. They must have encountered some sort of problem, and even the smallest problem out there is like the first in a line of dominoes falling. When the rescue ship—actually, we might as well call it a recovery ship—when the ship arrives on Titan, we should not expect any survivors. Our only hope now is that whatever catastrophe befell them, the information on the Pipeline Project is still intact."

None of the men moved or spoke a word for what felt like an eternity. After the pregnant pause, the president finally broke the silence. "Is there anything else, gentlemen?"

The Surgeon General looked to General Hodge, who gave an almost imperceptible nod. Dr. Cottman stood up and said, "If you'll excuse me, Mr. President, I believe that's my cue." He shook the president's hand, retrieved his disc from the DVD player, and quickly left the room.

As the door closed behind the doctor, the president and General Hodge were standing, facing each other. The general said in a low voice, "There is one other thing, sir…and this is for your ears only."

The president, looking rather shell-shocked, sat back down behind his desk as the general once again took the seat across from him.

CHAPTER FOURTEEN

Solar Space

A man in his early thirties stood in the ship with his arms folded, clutching a clipboard to his chest. A pen floated nearby. Surrounding him were banks of electronic and pneumatic instruments, displaying a multitude of indicators. The wall of instruments reached about a foot above his head, all the way to the ceiling of the Navigation and Control compartment, and stretched about five feet to his right, ending in an airtight hatch type doorway to the living quarters. The equipment continued another three feet to his left and then widened to a circular area eight feet across.

The man's name was Tony—a pale, ginger-haired Brit with an almost childlike freckled face. He observed as the lights and meters blinked and glowed from panels in the curved wall. A desk-like counter extended waist high from the circular wall all along its circumference, its surface ribbed with Velcro strips at regular intervals. The only break in the round countertop was where the equipment lined passageway from the living quarters emptied into the circular area. Any manual control of the ship and its functions, and all communications, came from this small round room, aptly named Nav-Con.

Tony often thought calling this area a room was somewhat of a stretch. After all, a room was purely a human notion. In practical application, this was a small round space in a massive machine into which two men had been inserted to perform minute duties.

The long, curved desk was littered with Velcro-backed books, manuals, pens and pencils, gadgets, a couple of tablet computers and a microphone. A second man sat at the desk where it met the passageway, typing on a tablet computer. A light from the top of one of the instruments in the center of the passageway lit the floor area at the Nav-Con entrance, illuminating the edge of the desk where the man was sitting. Tony, who was still observing the instruments in the passageway, shifted into the light as he leaned to one side and tapped on a meter, casting a shadow on the other man's work area.

The man at the desk set his tablet on a strip of Velcro, leaned his elbows on the desk, and cupped his chin in his hands. He looked up at Tony, standing in the passageway drumming on the meter.

"Get out of the damn hallway…you're blocking my light," Lou mumbled. He ran his fingers through his dark brown hair which had just recently started to gray at the temples—a side effect of this mission, Lou was certain. It had been a long day…or night…or whatever it was back home. Out here, it was difficult to keep track. But Lou thought it was important to at least try to keep tabs on what time of day or night it was wherever you came from on Earth. At least that's how you start off. For the first few days, you actually know what time of day it is back there, and you imagine all the people you know doing things they normally do at that time of day. Then after a few weeks it starts to slip, and after a couple of months you're lucky if you even know if it's day or night. That is without checking the instruments, which is cheating. It didn't count if you checked the instruments. He was so exhausted he felt half drunk. Locking his fingers behind his head and turning his bloodshot eyes up to the ceiling, he let out a huge yawn. What was important was to try to keep it straight in his head. Even if he was wrong, it kept things from getting too monotonous and running all together into one long, unending night.

"You talking to me, mate?" asked Tony, absentmindedly, in his unmistakable London accent. He stopped tapping on the face of the meter, convinced it wasn't sticking, and made the proper check mark on his clipboard. He had heard Lou perfectly well, but it was a little inside space joke. After all, when there are only two of you in a spaceship and the other guy asks a question, he had better be talking to you.

Lou grinned with his sarcastic, lopsided smile. "If I'm not talking to you, you'll probably get some kind of medal when we get back for flying halfway across the Solar system and back, locked in a tin can with a madman."

"With a dead man, you mean!" scowled Tony. "I'm not putting up with that bollocks. So help me, Lou, you go stark raving bonkers on me this early in the game, I'll just kill you right quick and put us both out of our misery."

Lou rubbed the grayish brown stubble on his chin and looked up at the ceiling as if recalling something.

"You know, Tony," he said after a short pause, "when they told me the co-pilot on this mission not only held impressive credentials as a laser-physicist but was an M.D. as well, it gave me kind of a reassuring sense of security." Lou looked down dejectedly at the desk and shook his head. "With that last comment of yours, I'm afraid that feeling has faded."

"Are you implying my bedside manner is lacking?" asked Tony.

"Lacking?" said Lou. "No, it's not lacking...it's missing! I thought doctors were supposed to be kind, caring, sympathetic souls. You know, all that Hypocritic stuff."

"That's Hippo*cratic*, you twit!" Tony said with a frown. "And just what do you think now?"

Lou leaned forward on the desk, looking into the passageway at Tony. The light Tony was partially blocking fell across Lou's ruggedly handsome face as he leaned into it, the shadows creating a sinister effect. "I think, my dear Englishman, that if I took a closer look at your family tree, I'd probably find Jack the Ripper hanging from it."

Tony, clutching at any form of entertainment he could get out in space, happily played along. He put on his best stunned face and responded with, "Well, I'm insulted I tell you...absolutely insulted!"

"Okay then, will you please get your insulted ass out of the hallway and out of my light so I can see what I'm doing," Lou responded.

"Aren't you the bleedin' romantic!" Tony said with a smirk.

"I'm not even a healthy romantic," said Lou, turning his chocolate eyes back to his tablet screen.

"You are too a romantic," insisted Tony. "Case in point: you just called this a hallway. Hallway? What hallway? Here I am, standing in a narrow slot between piles of bloomin' apparatuses blinking away at me, and you call it a hallway!" Tony shouted, his neck breaking out in red splotches as it always did when he lost his temper.

Lou turned his face slightly away from Tony to hide a grin. He'd done it, now. And he was glad. He loved sending Tony over the edge. It was much more entertaining than any movie or video game he had stored on his computer. Like lighting the fuse of a firecracker, there was no turning back once you ignited Tony. There was nothing to do now but sit back and enjoy the show.

Tony was already off. "Just where do you think you are, anyway?" he was saying, "back in your split level California condo with your two kids and a three-and-a-half car garage?"

"That's three-and-a-half kids and a two-car garage," Lou retorted. "And I don't live in California."

"Don't be ridiculous…all Americans live in California. Everybody knows that," Tony quipped.

Lou stifled a laugh and stared calmly at his tablet—which made Tony even crazier. "Not me…I'm from New Jersey," he said casually.

"New what?" asked Tony.

"Jersey," repeated Lou. "New Jersey." "Bunch of bloody thieves at that," Tony mumbled.

"Wait…what?" Lou said, looking up.

"You stole it, you know," Tony complained. "Stole what…New Jersey? Well, if it was Britain's, you can have it back," said Lou, decidedly. "And New Jersey, is it?" snapped Tony, his accent growing thicker with each comment. "A lot of nerve, you Yanks! What was wrong with the old Jersey? You know, there's this island we've got in the Channel called Jersey. Been called Jersey for millions of years, sittin' there doing quite fine, 'til you blokes come along and filch its name."

Lou was enjoying this. "Don't look now, Tony, but your Cockney's showing," he hinted.

Tony ignored him and continued his rant. "Now you've got to have a New Jersey. Matter of fact, *our* Jersey had been sitting there doing just fine up 'til you stole your whole damn country from us!"

"Who, me?" said Lou, attempting to mask his amusement. "I never stole anything in my life."

Tony kept going. "It wasn't right. That should have been ours. If you Yanks hadn't been so damn impatient, that silly country of yours would be part of the British Empire!"

Lou turned back to his tablet and started typing. "Yeah, I know. It was a real shame to have missed out on all that bankruptcy." Lou knew that was a good shot and braced himself for Tony's return fire.

"Well, if you damn colonials are so fabulously resourceful, why couldn't you come up with a more original name for the place where you live other than New bleedin' Jersey?" blurted Tony.

"Settle down, buddy," Lou said steadily. "If there's anything worse than being cooped up with a raving madman, it's being cooped up with a raving Englishman."

"We'll see who's mad when we get to that rock called Titan," Tony challenged, bobbing his carrot-topped head from side to side. "I still say all we're going to find left of that Polarizer Project is a bloody big hole in the ground!"

"Well, at least that will prove it works," smiled Lou, as he stood up from his seat and pushed past Tony to head for the living quarters.

"That's not funny," said Tony, talking to Lou's back. "But if it's any consolation to you, those poor bastards probably did get it working and polarized the daylights out of themselves!" He paused, glancing down at his clipboard. "Bloody Ray-Gun," he continued. "What's wrong with a shovel, anyway? It was good enough for my great-grandfather. He worked in the coal mines, you know."

Lou looked over his shoulder at Tony. "Well, working in the coal mines was good enough for your great-grandfather, but I notice you didn't choose to follow in his footsteps."

"The hell I didn't!" Tony shouted. "I may be standing here in your imaginary hallway, halfway to Saturn, hundreds of millions of miles from anywhere, but for all that, where am I headed? A bloody mine!"

Lou snickered as he grabbed a towel and a bottle of shampoo from a panel in the wall near the living quarters.

"Be careful of that stuff, mate," said Tony, pointing at the bottle with a grave face. "Especially out here in space. No telling what might happen."

Lou paused. He knew he was being set up, but he had to ask. Tony's stories were some of the strangest tall tales he'd ever heard. "What are you off about now, Tony?"

"Didn't I ever tell you about what happened at me girlfriend's flat?" asked Tony, raising his eyebrows.

"Nope," said Lou. He figured this would be interesting.

"Ah! Well, you had better read the ingredients on that bottle, mate, before you go uncorking it out here," he warned. "One day, I'm at my lady's place and I decide to take a shower to freshen up a bit, you know. To get in the shower, I have to climb over all these damn plastic bottles with no tops, and they're all scattered round the edge of the tub, see. I just want some damned shampoo, so I'm picking up all the bottles and finding conditioners, pre-conditioners, rinses, pre-rinses, all this special stuff that takes the oil out of your hair, other stuff that adds it back in; one adds life, another adds body.

"Finally, I find the shampoo; but it's not just any shampoo, oh no, it's *much* better because it contains amino acids, it says on the label. 'Amino acids?' says I. 'That's the basic molecular building block of living matter from which cells form. What are they trying to do, wash hair or *grow* it?' Well, in the excitement of the moment, I slip in the tub and drop the shampoo bottle. It hits the other bottles and they all dump out together into the tub in a big swirling mess. It bubbles up 'til the suds fill the tub. Next thing I know, some creature comes climbing out of the suds, says his name is Rodney. I don't know what the bloody hell it was…but I can tell you this. It had great hair!" Beaming from ear to ear, Tony waited for Lou's response.

Lou just shook his head with a quiet chuckle and ducked into the living quarters.

CHAPTER FIFTEEN

Bad to Worse

The night rain streamed across the windshield as Driscoll drove home alone. He decided not to use the limo and the driver today because he needed to think, and he found it easier to contemplate with his hands gripping a steering wheel. As he gazed ahead at the dark road glistening in his headlights, the patter of raindrops on the roof and the steady rhythm of the windshield wipers helped him concentrate.

The trouble with riding home from work in the limo, he thought, is that the next morning it would be there to take him back. And if the limo were out there waiting in his driveway at seven o'clock sharp, Driscoll wouldn't be able to talk himself out of going to work tomorrow.

In fact, if Carol was agreeable—and why not, she'd been after him for months to get away with her—he was seriously thinking about taking a short vacation. Why did that seem so indecent? He shouldn't feel bad about it... Shit, they really needed a vacation.

A tropical getaway might be just the thing to lift Carol's spirits, he thought with a pang of sadness. Of course, from the outside looking in, he and Carol seemed like a perfectly happy couple...and for the most part, they were. After their wedding nearly eight years ago, they had purchased a luxurious West Hollywood mansion complete with five thousand exquisite square feet, marble floors, a gourmet kitchen, and an oversized heated pool. But their lavish home was lacking the one thing that Carol wanted most: the pitter-patter of little feet. For years, the couple had been struggling to have a baby, and Carol had dabbled in everything from acupuncture to fertility drugs. But nothing worked. Although Carol had never shed a single tear over the matter, at least not in front of Driscoll, he knew she was heartbroken. For the past couple of months, she had thrown herself completely into her work—a distraction tactic. Dammit, she needed a break. Maybe if they just got away for a few days…

But for some reason, the thought of sipping cocktails on a pristine beach while the rescue ship approached Titan made him feel guilty as hell.

Well, there was nothing he could do for them. Nothing at all.

The rescue ship—who were they kidding calling this a rescue mission—wouldn't return from Titan for almost a month. And if he spent the next four weeks pacing his office floor and wringing his hands, he'd be talking to a basket of fruit in a padded room by the time the ship returned. Anyway, he knew they wouldn't hear any new news until after General Hodge and his team had finished sifting through everything they brought back.

There was even less he could do about this now than when General Hodge had given him some other disturbing news over a year ago. "The mining aspect of the operation is being put on hold for a while," the general had informed him matter-of-factly.

The mining aspect? Just what the hell was this operation if not a mine? Wasn't that the whole point of Project Pipeline? And anyway, they couldn't just put it on hold like a damn phone. Maintaining a major mining operation over eight hundred million miles away only worked if everything happened right on schedule, and putting things on hold was not part of the plan.

When Driscoll raised these issues with Hodge, the general gave him a simple two-word explanation: "Medical reasons." That was all Hodge would—and *could*, he swore to Driscoll—say about the matter.

"It's the Polarizer, isn't it?" Driscoll guessed.

But the general had remained tightlipped. "I am not authorized to give specifics," he said shaking his silver head. "I'm sorry, but I'm not at liberty to say more right now."

"What a load of bullshit," Driscoll said aloud to his empty car, his blood boiling as he glared at the slick road ahead. "If they can't even tell me, the guy who's running their damn mine, then who *can* they tell?"

Driscoll tried to relax, loosening his tight grip on the steering wheel. Rehashing all this in his mind wouldn't do any good. At the time, he figured he'd hear about the Pipeline Project medical issues on the news before anyone told him about it. But he didn't. In fact, he never found anything more than a short press release buried on some obscure website announcing that the mining operation on Titan was being "temporarily delayed for technical reasons."

That didn't sound so bad if it was said fast enough. Of course, the mainstream media was too busy covering yet another celebrity drug overdose or the latest politician's scandalous affair to pay any attention to a mining operation on Titan. Driscoll figured the majority of folks had never even heard of the Pipeline Project anyway.

After Hodge gave him the on hold news, Driscoll contacted the folks at National Dynamics, the contractor that would eventually convert the ore to metal and deploy it. But even Pete Teegan, the head of the company, claimed to know no more than Driscoll did. They weren't quite as upset over there, considered Driscoll, since their phase of the operation hadn't really begun yet.

This was more like in limbo than on hold. He didn't know what to think or which way the project was going. Most of the Driscoll Mining people were sent back home immediately. But according to the ones who had returned, there was still something underway on Titan…some kind of work or tests.

Driscoll hadn't heard much else after that—not until today. Today he had learned that things had suddenly gone from bad to worse. In fact, things couldn't get much worse. "We've lost all contact with the operation," General Hodge had informed him solemnly over the phone. "A rescue ship is on the way to Titan."

At least now he knew which way the Pipeline Project was going. He swung the car into the long driveway leading up to his massive home. Straight to hell.

He pulled into the garage and shifted his thoughts to Jamaica, imagining the picturesque villa he and Carol liked so much. A memory of his wife in a tiny green bikini with her beach-tossed red hair shimmering under the sun brought a smile to his face.

As he put the car in park, something on the local radio station, which he hadn't been paying attention to until now, suddenly caught his ear. He could have sworn the reporter had just said the words, "General Raymond Hodge…" Driscoll turned up the volume and leaned forward in his seat, the color draining from his face as he listened.

Chapter Sixteen

KUX Radio, Twelve Miles Away

The place was so boring at night. Then again, George enjoyed working at the station when it was quiet. During the day, all the sales people got on his nerves. Stifling a yawn, he pushed down a slider on the soundboard with his left hand. At the same time he was increasing the volume on an identical control, a little farther down the board, with his right hand. As the music faded and the news jingle came up, the bright green digital lines on the VU meter at the top of the board lined up perfectly in the middle.

Damn, he was good. He had perfected this art because he'd been doing it at stations just like this one up and down the west coast since he got out of the Navy. Before he deployed to Iraq, George received electronics training, and he considered himself lucky. Most of his buddies, at least the ones who survived the war, came home with nothing—except for maybe a brand new prosthetic limb or a nasty case of PTSD. At least George had learned a useful skill. Working in radio stations hadn't made him rich, but it kept him employed and he enjoyed it.

That's why he took it so seriously when things got screwed up. Especially if it was a programming screw-up and not an engineering mistake—the programming stuff was completely out of his control, but it made him look bad when things went wrong. And tonight, something told George things were about to go wrong.

He quickly glanced around. There were only three of them in the station, as was usual for this time of night. It was just himself, DJ Bobby, and the newsman…er, newswoman. He was never exactly sure what to call Gwen, the tall, thin rocker-looking chick with short blonde hair.

She always wore chunky high heels or knee-high boots with a mini skirt and a mid-drift bearing shirt—black being the predominant color in her wardrobe—and her tiny diamond nose ring sparkled under the studio lights. More like news-hottie.

He watched Gwen slide into the chair with her hourly five-minute world and local news report as DJ Bobby exited the studio. The studio had its own board of course, a newer one, but George liked to run his own from the outside when he was there. That way, all the talent had to do was talk.

In his soundproof engineering booth with his headphones on, he hadn't heard the news bulletin alarm that sounded during the news intro. It was the look on DJ Bobby's face that tipped George off to the impending screw up.

Bobby Rooney never got excited about anything.

In fact, George had never seen Bobby when he wasn't either hung-over, stoned or sound asleep. But without fail, when the on-the-air light came on, Bobby came to life. He was an awesome radio personality that all the listeners adored. He must have had some kind of multiple personality disorder.

But now, even though he was off the air, Bobby looked positively alert. With a small piece of paper in his hand, he barged back into the studio and handed it to Gwen, the news reporter. That was it. She liked to be called a news reporter.

Suddenly Gwen and DJ Bobby ran out of the studio toward the newsroom. George leapt up from the board, his eyes opened wide, as he watched through the glass. "The intro's almost over...where the hell are you going?" he said out loud, although he knew they couldn't hear him. Then Gwen ran back in the studio holding the same piece of paper she'd run out with, but Bobby stayed behind in the newsroom. The news intro ended with the required fanfare, George turned up the studio mike, the on-the-air light flashed on...and nothing happened. Silence. George looked up from the VU meter, which should have been bouncing with the words: "Good evening. For KUX Radio, I'm Gwen Jones, and here is the news." Instead, at the end of the jingle, the meter just dropped back to zero like somebody had shot it.

But it wasn't an engineering malfunction. Gwen Jones just wasn't saying anything.

She seemed to still be reading the slip of paper. When five seconds of silence in the real world goes by you rarely notice it, but five seconds of dead air on a radio station seems to last forever. How long can it possibly take to proofread a half page of paper anyway? "Say something, blondie!" George yelled so loud in his soundproof booth that DJ Bobby heard him all the way down the hall in the newsroom.

Gwen looked up and through the two slanted panes of glass that separated the studio from the engineering booth. She looked at George, then back at the paper, then back at George, then at the microphone that she seemed to notice for the first time.

"Uh…I've just been handed a breaking news bulletin…" she began awkwardly.

He had to admit that Gwen was one of the better small station news reporters he had encountered in his career. In his opinion, she was usually extremely professional and smooth. She had a definite future in this business, George figured. In fact, she was probably good enough to make the switch to television news, which he assumed she was aiming for. Of course, she'd have to lose the nose ring.

"This is Gwen Jones for KUX Radio," she began again, remembering the routine. "We have just received a news bulletin from The Associated Press." Then she looked down at her paper and read: "General Raymond Hodge of the United States Defense Department has confirmed to reporters that the U.S. radio telescope installation on the moon has received communications from…an alien source." She paused and swallowed, as if those last three words took an extra effort to say. She continued, "General Hodge made this admission at a news conference held in Washington tonight, concerning the controversial Pipeline Project, after a reporter from the Washington Post presented a document citing multiple contacts." She paused again. Then she added, "We'll have more details as they become available. For KUX Radio, this is Gwen Jones."

If it had not been for George's completely automatic response there would have been more dead air. But without looking, his hand reached out and pushed a button and a sixty-second PSA began. Something from the Humane Society about spaying your cat. It wasn't supposed to be funny, but it sounded absurd following that last little item, George thought absentmindedly. He was staring into the studio. Gwen Jones was staring at the five-minute world and local news report she was still holding in her other hand but had forgotten completely about. It now seemed like so much senseless drivel. She tossed it into the wastebasket.

Twelve miles away, Jeff Driscoll sat back in his leather car seat and began to consider the implications of what he had just heard. A lot of things started to fall into place in his mind, but he decided to go inside and tune into CNN before he got himself too worked up.

He climbed out of the car and raced into the house. It was late, and the house was silent. Carol was probably already asleep in their bedroom upstairs. Driscoll crossed the vast living room, grabbed the remote from the coffee table and pointed it at the huge flat screen hanging over the fireplace. The very first image he saw was a reporter standing in front of the White House, cupping his hand to his ear as people scurried by with microphones and cameras. When he saw the subtitle, "Alien contact!" Driscoll knew the local radio report had been no hoax.

Well, it was out. He slowly walked to the room's huge bay window that overlooked the expansive front grounds of their home. He stood with his hands on his hips and looked up at the night sky. The rain had stopped, and the clouds were quickly parting, creating small openings where he could see the pinpricks of light appearing—the same stars he had contemplated millions of times before. "What the hell is going on up there?" he whispered, fogging the window glass with his breath.

The stars said nothing.

CHAPTER SEVENTEEN

Eight Hundred Million Miles Away

At the precise moment that Driscoll was staring up at the stars from his living room window, eight hundred million miles above Tony and Lou were throwing switches and pushing buttons on the rescue ship. The two men tried to relax as the ship began its mostly automated descent to Titan, which appeared to be bright orange from this distance.

"How's your stomach?" asked Tony.

"Fine," Lou answered. "Anyway, it should be a smooth touchdown."

"That's not what I mean, mate," Tony said. "I mean, whatever we find down there, it ain't going to be pretty."

Lou took his mind off the landing process for a moment. "Oh," he said stiffly, anxiously rubbing his face stubble. "If you're asking if I'm gonna be at ease around a bunch of corpses, then the answer is no. But I'll be alright…thank you for your concern, Dr. Death."

"Lucky for us, there's sure to have been no air in there since the poor bastards…" Tony trailed off, turning his pale, freckled face toward Lou. "Well, you know."

Lou hadn't thought about it before, and he wished he wasn't thinking about it now. But a small dome filled with seventeen dead men and air for this long would be particularly gruesome. He supposed if he had to deal with HR's (or Human Remains, as they were officially termed) that the all-preserving vacuum of space was, in this particular case, a major point in his favor. And he was glad it would be the men with the follow-up mission who would actually have to examine the bodies and possibly bring them back to Earth. All the way back with a load of HR's. That was a long trip. But at least those guys would have a bigger ship.

"I mean," Tony continued, "even if life support was still functioning when whatever happened happened, it probably only kept working for a day or so before it conked out, because you know...no one was around to keep the bloody thing running."

Lou refused to sit there and try to figure out just how much a dead guy could rot in a day and said, "Could we please change the subject? Let's think of something more cheery, like our chances of being bashed to bits in the next few minutes."

"Never happen, mate," smiled Tony as he patted the wall of instruments alongside his seat. "This crackin' beauty is still under warranty."

Lou relaxed a little and leaned back in his seat. "Well, whatever happens out there," he said, "we're going to do this quick. In and out. Those are our basic orders, anyway. Unless, by some miracle, we find anyone alive, we don't touch anything..." He paused and added, "Or any*one*, that we don't absolutely have to. Just collect all notes and computers and get the hell out of there."

"Alright, chap. And then back home we go," added Tony.

"Yep," agreed Lou, "then back home. And like the orders said, under no circumstances are we to remove our shield-suits," Lou quoted in a sarcastic tone.

"Now that was a brilliant bit," quipped Tony. "Just what the bloody hell do they think we're going to do...pop off our helmets for a nice, big breath of fresh vacuum? Even if there was any air, knowing the shape it would be in by now...I'd rather suffocate."

As the surface of Titan approached, Tony and Lou peered through the window of the small ship. They could just begin to make out the site of the mine. Not much of a mine, Tony thought. It was obvious that work had only just begun when it was halted. As the ship continued its descent, they could clearly see the two domes connected by a long tunnel. The smaller dome, they knew, had been the living quarters and the larger of the two was the laboratory, which also housed all the communication and life support facilities.

Now that the domes were in view, they knew three things for certain: there had been no miracle for the workers there, there certainly was no air left to breathe, and there was no "bloody big hole in the ground" as Tony had predicted. But there was a bloody big one in the lab dome.

Eight hundred million miles away, General Raymond Hodge sat in his office and waited for Tony and Lou's report.

CHAPTER EIGHTEEN

Titan

Outfitted in their unwieldy shield-suits, Tony and Lou stood at the air lock of the small ship. "You ready, mate?" Tony's voice crackled through the small speaker in Lou's ear.

"Ready as I'll ever be," Lou answered drily. He looked over at the glass face of Tony's helmet, but all he could see were the ship's instruments reflected back at him. Although he couldn't see his expression, Lou knew Tony was grinning ear to ear with his toothy British smile. Tony gave him a thumbs up signal with his stiff glove and shouted cheerily over the radio, "Tally ho, chap!"

Rolling his eyes, Lou pressed the red button next to the air lock, and the door slid open with a *whoosh*.

With only a few minor jolts and bumps during the landing, the ship's state-of-the-art computer had placed them only steps away from the large laboratory dome. Now, as the two men bounded gracelessly toward the dome's airlock entrance, Lou braced himself for what would be waiting inside.

"Bollocks!" Tony exclaimed over the radio. "I can barely walk in this bleedin' big suit."

Lou glanced from side to side and took in the ice-covered, rocky terrain of this strange moon. "Some hell of a place to die," he mumbled.

"What's that, mate?" Tony responded. "Nothing," Lou said as they took their final awkward steps toward the dome's airlock. When they reached the door, Lou pointed to the keypad. "What's the code?"

"Ah, yes," Tony's voice crackled. "Rupert, display Project Pipeline laboratory entry code," he ordered his suit computer.

"Rupert?" Lou asked. "You named your computer *Rupert*?"

"What?" Lou said defensively. "He was a dear friend of mine back in London." He glanced down at a tiny computer screen just below the glass face of his helmet. "Anyhoo, the code is 4-0-3-5-5-2-8."

Lou punched the numbers into the keypad, and the airlock door slid open, offering them entry into the dome. The two men glanced at each other through their glass helmets. This time, in the semi-darkness of Titan backlit by the laboratory's still-glowing lights, Lou could easily make out Tony's calm face under his shock of red hair.

"Okay, then," Lou said. "Let's do this." "Rightio, mate," Tony answered.

As soon as they passed through the airlock and entered the laboratory, Tony and Lou fell silent. Dead bodies were scattered throughout the dome. The corpses were shriveled and frozen—almost mummified—and their skin had taken on a gruesome gray hue. Noticing the gaping hole on the opposite side of the dome, Lou silently wondered just how long it took the workers to expire inside the airless laboratory once it had ruptured. He shuddered at the thought.

"I bet it was quick," he commented out loud. "Once that hole was blasted and the air escaped, they probably died within a matter of seconds... don't you think?"

Tony, completely mute for once, was too busy studying a body next to a nearby desk to answer.

"Someone you know?" Lou asked hesitantly.

"As a matter of fact, it's someone we both know," Tony said. "It's Dr. Klavin...and he looks like hell."

"Of course he looks like hell," Lou said, grimacing behind his glass helmet. "He's dead!"

"No, look at him, Lou," Tony said earnestly. "He looks...old."

Lou took a quick sideways glance at the doctor and noticed that only a few strands of white hair remained on his crinkly, liver-spotted head. He hadn't remembered Dr. Klavin being quite that bald and wrinkled, but he didn't want to come in for a closer look. "Yep, looks like a dead old man."

"No, you dozy wanker...you don't get it," said Tony, still inspecting Dr. Klavin's frozen face. "Come take a closer look..."

"Dammit, Tony," Lou snipped, as he bounded in the opposite direction. "I swear, I'm gonna blow chunks in my suit if you force me to get up-close-and-personal with a dead space corpse. You can brief me on Dr. Klavin's appearance later." Attempting to avoid contact with any other corpses along the way, Lou busied himself with collecting computer tablets and notebooks, most of which were still securely attached to counters and desks throughout the laboratory. When he had gathered every piece of physical data he could find, he made his way to the other side of the lab, where Tony was inspecting a row of mouse cages attached to a long, narrow counter.

"How did the rodents make out?" Lou asked, dodging a desiccated corpse resting just a foot from his boot. As he approached Tony and the cages, Lou decided he'd much rather take a look at a dead mouse that had succumbed to the vacuum of space than a human.

"Not bloomin' good, considering they're all belly-up," Tony said in an unusually serious tone. Lou looked and noticed that each cage held five or six dried up little mouse corpses. "But look here, mate," Tony added. "The little fellas in this cage have completely deteriorated."

Lou peered into the glass cage Tony was pointing to and saw nothing but a few bits of dust, bones and fur.

"Absolutely fascinating, Doctor," Lou said. "Now let's get the hell out of here. I've got all the tablets and notebooks, so our mission is complete… it's not our job to examine the bodies."

Tony reluctantly turned away from the mouse cages and gazed at the jagged, cavernous hole in the opposite wall of the dome. Right next to the punctured wall, a table had been upended and three broken chairs were scattered across the floor. Another shriveled, white-haired corpse lay right next to one of the shattered chairs. Tony bounded over and took a closer look at the body. "What the bloody hell happened in here?" he whispered pensively.

"Whatever the hell happened, there's no saving these poor bastards now," Lou quipped. "Now let's get back to the goddamned ship, Tony. Come on!"

As the ship lifted off, Lou and Tony braced themselves for the acceleration. Although it was supposed to feel unpleasant, Lou thought it was a welcome change from weightlessness. At least it made you feel sort of solid for a while, he thought.

After they were satisfied that the computer was taking good care of them and had properly aimed their ship back at Earth, Tony and Lou just sat for a few minutes considering what they had seen back in the dome.

"Well," said Tony at last, "was it everything you always dreamed of?"

"It wasn't even a nice place to visit," Lou answered.

"So you were disappointed?" Tony asked. "Now don't get me wrong," Lou said, "but I really did expect a bit more of a disaster. Most of those poor fellas looked like they didn't know what was happening. I know I don't have your practiced medical eye, Doctor…but it looked like they were fine one minute and dead the next."

"Lou, those blokes didn't look fine to me," remarked Tony.

"Most of them looked okay," said Lou. "Or at least they were okay until that dome blew, that is." "Rubbish. That bloody dome didn't just blow, Lou," Tony said seriously. "That was no accident, and you know it. From the looks of it, there had been some kind of struggle or an outright brawl in there. God knows why or what about, but maybe some of this stuff will tell us." Tony pointed to the stack of tablet computers that Lou had collected back in the dome. They were already transmitting the computer data back to Earth.

"Besides," Tony continued. "You can't tell me Dr. Klavin looked okay to you."

"Hell no, Tony. He looked dead," said Lou. "I know he looked dead, Lou. They all looked dead. But it was more than that." "Isn't that enough?" asked Lou.

"You saw him, Lou. He looked exceptionally *old*." Tony said the last word slowly and repulsively.

"He *is* old…*was* old," Lou corrected himself. "Dr. Klavin was older than the others, sure, but he wasn't that old, Lou…and you know bloody well what I'm talking about. I bet the chap wasn't a day older than 55. And his assistant, too…that Dr. Willerstedt. He also looked much older than I remember…and he seemed to be involved in some kind of fiasco in the lab when it blew. The poor bloke was right next to that damn hole, over there in the middle of all those broken chairs. And did you see those abrasions on his face?"

Lou looked at Tony but said nothing. He moved over to a pile of computer tablets on the circular desk and began to sort through them.

"And the mice," continued Tony. "Most of them looked normal...well other than being dead, of course. But there was that one cage. How could the bodies of those mice have deteriorated like that if there was no damn air in the dome?"

"Unless they decomposed before the accident..." Lou speculated.

"Don't be ridiculous," said Tony. "It would have taken them weeks to get to that state. And who the hell would keep a cage full of rotten rats around?"

"Nobody would," said Lou. "But I meant what if they decomposed like an hour or so before the accident?"

Tony stared at Lou. "You mean all at once," he said, horrified. "As if they went from healthy to decomposing in a bloody hour?"

"Well, you said it yourself, Tony. They couldn't have deteriorated after the accident because there was no air."

Tony contemplated this quietly for a few moments before adding, "And it couldn't have happened too long before the incident or we would have certainly been informed in the automatic telemetry transmissions of medical data...but we weren't." Tony paused. "Come on, mate. We've got a bloody dickens of a report to write up."

Some time went by in silence as they read through documents and notes on the computer tablets they had collected. But Tony couldn't stop thinking about the two old-looking scientists.

Suddenly, he put aside a notebook he had been paying particular attention to and asked with a note of urgency, "Quick, Lou, run that bit of yours by me again—about how the Polarizer works."

"What?" Lou was startled by the abrupt sound of Tony's voice. "Why?"

"About what it does to the rock," insisted Tony. "Well," Lou began leaning back in his seat, "the rock surrounding the allidium ore is highly magnetic but very brittle, and highly susceptible to electromagnetic manipulation. The Polarizer rearranges every molecule in this brittle rock into conflicting magnetic patterns. This causes stress between all points within the rock. As soon as the stress is established, which is instantaneous, the Polarizer reverses the pattern, and then back again, over and over. But all this happens in a fraction of a second. The effect is similar to bending a soft piece of metal back and forth until it breaks. Within seconds, the brittle magnetic rock pulverizes itself into dust. The allidium deposit is left standing free and clear," finished Lou. "But what exactly are you…"

Tony grabbed the tablet he had been reading and interrupted Lou. "Listen to this, mate." He read an excerpt from a file:

"Over-propagation of cells occurs only when the opposite poles of two or more cells interact at the molecular level.…causes can be chemical, such as glandular malfunction, or nuclear, such as electro-magnetic radiation. Blah, blah, blah… This is not normal in natural growth patterns where cell growth occurs at the biological level…therefore, preventing or stopping over-propagation of cells must take place at the molecular level."

"Wait, over-propagation of cells?" Lou asked, wrinkling his brow.

"Those blokes were playing with cancer, mate," Tony said.

"Playing with it?" asked Lou.

"Well, trying to cure it, I presume," Tony clarified.

"Cure cancer?" Lou blurted. "What, with the damn Polarizer? What the hell ever gave them the idea to do that?"

"They must have had a bloody good reason, Lou. After all, this was probably what halted the Pipeline Project. I bet it's all in these damned computer files someplace." Tony gestured at the stack of tablets. "You would think they might have bothered to tell us what the hell was going on up here before we left Earth," he added.

"Nobody ever tells us anything," mumbled Lou, thinking about the two ancient looking scientists in the dome.

"Well, somebody's telling us something now, mate." A chirp was sounding from the far end of the instrument panel, notifying them that they had received a message. Tony stood up, stretched, and walked down the passageway toward the ship's communications screen. It was the first message they had received from Earth since their lift-off from Titan. Purely routine. But it wasn't.

"Hey, Lou," Tony called loudly from down the hallway. "Who are the bleedin' Kabrini?"

CHAPTER NINETEEN

The Waiting Game, Washington D.C.

General Hodge was exhausted and knew he needed sleep, but he needed something else even more. He desperately needed every scrap of information that could be gleaned from the report that would be sent to his office within the next few hours. It wouldn't tell him everything he wanted to know right away, but it would tell him enough.

He had to come up with a date for the resumption of the Pipeline Project, and fast. He cursed the memo addressed to himself (which he had never even received) with the president's signature on it. The president's own damn signature, signed in real ink. He still couldn't believe it. Hindsight is no great asset, he knew, but you didn't have to be a genius to know that it was an idiotic thing for the president to do. Hodge figured that's probably why the president hadn't come down on him too hard about that embarrassing news conference.

Not for the first time did the general consider the possible political motivations for the "accidental" misplacement of the president's memo. After all, the general thought the president seemed too well organized and professional to have made a blunder like that. But the shit would all hit the fan eventually, and so it would be in the president's best interest to be able to claim in the next election that he wanted the people to know the truth. Was that what led to the untimely release of the memo?

The general didn't really trust any politicians, and he thought he had been in Washington long enough not to be anybody's pawn. But he kept forgetting how treacherous and cutthroat it could be in this Godforsaken town. General Hodge much preferred battle to backstabbing.

So now the public was pissed, and guess who they were pissed at? He frowned as he ran his hand through his silver hair. The press had quickly put two and two together, and they all came up with four million questions to ask him about the Pipeline Project—including the project's now obvious connection with the Kabrini contacts.

He heard the phone ring outside his private office. The intercom buzzed and his secretary's voice announced, "The president is on Line One, sir."

Shit. He quickly regained his composure and picked up the phone. "Hello, Mr. President," he said calmly. "No, sir. Not yet, sir."

He listened patiently as the president peppered him with questions from the other end of the line.

"Well, they don't have all the facts, sir," Hodge continued. "They don't understand. They think we've been sitting around on the goddamned moon talking to these Kabrini guys about the price of rice on Neptune or something. They don't know that we can't talk back yet. But the longer we keep that quiet, the better. Or at least"—he leaned back in his shiny leather chair—"at least until the Pipeline Project is back on line."

Hodge sat silently for a few moments before saying, "Okay, I will sir. Good evening, Mr. President." He hung up the phone.

Damn. He leaned forward, cradling his forehead in his hands. Another couple of months and they could have made the announcement as planned— after the means for two-way communication had been established or at least was well underway. The U.S. was certainly far ahead of anyone else's ability to establish that kind of intergalactic communication, and that's what mattered most. So far this operation had not become another Space Race, and the general still hoped to keep it from becoming one.

He heard the phone outside his heavy wooden office door ring again. "Mr. Driscoll on Line One, sir," his secretary chirped over the intercom.

"Poor son-of-a-bitch," the general mumbled as he hesitated to reach for the phone. Driscoll had been taking all of this rather well. He could have been another thorn in the general's side, but he wasn't.

The general finally picked up the phone. "Hello, Mr. Driscoll."

"No sir, not yet," he answered. "But any time now."

He nodded his silver head as he listened.

"Yes sir, I certainly will….okay then. Goodbye, Mr. Driscoll."

Just as the general started to hang up the phone, his secretary buzzed him again and said tersely, "Line Two, sir. It's Lunar-Comm."

The general fumbled with the phone and almost dropped it. He recovered the phone, put it back to his ear, and stabbed the button for Line Two. "This is General Hodge," he said anxiously. "Please go ahead."

There was a three-second round trip delay due to the distance between the Earth and the moon. But even this relatively short pause seemed to the general too long to tolerate right now.

Hodge squirmed impatiently in his chair until he finally heard the words, "We've begun receiving the computer data from the ship, sir. We're relaying now."

"Thank you," said the general, and once again he hung up the phone. He figured it would take about twelve hours to convert the digital data to humanly understandable information and get the pilot's report. So within twenty-four hours he would be able to make some hard announcements—and then finally, get some sleep.

Hodge pressed the intercom button and called to his secretary, "Kate, get me the president again."

"Yes, sir," her voice twittered. "Calling his office right now."

Chapter Twenty

Jamaican Getaway

Carol Driscoll sat on the veranda outside the bedroom of their private Jamaican vacation home. Perched regally on a mountainside, the stunning stone villa included a sprawling master suite, an indoor and outdoor kitchen, and a dramatic vanishing edge pool that appeared to dip off into the Caribbean below.

Carol replaced her coffee cup on the table as a tall, bronze Jamaican server refilled it.

"Thank you," she said, brushing a stray crimson wave from her freckled forehead.

"More coffee, Sir?" asked the Jamaican in his lilting accent.

"What?" said Driscoll, suddenly roused from deep concentration. "Oh, yes, please." He leaned forward in his chair and watched as the server carefully filled his coffee cup.

Carol adjusted her sunglasses and titled her face up toward the warm, tropical sun. This is nice, she thought to herself. We needed this.

As she directed her gaze toward the Caribbean, she said, "Now, that's what I call a view." She let out a long, relaxed sigh and watched a flock of Wave Runners flit across the turquoise-blue surface in figure eights, leaving a white trail behind them. From her vantage point on the side of the hill, they looked like talented water bugs putting on their daily early morning show. Of course, they were actually talented employees from a nearby hotel attempting to attract tourists to the water sports rental hut on the beach.

Carol looked across the table to Jeff, who was once again lost in deep thought. She admired her husband's ruggedly handsome face. Other than a few specks of salt and pepper in his thick brown hair and a couple of crinkles at the corners of his intense blue eyes, Jeff looked exactly the same as the day she'd first met him on this very Jamaican beach. Her heart swelled as she reminisced about that day. Somehow, it seemed like an eternity had lapsed since then—yet she could still remember every tiny detail as if it were yesterday.

Oh, excuse me, ladies...is this seat taken? Jeff's younger voice echoed in her mind. She remembered the way he ran his fingers through his unruly hair and flashed an adorable smile at her that scorching afternoon. He reeked of the previous night's alcohol, and she could clearly see that he was hung over as hell—but Carol didn't care. She found it somewhat amusing, charming even. From the moment Carol laid eyes on Jeffrey Driscoll, she was immediately magnetized to him...as if the universe was demanding that they would be together.

Snapping back to the present, Carol's face melted into a secretive little grin as she reached across the table to grab her husband's hand, which was hanging loosely in his lap. They'd been to hell and back during their long struggle to get pregnant, but she still loved him more than she could ever explain. She simply couldn't imagine life without Jeff.

Noticing his increasingly pensive expression, Carol felt certain that her husband was about to explain a great deal more about the Pipeline Project than she cared to understand just now—but after living with Jeff for nearly a decade, she knew this was a crucial part of his thinking process. Thinking out loud to Carol allowed him to organize his views, gain fresh perspective, and get things off his chest. Of course, she did have some questions about what had recently happened, but he hadn't been ready to talk about it until now. In fact, after his long phone conversation with General Hodge, Jeff had immediately picked up his cell phone and dialed their travel agent.

All Carol knew for sure was that the folks in D.C. had set a date for the resumption of work on the Pipeline Project—nearly a half a year from now. So they had almost six months to kill before Jeff would have to get personally involved with the venture again. Carol was glad he had decided to sort things out here in Jamaica, and she hoped he would take all the time he needed.

"The way I see it..." Driscoll broke the silence at last.

Carol poured herself another cup of stout coffee and reached for the creamer. She loved the rich, robust flavor of this local delicacy. She often bought the Jamaican brands at home, but they were never quite the same as the coffee they served at the villa.

Driscoll was sitting alongside the table looking toward, but not at, Carol was sure, the picturesque view.

"I saved them a lot of time," he continued. "They wouldn't have stumbled across their first Kabrini message for years without me."

Carol quietly sipped from her steaming cup and wondered where this was going.

"I'm the one who had the information from the Oracle…the celestial coordinates we found during our dig in Delos. The Oracle was carrying a message intended for any civilization smart enough to use it. It told of the Kabrini message and how to capture the signals in space. The Kabrini were broadcasting it even back then. Well, I mean the signals were reaching Earth even back then; who knows how long they'd actually been sending them. The Oracle's note gave the precise coordinates for where to aim our antennas to receive the message. I guess the coordinates must have been corrected for each planet the Oracle visited."

Driscoll paused and reflected for a moment. "Damn, at least I hope the poor thing got around the universe some before it got stuck on this rock."

Carol let out a nervous giggle before asking, "So was the Oracle one of them…a Kabrini?"

"I doubt it," Driscoll said, adjusting in his seat. He pulled off his sunglasses to wipe a bead of sweat from his furrowed brow, and Carol caught a glimpse of his squinted eyes sparkling in the sun. "I don't know who or what that creature was, or where it came from, but there are stars just a few light years away…although that's still too far for any kind of practical travel. Gregory believed it must have been in some kind of biological suspension for many years until it neared a planetary system. I wish Gregory had found something, *anything* left of the Oracle, so we could know for sure. But we found enough, I guess."

Driscoll paused as he slipped his sunglasses back over his eyes. "Anyway, with my coordinates, the Lunar dish installation immediately began picking up same batch of what appeared to be intelligently organized impulses, over and over. It didn't take long to translate because, along with the message, the Kabrini sent signals with every possible conversion key…a little cheat-sheet to help anyone easily translate it to their own digital computer language. So the folks at the Lunar station translated it…and the message told of an incredible network of solid rods in space, covering mind-boggling distances. According to the Kabrini, these rods…"

"Back up a bit, Jeff," Carol said, the sunlight glinting off her fiery red hair. She gently set her coffee cup on the table and leaned into her husband. "Exactly who are these Kabrini?"

Driscoll sipped his coffee. "At this point, maybe we should be asking, who *were* the Kabrini? The distances we're talking about are so immense, the signals that they are receiving now on our moon were first sent when… well, when our ancestors' idea of technology was a longer stick for knocking fruit out of trees."

Carol smirked at her husband's joke, but she still couldn't believe what she was hearing.

"So the Kabrini might not even exist anymore," he said, thinking about the Pipeline Project. "I guess we'll find out soon enough."

"Okay, so…who are—or *were* they?" Carol asked, absolutely engrossed now.

"Well, we're not sure," Jeff answered, placing his forearms on the table and making a little tent with his hands. "The word Kabrini is just the way it translates through our computers. We have no way of knowing what they really call themselves or exactly what form of life they really are. Not yet anyway."

He reached for his plate and picked absentmindedly at a small chunk of fresh pineapple. "But whatever they are, the Kabrini claim to have been in contact with other star systems for as long as they can remember, using this network. They also say they are not the only ones spreading the message…but theirs seems to be the only one we've come across, so far." After a short pause, Driscoll corrected himself. "Well, no, I guess the Oracle's message was the first, but it was pretty much meaningless at that point…people just weren't advanced enough to understand it back then."

"I wonder…" said Carol thoughtfully, allowing the almost overpowering presence of Jamaica to fade into the background of her awareness for just a moment. She pulled her sunglasses on top of her hair like a headband, sweeping her long wispy bangs from her green eyes. Looking intently at her husband, her porcelain forehead wrinkled slightly as she said, "Think about all those UFO sightings down through the ages. Maybe it was always the same message being sent by different species…in different ways. Maybe this is just the first one we've been able to interpret correctly."

"Wow…that's an interesting concept," said Driscoll, a little taken aback. He was always impressed with his wife's ability to quickly absorb complex information and then introduce a fascinating new perspective he'd never imagined. "That's entirely possible," he added, raising his eyebrows above his sunglasses. "Anyway, so the Kabrini claim that this network of rods exists all through space between star systems suspected of having, or someday having, life supportive planets."

"Did they put the rods there themselves?" Carol interrupted. "The Kabrini, I mean?"

"Probably not," said Driscoll. "According to them, the network has always existed. At least 'always' is how the word translated…but come to think of it, I'm not really sure exactly what they meant by that. They also said the network is 'always' expanding." Driscoll paused a moment, rubbing a whiskered cheek with his tan fingers.

"It seems," he continued, "that the Kabrini believe space travel involving thousands of light years is, was, and always will be completely impractical for living beings. And as far as we've ever been able to prove, they're right. Shorter distances, like a few light years, may someday be possible for us. But even that's pushing it. That's probably what the Oracle was doing; just cruising the neighborhood. But the Kabrini are talking about distances of galactic proportions, maybe even intergalactic."

"Well, they should know, I guess," said Carol. "But then, who could have accomplished such an enormous feat?"

"God only knows," said Driscoll. "The universe is so old we can scarcely imagine the countless civilizations that may have come and gone before our Sun even existed. We've always believed there must be other folks scattered throughout our galaxy. And what the Kabrini Message is saying is that although they can't visit yet, they can talk. Well, not exactly talk, but exchange information—and just think of the things we could learn from an ancient, advanced civilization like theirs!"

Driscoll leaned back in his chair, locked his fingers behind his head and looked up at the seemingly endless blue sky. As a single puffy white cloud floated directly overhead, his mind went spinning back to his childhood and college days, back to the countless hours he spent gazing at this same sky, contemplating the stars, feeling—no, *knowing*— that some other species was out there. And somehow, deep in his bones, he'd always felt like it was his duty to confirm it.

Carol eyed her husband as he stared up at the sky, and she realized that he was a hair's breadth away from realizing his lifelong dreams. He was meant to do this. Maybe it was a good thing that they'd never had a child, she considered a little sadly. Maybe a baby would have slowed him down, gotten in his way.

Jeff suddenly sat upright and leaned against the table again. "The catch is, we're responsible for constructing our own link from a point in space near Earth, out to the nearest rod—which is certainly no stone's throw away, but we can do it."

"And then what? We sort of tap into it, like a phone line?" Carol asked. Her cup of coffee sat untouched in front her. She was too engrossed in Jeff's explanation to even reach for it.

"Something like that, I suppose," Jeff answered. "We'll find out exactly how it's going to work when the Barge gets there." After a short, thoughtful pause, he added, with just the slightest trace of disappointment, "But that will be a couple more years from now."

"I don't get it," Carol was saying, idly replacing a spaghetti strap of her flowered sundress that had slid down her freckled shoulder. "If these people could come from so far to put this rod in place, why didn't they drop by Earth…or at least leave a note?"

"No, they were never here," Driscoll answered, staring out toward the small waves gently lapping at the powdery white beach. "Whoever started this incredible work apparently did so from some central point, probably hundreds or even thousands of light years from here. We think from that location, they extended these rods out in all directions. It probably took billions of years—which seems fantastic to us, but it's a blink of an eye in the life of a universe."

Carol could hear the passion and curiosity in her husband's voice… she had never seen him this spellbound.

"And as far as them leaving a note," he continued, looking over at his wife, "well, that's exactly what the Kabrini Message is. It's sort of a 'To Whom It May Concern…please pick up the damn phone!'"

Driscoll sat back in his chair again, looking out at the Caribbean. A cruise ship was ambling into view on the horizon, but Carol figured he didn't really see it.

"So that was the real intention of the Pipeline Project all along?" Carol asked, fiddling with a napkin on the table. "To make this connection to the Kabrini signals? Sort of like hooking up to a party line? Wow…Party line…Now there's a throw-back"

"But that's it exactly," said Jeff. "But the only way we could get the project underway, before the rest of the world found out what was going on, was to use the Polarizer…which still had a few bugs in it, I guess."

"Bugs?!" remarked Carol, her eyes widening as she glared at her husband. "Don't you think that's a bit of an understatement, babe?"

"Maybe so," he said, displaying a small grin for the first time all day. "Really, it's pretty damn ironic. The General's 'Fountain of Youth' turned out to be one of the most horrific ways to kill yourself anybody has ever dreamed up."

"Good God," Carol said, her voice trembling. "What exactly did it do to those poor men?"

"Well, it certainly didn't cure cancer or extend life. It just enhanced cell growth—which basically simulated almost perfect health for a few years. Of course they soon learned that eventually, the Polarizer does the same thing to living tissue that it does to the rock…it disintegrates it. But exposure takes a few years instead of just a few seconds to destroy a human—or any living tissue, for that matter. That's why their test mice lived three years longer than they should have—it almost doubled their lifespan. But suddenly one day, poof! The poor little rodents disintegrated."

Carol slowly shook her head, and looked down at her hands.

"Unfortunately, in the early days of testing, Dr. Klavin and his associate, Dr. Willerstedt, were exposed to the Polarizer, but they didn't experience any negative effects. Well, not in the beginning anyway. What we've learned since then is that in humans, the brain cells are the first cells to go—and it happens fast."

"H-how did they figure *that* out?" Carol asked in an unsteady voice.

"Well, the Brass believe that Dr. Klavin…" "The Brass?" Carol interrupted.

"The military officials—General Hodge and his minions—they believe that Dr. Klavin knew what was happening but was able to control it for a while. I guess they read his journal entries, and they could tell that something weird was going on in the doctor's mind. His writings showed signs of paranoia, irrational fear, even multiple personality. But the other poor fellow, Willerstedt, apparently went full-blown postal—and in his wacko state decided to destroy everything in the lab."

"I'd say he did a pretty good job of it," Carol said dryly.

"Yes, he did," agreed Driscoll. "Knocked a hole big enough for a tractor trailer to drive through in that damn dome. So obviously…knowing what we know now…we'll be using robotics the next time around. The Polarizer has to be used, but not around people."

Driscoll squirmed in his seat with a scowl on his face, and reached for his coffee cup. All joking aside, Carol knew that her husband was haunted by the people who died up there on Titan. He had a tough exterior and certainly put on a good show, but she knew Jeff well enough to know he was deeply disturbed by those casualties as well as the sinister events that led up to that day. He'd mentioned to her a few times how terrible he felt for their families.

"Anyway," Jeff added, "thanks to that damn news leak, the word is out about the Kabrini Message, and the United Nations has gotten involved. So now this project is going to be more of a worldwide effort."

"What exactly does that mean?" asked Carol as she watched a young couple struggling to launch a kayak in the surf.

"That means that we pay for it, but the whole world gets the credit," he answered.

"So what else is new?" Carol said with a half grin. She paused for a moment, and glanced up at the sky. "But you know, that's probably what the Kabrini had in mind anyway," she said, thoughtfully. "It's not the kind of thing you should keep to yourself. After all, they want to be in contact with our entire species, our whole planet…not just one country."

"You're right," he said. "But the General couldn't resist getting the jump on everyone else…and I guess he accomplished that much."

With that enormous weight off of his chest, Driscoll sat back in his seat again—and this time, he actually took in the view. The Wave Runners continued to weave their patterns in the brilliant blue water, only not quite as elegantly now as some were occupied by rookie tourists. He glanced over at his stunning wife and truly saw her for the first time this morning. Carol had placed her sunglasses back over her eyes and was leaning back in her chair, dreamily twirling a ginger wave around her pointer finger as she admired the view.

Driscoll intended to fully enjoy this vacation—and maybe a couple more—before he resumed work on the Pipeline Project. He stood up from the table, stretched and said, "You ready for the beach, beautiful?"

Carol snapped out of her reverie and turned toward her handsome husband with a sly grin. "Later," she said smoothly as she stood, sauntered up behind Jeff, and wrapped her arms around his chest.

They discovered a new route to the beach, via the king-size bed in their private villa. The sand and surf could wait.

CHAPTER TWENTY-ONE

Saturn Space, Three Years Later

The Barge was immense. Not only in its linear dimensions (passengers had to drive, not walk, from one end to the other), but also in its sheer bulk. It required an extraordinary mental effort just to look at it and understand that it was a vehicle designed for space transportation. A ship. The human mind instinctively rejected the thought. It was just too big! It didn't even remotely resemble the romantically streamlined rocket ships and shuttles that everyone had grown accustomed to seeing in space.

Unlike those sleek ships, this vessel was born in space—and it would never have to negotiate a planetary atmosphere, thus completely eliminating any need for aerodynamic features. In less than a year, a team of the world's most brilliant rocket scientists, engineers, contractors and robots had designed and built the Barge from scratch, in orbit, far above the Earth's nagging gravity, where structural considerations of weight and stress could not dictate or limit man's creations. In space, size meant nothing. Nor did shape.

So the Barge looked like a truck—a mammoth truck. And it would fly about as well as a truck in the Earth's atmosphere, but this ship was never intended to accomplish that feat. The colossal space Barge was intended simply to move when pushed, in a more or less straight line, from here to there in space. And the two massive nuclear engines on either side of the ship gave it that push.

Its history-making journey had begun two years earlier when the giant engines nudged it gently out of Earth's orbit and toward Saturn—a billion mile trip. It would take another year to return to Earth's orbit. The UN had aptly named the Barge's revolutionary mission "Legacy."

The rear two-thirds of the Barge encompassed a gigantic ore-processing plant, and the front third of the ship contained a city. Covered by an enormous, multi-faceted Plexiglas dome, this sprawling residential and working area was affectionately called The Crystal City. The U.S. military officials in charge of this mission decided there was a psychological advantage to using the term "City," as opposed to "Barge." For the workers on board, the thought of spending the next three years on a barge was depressing. The Crystal City, on the other hand, sounded exciting, elite.

The Barge had been loaded with enough allidium ore to build a small moon. In the processing plant, the ore was being smelted down to liquid and would soon be shot from a nozzle in the rear of the ship at a speed exactly matching the forward speed of the Barge. The hot liquid allidium would freeze instantly in the icy cold of space, forming the rod—the rod that would allow mankind to communicate with the Kabrini.

Once its mission was complete, the Barge's speed would no longer be limited by the allidium rod ejector, so its return trip to Earth's orbit would be shorter—approximately one year. A few days earlier, the mine on Titan had been closed down, and the Driscoll Mining personnel were transferred to the Crystal City. For the next year, they would live there, along with the National Dynamics people and the UN personnel, bringing the city's total population to 306.

On this momentous day, things had reached a fever in the Crystal City. Workers were buzzing as they made the final preparations to begin the historic allidium ejecting process. Within the next few hours, if everything went according to plan, the rod would be complete—and the people of Earth would soon be in direct communication with the Kabrini.

The Barge lazed in its orbit around Titan, awaiting resumption of its journey. From one billion miles away, the world watched.

In California, Jeff and Carol Driscoll watched. In Las Vegas, Mondo watched. In London, Gregory watched. In Cairo, Mohammed watched. In New York City, Goldstein watched.

And in The Crystal City, Tony and Lou watched. Saturn retreated slowly from their view as the two men brought the Barge's massive engines up to full power.

"Well, this should be something," said Lou from the Pilot's seat, his eyes focused intently on the control panel. "I'd say a couple of dopes like us are pretty lucky to be a part of this moment in history."

"You're damn right, mate," replied Tony in his typical good-natured sarcastic tone, a smile plastered on his pasty freckled face. "Just think of it: clear across the solar system in a bloomin' big dump truck full of dirt. You can't beat that with a bloody stick!"

A billion miles away, Driscoll stood in the center of his family room, his whiskered face illuminated by the flat-screen TV on the wall. His icy eyes were intently focused on the image of the largest craft ever built by man, trailing the extruded rod behind it.

"Just think," he said, "Legacy is the first space effort—shit, really the first effort of any sort—involving *all* of mankind." He turned to Carol, who was standing ramrod straight next to him, her cherry lips agape as she watched the newscast in amazement. Driscoll grabbed his wife's delicate hand and gave it a little squeeze. "This is only the beginning," he whispered, a boyish grin spreading across his face.

PART THREE

The Crystal City

Six Months Later

CHAPTER TWENTY-TWO

Deep Space

Mark Ranier winced as he watched his shuttle, the last shuttle for the night, roar silently away without him. He turned from the portal near his station's air lock at the rear of the space Barge and headed for the lounge. As Chief Extrusion Technician, Ranier had enough clout to hold a Reserved Seat Pass on the shuttle back up front to the City—but apparently not quite enough for the shuttle to wait for him.

"Damn," he muttered. Now he'd either have to wait for the next shuttle in the morning or take the inside tram back. "All the way back," he thought. It was a boring and demeaning trip. He decided to take the shuttle in the morning, partly so that he'd still be here and still be mad enough to give the shuttle people some early morning hell. "After all," he thought, running his fingers through his overgrown brown hair. "I do have some seniority around here." Ranier had been with the Legacy project since its inception. He had helped design the extrusion housing for the rod, and Mr. Driscoll himself had picked him for this spot—and he had beat out plenty of competition, too; not only from the Driscoll Mining folks, but from the National Dynamics team as well. And besides, he had called the shuttle terminal earlier and left a message saying he might be just a few minutes late. "A lot of good that did," he thought with a childlike frown. "Typical."

It probably wouldn't have mattered much to him any other night; he'd spent plenty of overnights by choice here at the extrusion station. Oftentimes, he just didn't feel like traveling, by whatever method, all the way back to the City, just to go to sleep for a few hours, then get up and travel all the way back.

But that was before he had met Marla. She worked in the labs up in the Crystal City. Now, he would have to call her and cancel their plans for tonight. "What a damn SNAFU," he said aloud to absolutely no one. Even if he took the tram, he'd get back far too late to catch the movie they were planning to see with Barbara and Allen in the Crystal City Cinema. So he strolled toward the lounge, where he'd call and tell Marla to go without him. Of course, he knew she would say no. She'd probably say something like, "No way, Punkin' Pie" (He had once told her he thought pet names were silly. She wholeheartedly agreed, but ever since then, she'd made a point to come up with a disgustingly sappy new name to call him every day. It always made him laugh). "I'd rather wait and see it some other time with you." He smiled. She was like that.

Mark thought back to the morning when he'd first run into Marla—literally. He was walking side by side with Lou, completely engrossed in a captivating conversation about the Kabrini, when he bumped shoulders with Marla, causing her to drop an entire tray of test-tubes on the floor. Marla immediately squatted down and started scooping up the glass tubes, which had scattered across the hallway. "Oh shit," Mark said as he bent down to help her. "I'm so sorry."

"No, no, don't worry about it," she said in her distinctively throaty voice with just a hint of a Southern accent. "They're all empty, so there's no need for alarm. We're not all contaminated with the Bubonic plague or some other weird disease!" She released a nervous giggle as she glanced up at Mark, peeking over her black-rimmed glasses. As he handed a test tube to her, Mark finally caught a glimpse of Marla's enormous blue eyes—and for the first time in his life, he found himself at a complete loss for words. Assuming his silence meant he thought her plague joke was stupid, Marla quickly averted her gaze, blew a strand of hair out of her face, and got to her feet. Mark stood up too, and he now towered over Marla.

"By the way, I'm...I'm Mark," he finally managed to stutter. "I'm Marla," she said. Balancing the tray of test tubes on one hip, she held out a rubber-gloved hand to him. "I work in the lab, in case you hadn't guessed! I mean, I know the lab coat is quite fashionable and all, but I wouldn't necessarily choose..." her voice trailed off as Mark took her small, delicate hand in his big, strong one.

As they shook hands, he felt sparks fly through his fingers and all the way down to his toes. Marla was a gorgeous, petite creature with long, wavy black hair and skin so pale it almost appeared translucent. And Mark couldn't help but stare at those striking eyes again…two vast pools of such a calming deep blue that he wanted to dive in and take a swim. "She looks like a damn fairy," he thought. "Like a gorgeous, geeky fairy." Mark had asked her out on a date right then and there, and she'd accepted. They'd been together ever since—almost a year and a half now.

And now Mark was trapped in the extrusion station instead of sitting next to his beautiful girlfriend in the movie lounge, holding hands and munching on popcorn. "You should look for something closer," Marla had said just that morning over breakfast, as she straightened her glasses and flashed her quirky grin. It was a joke, of course. In the first place, when you're on a spaceship so far away from Earth that the Sun is just another star in the eternal night sky, there aren't a lot of other places to look for a job; and secondly, since Mark had been specially trained to maintain a device that is the only one of its kind in the entire…

Ranier interrupted his own thoughts, pausing to scratch a clean-shaven cheek. He wanted to say it was the only device of its kind in the Universe, but that was obviously not true. After all, here he was in the back end of the biggest spaceship man had ever imagined, designed for only one purpose: to smelt down a small mountain of allidium ore, extrude and deploy it as a solid rod through a vast distance of space, and then connect it with a recently discovered communications network of similar rods, stretching out to the infinite, put there some time ago by…somebody…with a device perhaps not unlike the one in his charge.

"Yeah, right," he thought to himself as he continued his slow stroll down the corridor. That idea, while comfortingly noble to consider, was a bigger load of dirt than the one they'd hauled out to the Terminal in the first place. He knew the civilization that had established this incredible network must be far advanced beyond this ridiculous flying dump truck and ore smelting factory, even with its state-of-the-art Crystal City up front. In fact, if the Kabrini were watching right now, they were probably getting a real kick out of this uncivilized show.

But on the other hand, the giant space Barge had done its job, and pretty damn well too, thought Ranier. And now, they were on the long road home. "If we ever make it back," Mark thought with a spasm of panic. He rarely let himself think that way, but he occasionally had a creeping feeling that the ship would not survive its long trip back to earth. There were so many dangers in deep space, so many things that could go wrong. Of course, as the Chief Extrusion Technician, Mark knew how to play the tough guy, and he always exuded complete confidence in front of his team and colleagues. He would never reveal this nagging fear to anyone… except for Marla, of course. For some reason, he felt comfortable sharing things with Marla that he wouldn't dare reveal to anyone else. On this strange ship in the middle of the deepest depths of space, Marla felt like home to him.

Passing another view portal, he paused. Mark preferred watching the stars from the Barge instead of the Crystal City. The City rotated on its single giant axis coupling, which connected the huge Crystal dome with the Barge. This was necessary to simulate gravity within the City, especially along the outermost edges where the gravity was the strongest; not quite as strong as Earth's, but not bad. It was there, along the edges of the dome, where the living quarters, entertainment and recreational facilities were located. The labs and offices occupied compartments in the inner sections of the City, where gravity was not quite as strong. In fact, some of the City's scientists had chosen to put a few specialized labs close to the center of the dome because of the almost complete lack of gravity there.

But the rotation of the City caused the stars to drift by in an endless procession. And while beautifully hypnotic, it definitely made it difficult to concentrate on any particular group of stars.

But because the Barge did not rotate, here the stars remained relatively stationary. They were inching slowly past the portal, of course, as the Barge's enormous engines pushed the ship forward, but this movement was barely perceptible to the human eye, due to the even more enormous distances involved.

Mark Ranier looked across that immense distance. "The Sun is getting brighter," he thought. And brighter meant bigger, and bigger meant closer. Closer to Earth. Closer to home. "Damn, it will be good to get back," he thought as he widened his amber eyes and peered out the window. Not that he minded life in the Crystal City. Nor did Marla. But he'd like to get back on solid ground, maybe ask Marla to marry him. And who knows? Maybe they'd even have a couple of kids one day.

They would be heroes when they got back, he realized. All of them. "Hell," he thought, "we're heroes already!" After all, the Legacy mission had been a complete success. They had made contact with the Kabrini.

And the world would never be the same.

Chapter Twenty-Three

Kabrini Communications

Jeff Driscoll sat on the edge of the black leather couch, pointing the remote at the massive flat screen TV on his living room wall. Carol was curled up next to him, her wavy hair pulled back in a loose ponytail, completely absorbed in a mystery novel on her e-book reader. After flipping through what seemed like hundreds of channels, Jeff finally landed on CNN, which was airing an update about the Kabrini communications project.

"The UN has confirmed that initial contact was made with the Kabrini after the space rod construction was completed in March," the attractive brunette anchorwoman reported, wearing a shockingly low-cut shirt and her most serious journalist face. "However, sources say the UN has exchanged only a handful of messages with the Kabrini since that time. A UN representative says they will release these messages to the public within the year. And now for the weather," she chirped, her face suddenly breaking into a playful smile. "John? What's up with that heat wave in the Midwest?"

"Bullshit," Driscoll muttered as he switched off the TV. Carol gently lowered her e-reader and raised a single red eyebrow at her husband. She knew he was growing increasingly impatient. It had been three months since the rod was completed and the UN had begun direct communications with the Kabrini…and Driscoll had not been involved in a single conversation.

He ran his fingers through the unkempt nest of his thick hair, which had grayed quite a bit in the past year, Carol noticed. She took one look at the purplish skin under his eyes and guessed that he probably hadn't slept in days.

"I know damn well that the UN's 'special team' of scientists, doctors, military officials and whoever the hell else they've got are holed up somewhere…and they're probably having a goddamned gabfest with the Kabrini," he said, glancing towards his wife. "Dammit, I'm the one who handed over the celestial coordinates and got the ball rolling on this entire thing. How the hell could they cut me out of the loop?"

Carol reached over and rubbed one of Driscoll's sturdy shoulders, wondering what she could possibly say to extinguish his fury.

"Have you heard from General Hodge recently?" she finally attempted in her most soothing voice.

"I've called the asshole's office every day for the past three months," Driscoll said. "He finally took my call last week and claimed he was trying to get me access to the SCIF."

"What's the SCIF?" Carol asked as she slid behind Driscoll and started to massage both of his shoulders, which felt like two taut cables.

"It stands for Sensitive Compartmented Information Facility," Driscoll replied as he allowed himself to relax just a little under his wife's touch. "Basically intelligence speak for a classified clubhouse…and this one apparently has a sign on the door that reads, 'No Driscolls Allowed!'"

Carol stifled a giggle as she firmly pressed the heel of her hand into Jeff's rigid muscle, attempting to grind away the tension.

"Ahh…that's good," he mumbled, and Carol felt his shoulders slacken a little. At that precise moment, Driscoll's smartphone burst into a ring. Carol felt her husband's shoulders immediately tighten at the sound as he grabbed his phone off the coffee table.

"Jeffrey Driscoll," he answered briskly. He remained perfectly still for a few moments as he stared intently at the floor. After what felt like an eternity, he grinned up at Carol, still perched on the couch next to him with an eager look on her face. "Who is it?" she silently mouthed.

Driscoll looked away from her and said into the phone, "Well, it's about damn time. Thank you, General. I'll meet you at the airport on Monday."

He gingerly pressed the End button on the face of his smartphone and slowly looked up at Carol. The boyish smile had returned to his face and his blue eyes glistened with what appeared to be tears.

"I'm in," he whispered. Carol just looked at him with a questioning face, not certain what he meant. "Carol, Hodge got me access to the SCIF!" She let out a burst of excited laughter and threw her arms around his neck. Driscoll picked up his wife and spun her around the room, as she shouted, "Welcome to the clubhouse, kid!"

Less than a week later, Driscoll found himself more than 6,000 miles away from his Los Angeles home as he and General Hodge approached a formidable building in the heart of Austria. "Welcome to the United Nations Office at Vienna," Hodge quipped. The general was looking quite distinguished as usual, clad in full dress uniform, his silver hair and brass medals glinting in the sun as he held open a huge glass door for Driscoll.

As they slowly made their way through the sprawling facility, Driscoll and Hodge stopped at eight different security checkpoints, where they were required to present their photo identification and passports. Each station was manned by an increasingly intimidating guard, who scanned their passports and IDs with a hand-held laser and then waited for approval from his desktop computer to give them access to the next part of the building. At each checkpoint, Driscoll was presented with a series of name tags and badges, which all jingled from his neck like a gaudy necklace. When they finally reached what Driscoll assumed was the back wall of the building, he glanced up at the general with a confused look and said, "Where to now?"

General Hodge gave Driscoll an arrogant little smirk as he flipped open a hidden compartment in the wall, revealing a key pad. "Now, we go underground," he said as he punched in a series of no less than fifteen numbers. A previously concealed door in the wall suddenly slid open. "After you, Mr. Driscoll," Hodge said with a smile as he stepped aside and held out an arm. Driscoll walked into the secret hallway and Hodge followed one step behind as the door slid shut with a *whoosh* behind them. They continued down the silent, dimly lit corridor for the length of a football field until they finally ran into another dead-end—but this wall held a conspicuous black box at eye-level. General Hodge flipped open the lid of the box, revealing another keypad. He entered another series of numbers and then placed his chiseled, clean-shaven face on a small chin rest at the front of the box. Driscoll stood with his mouth agape as he watched a red laser scan the general's right eye. "Access granted," the computer stated in a sultry woman's voice.

"You gotta be kidding me," Driscoll muttered as another hidden door slid open, revealing an elevator. "This shit is straight out of a movie," he said as he poked at the eye scanner box. Hodge breathed an annoyed sigh and nudged Driscoll into the elevator. "Come on, Mr. Driscoll…we don't have time for all the dramatics."

The general punched the only button on the elevator wall, the doors slid shut, and the small metal vessel started with a jolt as it began its descent. After they rode the elevator down for at least a full minute, the doors reopened. Driscoll followed General Hodge down one last dark hallway, which eventually opened up into a massive, windowless room illuminated only by a handful of desk lamps and the blue glow of computers. When his eyes finally adjusted to the low light, Driscoll saw that there were about a dozen men and women scattered throughout the room, each sitting in front of what appeared to be floating computer screens. The men and women could simply reach into the air and grab at these holographic windows to switch views and move images, maps and virtual documents to wherever they pleased, all while quietly barking commands at their individual computers.

"Show Kabrini Message number four, dated April fifth," Driscoll heard one woman drone to her computer. A window instantly appeared in front of her face, and Driscoll leaned over her shoulder attempting to read the words…but it was impossible to make them out from his angle.

"Come along, Mr. Driscoll," General Hodge said brusquely, grabbing onto Jeff's elbow like an impatient father guiding his mischievous child. "I'll take you to my office…you can read all the messages there."

Once seated in General Hodge's office with the door closed, Driscoll asked, "So your team has been communicating with the Kabrini for more than three months now?"

"Well, yes…sort of," Hodge answered as he shifted in his leather chair. "When communications first began, the Kabrini established certain… guidelines. And we of course agreed to follow those procedures."

"Well, that's not too surprising," Driscoll said leaning forward in his seat. "I mean, obviously, they are a much older, advanced civilization, far more evolved than humans. We have a lot to learn from them."

"Sure…and more importantly, we didn't want to piss them off right off the bat," Hodge said. "Computer on," he commanded, and a series of floating screens came to life in the space directly above his desk. Driscoll stood up and walked over to Hodge's side of the desk, where he could read the series of transcripts on the holographic windows. Driscoll quickly scanned the first message, dated March twentieth:

UN: *This message is for the Kabrini. We are the people of Earth. We received your recorded message from our moon and constructed the communications rod as directed. Do you copy?*

Kabrini: *This is the Kabrini. Hello people of Earth. We are listening.*

As Driscoll digested this message, he felt chill bumps rise up on his arms and legs. The room began to whirl around him, and he had to grab onto General Hodge's desk to keep his balance.

"So," Hodge continued, seemingly unimpressed. Obviously, the newness of mankind's ability to communicate with aliens had worn off for him months ago. "We quickly acknowledged that the Kabrini are the superior race, and we agreed to tell them some things about ourselves before we started asking about their civilization."

"Right, that sounds reasonable," Driscoll responded, still gripping the side of Hodge's desk as he scanned through the messages on the screen, his piercing blue eyes as wide as two dinner plates. He still couldn't believe what he was reading.

"So we started off with the basics, explaining the history of mankind, our anatomy, necessities for survival, etcetera," Hodge continued. He reached up with one sturdy finger and tapped the holographic screen hovering over his desk. That screen promptly disappeared, and another screen displaying a new series of messages materialized. "And then we moved onto, well…more cultural topics. We thought that our explanation of our social, political and economic structures would, if anything encourage helpful suggestions from them. But it seems they were disgusted by the fact that we are still a conglomeration of individual nation-states…"

"Yep, down here on Earth, we're still slugging it out with each other to be King of the Hill," Driscoll interrupted. Hodge shot him a dirty look for what he perceived to be a cheap shot at his chosen profession. "So in other words," Driscoll continued, ignoring the general's sneer, "Unlike us humans, the Kabrini have transcended the petty, bickering stage of evolution."

"Yes, something like that," Hodge answered, still looking annoyed. "Apparently, they're at the 'one big happy family' stage." Hodge didn't even attempt to hide his disgust as he rolled his steely blue eyes. He reached up, tapped the current screen to close it and grabbed a new window of Kabrini messages entitled, *Social and Economic Discussions, May.* Driscoll immediately devoured the series of messages as he half-listened to General Hodge's explanation of them.

"Anyway, as you can see here, when we explained that there were poor, desert countries, unable to grow enough food to support their ever-expanding population, they sent us information on converting the abundant sunlight in these desert areas to electrical energy to run pumps for irrigation."

"But we already know how to do that," Driscoll responded as he continued reading the screen.

"Right...and that's exactly what we told them. So they sent us information on small nuclear power plants to furnish energy to those remote areas..."

"But we already know how to do that, too," Driscoll interjected. He looked away from the holographic screen and stared at Hodge.

"Correct, and we told them that. So they sent us information on low cost housing and synthetic food production..."

"And you told them we could do that, too," Driscoll interrupted again. He was now sitting on Hodge's desk with his arms crossed and a worried look on his face.

"Right. So now...well now, they just want to know what our problem is."

Driscoll turned back to the screen and scanned to the middle of the page:

UN: *Yes, we already know how to produce synthetic food.*

Kabrini: *Then why are you not doing these things? Is there a problem? Or are you a stubborn, uncivilized race?*

UN: *We are not stubborn. This is just how things are set up on our planet. Each country on Earth is responsible for its own people. Of course, some countries help out other countries from time to time, but in the end, each nation is responsible for its own political, social, and economic systems.*

Kabrini: *How could you possibly have developed the technology for space travel and the ability to communicate with an advanced alien civilization and still be so socially primitive? How can you not care for your own people? Do you not realize that you are all connected?*

Beads of sweat had materialized on Driscoll's brow, and he quickly wiped them away with his sleeve. "So they basically perceive us as a race of high-tech barbarians."

"I think they believe we already know too much for our own good," Hodge answered as he absentmindedly tinkered with the Newton's Cradle on his desk. He lifted a shiny metal sphere on the far end and let it drop, and the ball made a clink as it knocked it into the sphere next to it. This set all five spheres in motion, and they continued to swing back and forth in a hypnotic, rhythmic dance as Hodge continued. "When we told them that we are still fighting wars, they were dumfounded. They say they're surprised we humans didn't annihilate each other ages ago. Frankly, I've thought the same thing many times before…"

"Okay…so where do we stand now?" Driscoll asked, looking back towards the floating screen. "Where is the most recent series of messages?"

"That's it," Hodge replied grimly. "Their last message to us is on the bottom of that screen."

Driscoll's eyes quickly skimmed to the end of the transcript, finally resting on the very last message, which was received more than two weeks earlier:

Kabrini: *Until you can prove that you are a responsible race, we will cease all communications with Earth.*

UN: *We assure you that we are a responsible race. How can we prove this to you?*

Kabrini: *You must make widespread social changes to improve your people's general situation. Remember what we have discussed. The answers are right before you. We will reestablish communications if and when you make these changes.*

UN: *If we cannot communicate with you, how will you know when we have implemented these changes?*

Kabrini: *We will know. We always know. Until then, farewell and good luck.*

When he finished reading, Driscoll stumbled to the other side of Hodge's desk and collapsed in the chair. His mess of brown hair was now drenched with sweat, and he cradled his head in his trembling hands. "So basically, we're not worth the risk to them."

"I guess not," Hodge answered matter-of-factly. "Or at least not until we make some serious global changes. And as you can imagine, the UN Council is not about to roll over that easily."

Driscoll breathed a shuddering sigh and looked up at the ceiling, his face completely drained of color. He could feel his lifelong dream slipping away, all because of something completely out of his control—the inferiority of mankind.

Chapter Twenty-Four

Danbury's Doom

A deafening explosion shattered the early morning desert air with a quick crack, followed by a long roar and a thunderous boom. To Professor Danbury, the earsplitting blast seemed indecent and obscene in this landscape that had lain undisturbed for hundreds of years.

The few diggers remaining on Danbury's crew applauded and cheered. They loved the thrill of explosions. Danbury hated it. But he looked on these detonations simply as a means to an end, just another tool at his disposal to help him unearth mysteries and legends and long forgotten truths; and bring to light—and to his pocket—the proof of things Modern Man now believed to be only distant echoes of ancient stories and dreams. Things that, while interesting to observe in a museum, were surely of no practical worth in a modern world.

But Danbury had a history of proving the world wrong over and over again. Thanks to him, museums around the globe now contained treasures of old that many archaeologists had formerly believed never existed. Professor Danbury, who often conducted years of tireless research and detailed analysis before each dig, was always confident in his theories and successful in his efforts.

But this find was to be more spectacular than any of his previous ventures. He didn't know exactly what form the object he sought would take. But he felt certain it was something that had been of great importance to people alive at the time—something that had impressed humans enough that the legend had survived the ages. But what exactly was it? Danbury felt sure he would know soon; and he believed this discovery could have a huge impact on Modern Man. Thankfully, the handful of diggers who remained, still loyal to him even after his cash had run out a week ago, could provide enough manpower for his final excavation.

Danbury had financed this little project himself. He felt he had no choice. He couldn't risk telling anyone what he was after. Not this time. Certainly not the University. There would be forms to fill out, approvals to obtain, too many questions, too many investigations, too many people involved. No, this was his. All his.

He was certain of the spot. He had paid a pretty penny to the Egyptian government for the map, which was really just one small piece of an enormous puzzle that only Professor Danbury's peculiar expertise could piece together.

Not far under the bottom of the crater left by the last and final explosion, he knew there would be a roof made of a dozen large tree trunks, still preserved by the dry desert sand all these years. And under that—Danbury's pulse quickened at the thought of its nearness—under that would be the tomb!

The tomb of precisely what, Professor Danbury had no real idea. Some kind of being ranging between a local shaman and a god—or something else, perhaps not of this Earth. The possibilities had cost him many sleepless nights in nervous anticipation.

But what Danbury really wanted was the object that had earned the being its reputation: the legendary Cat's Eye Crystal. And more importantly, he wanted whatever it was inside the crystal that had amazed and enlightened mankind in ages past.

Yes, he thought as he rubbed his gray, sand-dusted beard. Enlightened. That's the key word. Danbury's mind was haunted by images of the Cat's Eye Crystal and whatever magical item it held at its golden core. He had been studying and obsessing over renderings of the crystal in ancient scrolls and age-old archeology books for more than a decade now.

He and his chap, Professor Gregory, had discussed the Cat's Eye Crystal over a few rounds of scotch and brews just a few months earlier.

"It's a bloody myth, Danbury," Gregory slurred to him that evening at the local pub. "I mean seriously, mate…a crystal that makes people smart? It sounds like something the bloomin' Tooth Fairy would keep in her enchanted bag of tricks. Preposterous!"

"Oh, shut your gob, you blithering fool," Danbury answered, muffling a hiccup. "It's not the crystal itself that enhances one's intelligence. I believe it's whatever is hidden inside the crystal. The age-old legend says, 'Those who gaze directly into the pupil of the Cat's Eye Crystal will gain unparalleled wisdom.' So there must be something inside that crystal... something bloody brilliant! And anyhow, haven't you read about the scientific significance of crystals?"

"No, regrettably I have not, but I'm sure you'll enlighten me," Gregory grumbled as he waved to the bartender for another round of drinks.

"Well, mate, some scientists believe that the Earth's core is essentially a massive crystal—or perhaps an aggregate of millions of crystals. You see, they were trying to figure out why seismic waves traveling between Earth's north and south poles move faster than those moving east-west. Turns out the iron alloys in the inner core of the Earth have crystallized in such a way that it's easier for energy to pass on the north-south axis than on the east-west. So Gregory, do you know what that means?"

Gregory grunted a barely discernible, "Wha?" through his scotch glass, which he was turning up and draining.

"It means that crystals are the bloody center of our Earth—a pretty damned significant fact, if you ask me. Especially seeing as how finding this particular crystal has become the center of my world. But anyhow, as I said before, the crystal is just the receptacle. It's whatever thing that's hidden inside the Cat's Eye at the core of the crystal that supposedly makes people smart as a whip. But based on the rock engravings I've studied from those times, it appears a person can only use the crystal three times. I can't quite figure that part of it..."

Before he could finish his lengthy explanation, Gregory's head had collapsed onto the bar, and he was snoring loudly. "Come on mate, you look knackered," Danbury said, helping his friend up from the barstool. "You should get back to your flat. I'll hail a cab."

Now, as Danbury baked in the scorching desert sun, he thought back to that refreshingly brisk London evening. Despite Gregory's skepticism, Danbury had always felt certain the Cat's Eye Crystal existed. But what exactly was it? And what the bloody hell was inside that damn Cat's

Eye? And why could it only be used three times? The familiar questions tortured his brain as they had since he had first begun his research, only they attacked his mind more acutely now as the moment drew nearer. He had to know.

And he would know, sooner than he thought. His head man called him loudly from the pit. They had struck wood.

CHAPTER TWENTY-FIVE

Athenium

"And that's when Danbury found the crystal?" asked Goldstein. He was slouched in a comfy leather chair in Professor Gregory's London study, which was tucked away in a small brick building on the university campus.

"Yes," replied Professor Gregory, whose head of perfectly coiffed hair had turned salt and pepper since the last time Goldstein had seen him. Of course Goldstein wasn't one to judge—he only had a few gray strands remaining on the top of his head, carefully combed over his shiny scalp.

Gregory stood and leaned against his massive wooden desk as he addressed Mondo, Mohammed, and Goldstein. He had wasted no time in tracking down the esteemed trio after his strange discovery. It had all started a few weeks earlier when Dr. Clemmins, a university administrator, had approached Gregory asking if he had any idea about what some very irate Egyptian government officials were rambling on about…something about Professor Danbury and some sort of crystal.

After listening to Dr. Clemmins' story, Gregory realized what had happened. His old chap Danbury had found it! Gregory was probably the only person alive who even knew about Danbury's secret dream of unearthing the Cat's Eye Crystal, but he didn't know Danbury had actually gone after it. But now it seemed his mate's dream had probably become a reality—and it may have cost Danbury his life.

"Where is this, ah…crystal thing…now?" asked Mondo, who had grown from a stick-thin, gangly young man into an adult. The midnight-black African had packed a few much-needed pounds onto his tall frame, which made him appear quite imposing—until his chiseled face broke into that familiar, child-like grin.

"Well, before I answer that," Gregory said, taking on a slightly sheepish tone, "let me first explain how it happened."

"Oh-oh!" said Goldstein, leaning forward in his chair. "I don't like the sound of this already." "From what I gather," Gregory continued, "Professor Danbury found what he was looking for—the ancient Cat's Eye Crystal—but nothing else. That suited him just fine, but all his hired help were expecting a bit more, like gold. Danbury must have made some kind of deal to cut them in on a share of the spoils, except there weren't any. Apparently, the diggers decided to settle for the crystal instead of gold or cash, thinking they could sell it. I'm sure Danbury put up quite a fight—there's no way in bloody hell he would have just handed the crystal to them. I know Danbury would have gladly given them all the gold or anything else he found there if he could have just returned with what he labored so long and hard to find. Poor old chap."

"And that's the last anybody heard of him?" asked Mondo.

"That's it," said Gregory. "When the diggers tried to sell the crystal to a museum in Cairo, the museum curator tipped off the authorities. The local police apprehended the diggers for questioning. They apparently spilled their guts, probably quite literally, and told them where they could find the site. The Egyptian authorities claim they returned to the spot in the middle of the desert, but found nothing but a hole. Danbury had disappeared."

"Desert is very good place to disappear in," said Mohammed in a serious tone. He had not uttered a word until now, and when he said this, he lowered his head in respect. Not for Danbury, but for the desert. Mohammed knew the desert. And he knew the desert cared nothing for discoveries or scientific achievement or money. In fact, the desert despised civilization, and it hated man. That's how it had always seemed to him, at least. The desert never compromised. It was absolutely unforgiving…and it quickly swallowed up any person who stumbled into its sandy grasp.

"If they left your Danbury in the desert," Mohammed said stiffly to Gregory, "then he is not lost. He is gone. Vanished. As if he never was. Do not waste your time looking for him. You will never find him. Never." Mohammed cocked a knowing eye at Gregory. "But you have in mind to look for something, my friend. Come, tell us how you lost this thing… this magic of the crystal."

"I was coming to that," said Gregory, "and it wasn't, I mean isn't, magic…and I didn't just lose it," he added hastily. "It was taken—stolen, that is—by terrorists!"

"Terrorists, humpf!" said Mohammed. "Always with the terrorists." Mohammed looked a little disgusted. "Tell me please, why is it that when a man commits crime in America, that man is criminal. But when same man commits same crime anywhere else in the world…then he is terrorist."

"An international terrorist," Gregory corrected and agreed. "It sounds even more dangerous that way."

"So what's a national terrorist?" queried Goldstein.

"Just a criminal," shrugged Mondo.

"Now you mock me!" said Mohammed, a little angrily.

"No, no, not at all, Mohammed," said Goldstein with as much earnestness as he could muster while still keeping a straight face.

"It's just that we don't know what the hell you're talking about," explained Mondo.

"Yes, that's exactly it," said Goldstein, nodding to his African friend. "Thank you, Mondo."

"Why, you're welcome, Goldstein," Mondo replied as a grin spread across his face.

Mohammed stood up, glaring at Goldstein. "You do mock me!" he said, instinctively clutching at the hilt of where his scimitar would have been in his earlier, more casually dressed days.

"Sit down, Lawrence," said Goldstein. "You ain't in Arabia anymore."

"Gentlemen, please!" refereed Gregory. There was a lull as Mondo, Mohammed, and Goldstein all froze and looked back at the professor. "Now, shall I continue, or would you two rather hack at each other with imaginary weapons?"

Mohammed had returned to his seat and was fumbling in his pockets. "I do not even have my dagger…" he mumbled.

"Thank God," whispered Goldstein to Mondo.

Mondo sat with his elbow propped up on the table and his hand over his face, shielding a silly grin. Goldstein stared straight ahead at Gregory with a dead serious face, as if the professor's explanation absorbed his total interest and nothing at all out of the ordinary had just happened.

Mohammed felt slightly embarrassed for letting Goldstein get to him that easily. He shot Mondo a stiff glance. "And you are no help," he said. Mondo never initiated any of the little confrontations between Goldstein and Mohammed, but he was always willing to aid and abet; no matter who started it.

"What did I do?" cried Mondo.

"Never mind," said Goldstein. "Gregory's starting to fidget."

The professor was standing in front of his desk, squeezing a stress ball with all of his might. "So you were saying…" Goldstein added, looking at Gregory.

There was a brief knock at the door.

"Oh, that would be Dr. Clemmins," said Gregory, placing the ball back on his desk.

"Who?" asked Goldstein. "You told me on the phone that no one else knew about all this."

Gregory crossed the room as he explained. "Well, no one else did— then—except for the chemist I mentioned on the phone."

"The dead chemist?" Goldstein asked.

"That's the one," said Gregory as he opened the door and Dr. Clemmins entered the study.

Dr. Clemmins certainly looked the part of a University Administrator with his perfectly pressed navy suit, glossy shoes and silver hair. A good bit older than Gregory and decidedly more business-like, Clemmins wore sophisticated looking glasses with tortoise shell frames. A bit stuffy, thought Goldstein. After Gregory introduced Dr. Clemmins to Mondo, Mohammed and Goldstein, he added, "Dr. Clemmins represents the authority around here—and the money."

"Well, that is, the university's money," Dr. Clemmins said in his snooty British accent as the five men took their seats around Gregory's office table. "And more importantly, I represent the university's image in the academic community. That is why I agreed to let Dr. Gregory try it his way first."

"I had to include Dr. Clemmins in our confidence," said Gregory. "It was the right thing to do, and besides, Dr. Clemmins was the only one with enough political clout to keep the real authorities away after they had finished their initial investigation. With the return of the serum formula to this university…"

"*Serum?*" exclaimed Mondo.

"Yeah," said Goldstein. "I thought you said it was some kind of gem; a crystal or something, Gregory."

"Yes, yes, it is a crystal," Gregory said, a little impatiently. He didn't like to interrupt Dr. Clemmins. "But hidden inside the Cat's Eye core of the crystal was a, uh, recipe, if you will, for a serum."

"The return of this discovery to this university," continued Dr. Clemmins, "for us to research and *carefully* present to the world for use in a properly controlled manner, would represent a great deal of money for the school in research grants alone. That is why we would like to handle this privately, if possible. Naturally, the university would make it worth your while."

"I dunno," said Goldstein, speaking as the financial advisor for the trio. "Our while is worth a lot."

"How about eight million dollars?" asked Dr. Clemmins, briskly without so much as a blink of an eye. "Four million now, and another four million when you return the Cat's Eye Crystal. I can guarantee it."

"Eight million bucks?" shrieked Goldstein, who had completely dropped his poker face. "What the hell *is* this stuff? Gregory, you never mentioned THIS kind of money!"

"I didn't know…" Gregory trailed off, looking genuinely stunned.

Mondo and Mohammed were visibly ecstatic, until Mondo suddenly came to his senses and repeated Goldstein's question. "Wait a minute. Gregory, could you make a long story short and tell us exactly what this stuff is?"

Mondo looked around for support and found it. Mohammed was nodding vigorously and said, "Yes, my friend. Tell us what is so important about item you seek…and is it dangerous?"

"Yeah, we ain't goin' after no radioactive shit!" Goldstein added quickly, as he rested his hands on his growing beer belly.

"Who do you think you're kidding, Goldstein?" chided Mondo. "For eight million dollars, you'd steal a mushroom cloud from an A-bomb blast."

Gregory looked to Dr. Clemmins, then to Goldstein, Mohammed, and Mondo and said flatly, "It's not radioactive, gentlemen, I assure you.

The crystal holds the formula for Athenium." He stuffed his hands in his pockets, turned his gaze to the floor and said nothing more.

"That is what we have come to call it around here," Dr. Clemmins picked up where Gregory had left off. "The Athenium elixir…and it is the closest thing to magic that I have ever seen."

"Yeah, and it's the closest thing to suicide that I've ever seen," said Gregory in a chillingly sober tone. "An alluring, tempting, guaranteed suicide." A pregnant pause filled the room.

"Okay, I get it," Goldstein broke the silence with a smirk. "This university is gettin' into the pharmaceutical business. Big money, especially if your drug can build a better boner. But how the hell did you lose the crystal, Gregory?"

"I told you, I didn't lose it," protested Gregory. "Yes, yes, we know," said Mohammed. "The terrorists took it. But my friend, tell us how you got crystal and found out about drug."

"Well, as I mentioned, the authorities from Cairo contacted Dr. Clemmins, and he notified me because of my association with Danbury," Gregory explained. "I frankly had no idea of what they were going on about," interjected Dr. Clemmins. "But when I spoke with Gregory and saw the effect the news had on him, I agreed to let him go to Cairo and straighten things out."

"Since the Egyptian government was obviously embarrassed about losing track of Professor Danbury…"

"You mean he was there legally," remarked Goldstein with mock surprise.

Gregory ignored the reference to their previous adventure on Delos, which was basically an illegal dig, and resumed his explanation. "Anyway, they felt bad about Danbury and agreed to let me bring the crystal back to the university."

"What does it look like?" Mondo inquired, his eyes growing round with curiosity.

"It is a beautiful sight," Gregory recalled, "like a giant marquise diamond—it's football-shaped and about as big as my fist, with a perfectly round honey-colored Cat's Eye gemstone in its center. In fact, the whole bloody crystal looks like a giant eye. The diggers who pilfered it from Danbury must have thought it a priceless gem…but they didn't realize there was something even more valuable inside the crystal's golden center. When we brought the crystal back to the university, we quickly discovered there was something etched in the Cat's Eye—a miniature inscription—the formula for some sort of elixir."

"And that's where the chemist came in," said Mondo.

"Ah, yes, came and went, I'm afraid," Gregory said apologetically. "I really do feel badly about Robinson. I feel responsible. I shouldn't have been so naïve, I guess, but if I'd had any real idea of the implications of Danbury's discovery, and certainly if I knew I had been followed by..." Gregory glanced toward Mohammed's general direction, "by...ah, those people," he stammered.

"Oh, you mean the terrorists!" Goldstein announced loudly. Mohammed grimaced, and Mondo looked away and stifled a laugh.

Gregory continued. "Anyway, I should have taken the matter more seriously—not that I was taking it lightly. But if I hadn't been so blinded by the extraordinary scientific aspects of this drug, I might have sensed the impending danger and requested some protection."

"What kind of protection?" Goldstein said. "The campus security patrol? Or maybe a few of your English Bobbies with their little sticks? These guys were killers, Gregory, not jaywalkers! You really can't blame yourself."

"Well, I might have done something," said Gregory. "But I left poor Robinson alone with the Cat's Eye Crystal. I should have at least stayed with him."

"But then you would have been killed, too!" said Mondo. "And where would we be now?"

Mohammed leaned forward in his seat toward Gregory. "He is right, my friend. There was nothing you could do to prevent this man's death, but now we can help you avenge it. Now tell me...who took crystal?" Gregory knew if Mohammed had his dagger with him, this would be his cue to pull it out and start toying with the blade. Fortunately, his intimidating Arab friend was weaponless today.

"Well, I never saw anyone following me," Gregory said a little nervously as he looked at Mohammed's leathery face. "I don't know where they picked up my trail, or who the hell put them on to me, for that matter. It could have been Danbury's bloody diggers—or who knows, maybe even the Cairo authorities. Perhaps they wanted to recoup their loss of what they must have known was a valuable find. When I met with Cairo police officials, I sensed they didn't really want to give the crystal to me…but I'm sure they were getting pressure from their government to cover up this Danbury thing at any cost. Maybe they sent someone to track me down… someone from another country, of course, so there would be no blood on their hands."

"Well, whoever the hell it was, it's a damn good thing they didn't catch up with you until after you got back to London," Goldstein quipped as he fidgeted with a Rubik's Cube he'd found on Gregory's shelf. "But it's too bad for that Robinson…unlucky bastard."

Dr. Clemmins adjusted his glasses and folded his hands on the table in front of him. "It was I who originally suggested that Gregory contact Robinson," he said before clearing his throat. "I take full responsibility for that. At least the poor chap had a few weeks to make some rather startling discoveries about the formula engraved on the Cat's Eye at the center of the crystal."

"The engraving was impossibly small, but the large crystal surrounding the Cat's Eye acted as a magnifying glass," Gregory added. "Once we translated the ancient script, we discovered it was the formula for Athenium."

"So this Athenium is just drug?" Mohammed asked. "There are many drugs in world. Why is this one so special?"

"Well, it's not really a drug," Gregory answered. "Not as we understand the word, anyway. It's more complicated than that."

"According to Robinson's lab tests, Athenium seems to temporarily complete an evolutionary process—but out of sequence," added Dr. Clemmins. "It emulates a process that would naturally occur in our brains eventually, but not now…somewhere far down the evolutionary road."

"In short, it makes you a bloody genius," Gregory said. "But only temporarily. For about forty-eight hours, to be exact. But for those forty-eight hours, whatever you're naturally good at, no one on Earth is better than you at that task."

"It makes you invincible," Dr. Clemmins added, with a barely perceptible trace of admiration. "At least, that is the psychological effect," he added more soberly. "You feel and you know that you are unrivaled! Unbeatable!"

"Unnatural!" Gregory said with a scowl. "Let's not forget, Dr. Clemmins, that this drug...or elixir, whatever you want to call it...it is deadly," he said before turning to Mondo, Mohammed, and Goldstein. "Because the physiological effect that occurs in the brain is produced so far out of the evolutionary sequence, our bodies have not had the time to produce the other physiological processes necessary to control the chemical produced in the brain by Athenium; and this chemical, by itself, is poisonous and cumulative. In our present state of evolution, the average human being can take this drug only three times. Then it kills you."

"So it's sorta like you get three chances...or three wishes to do whatever you want," Goldstein said dreamily. "Like a genie lamp or something. Maybe you should've named this thing the Genie Drug!"

Gregory rolled his eyes. "We named it Athenium after the great Athena," Gregory explained. "The goddess of wisdom, courage, inspiration...and of course, warfare. She is the perfect namesake for this enlightening yet destructive drug." Gregory paused and rubbed at his tired, bloodshot eyes. "However, I did briefly consider naming the drug Thoth."

"Thoth?" Goldstein said with a snort. "What kind of name is that? Gregory, are you sure you haven't been hittin' the 'thoth?'"

Mondo's thunderous laugh shook the table.

Gregory let out a long sigh and said drily, "Thoth is the Egyptian God of Wisdom, you daft plonker."

"Tell me, Dr. Clemmins," Mondo asked. "Are there no exceptions to the three time limit? Does the fourth time always kill you?"

"Well, not always—at least according to Robinson's laboratory research," replied Dr. Clemmins.

"But that only makes it worse!" said Gregory, as he pushed his chair away from the table and started to pace around his study. "Don't you see the immense danger here? There is always the slim, slight chance that a person could use it just one more time. Just once more. And even though the odds are stacked astronomically against you, eventually you convince yourself that you're the lucky one who can do it. And you end up killing yourself."

"Shit, Gregory," said Goldstein. "Aren't you being a little morbid? I mean most people aren't suicidal enough to take that risk."

Mohammed turned to Goldstein and said, "How can you say that, my friend? You are from big city where men die in street from drinking and taking drugs. What do you think will happen with this Athenium? They will kill themselves with it, just as they do now…but even quicker. I think Danbury should have left crystal buried."

"Yes, but beyond the social consequences of this drug, just think of the political implications," Gregory said, spinning around to face Mohammed.

"Jesus H. Christ, Gregory," Goldstein chuckled. "You are quite the drama queen today…"

"Perhaps we haven't made our point sufficiently clear," Gregory interrupted, casting an eye to Dr. Clemmins. "Dr. Clemmins' use of the term 'invincible' was not just a figure of speech. He meant just that. Just imagine what a group of organized, if not fanatical, people could do with Athenium…if they could become invincible."

"Oh, the goddamned terrorists again," Goldstein said for Mohammed's benefit.

"Stop that!" cried Mohammed.

"Oh, put a sock in it, you two," Gregory said, completely exasperated. "Let me put it in simpler terms: If Hitler and his bunch had gotten a crack at this stuff, they probably would have won the war."

"Oh," said Goldstein, quietly.

"In our case," Dr. Clemmins chimed in, "whoever took the crystal, not even knowing what it is, will likely sell it to a government that is somewhat less than cordial to us."

"And if it got into the hands of those people?" Mondo asked hesitantly.

Dr. Clemmins slowly slid off his glasses and began to polish the lenses with a handkerchief. "They could then probably accomplish political and military strategies that they are usually incapable of in countries like those; ultimately causing people like us, in countries like ours, to have to agree to social, political and economic compromises that don't particularly suit our fancy."

Goldstein turned to Mohammed and simplified, "In other words, these folks are usually too stupid to be dangerous…but if they get smart, we're in trouble."

"Yes, yes, I know what he means," grumbled Mohammed.

"Exactly!" said Gregory. "That is why it is imperative that we retrieve that crystal and the formula for Athenium before it leaves the country."

"Where is it now?" asked Mondo.

"Well, we hired a private investigator—without giving him many details, of course—and he discovered that the terror-...I mean thieves... are staying in a small hotel a mile from Heathrow airport," replied Gregory. "But before their flight tomorrow morning, you must get to them, retrieve the Cat's Eye Crystal, and place this satchel of drugs in their luggage." Gregory held up a brown leather bag.

"What kind of drugs?" Mondo inquired. "And why the switcheroo?" Goldstein added.

Gregory shifted uncomfortably in his seat and glanced at Dr. Clemmins. "Well, Dr. Clemmins managed to put the authorities off the track after the raid on our lab...and we'd like to keep them derailed for a little longer while we retrieve the crystal."

"I told them that a large amount of pharmaceutical cocaine, used in various animal tests and experiments, was missing," Dr. Clemmins added. "And it was...here it is." He gestured toward the bag. "Oh yes, and here is this," he said as he handed a large manila envelope to Gregory, who passed it to Goldstein.

"What's this?" Goldstein asked peeking inside. "Money, gentlemen, money," replied Dr. Clemmins. "Fifty thousand dollars in cash, American, to get you started. You will need this for immediate expenses, especially if this turns out to be a bit more of a goose chase than we anticipate. The rest of the four million—the first half of your reward—is distributed evenly on those credit cards, in your names."

Goldstein eyed the satchel and stroked his chin, then passed the credit cards to Mondo and Mohammed. "And I suppose we're just supposed to waltz into these guys' hotel room and ask them if they want to make a trade?"

"Absolutely not," Gregory barked. "They must not know that you have taken the crystal and replaced it with the..."

"Yeah, yeah, I know," Goldstein said. "I'm just trying to figure out how to make it happen."

"I have plan," Mohammed said. "Come now, I will tell you on way to hotel."

"Oh boy, I can't wait to hear this," Goldstein said, rubbing his forehead.

"Call me on my mobile immediately after you make the switch," Gregory said, "then get back here with the crystal as fast as you can. I'll call the police and report some sort of suspicious activity at the hotel. Hopefully, they'll move in quickly enough to recover the stolen drugs… if not, these guys will undoubtedly get caught red-handed whenever they try to breeze through Customs with a huge bag of coke."

"Okay then, let's go," said Mondo as he stood up and looked around. "Unless anyone has any objections?" he added.

"Yeah," said Goldstein, "I object on the grounds that I'm getting too old for this shit."

"I do not believe my ears!" cried a shocked Mohammed as he stood and walked toward Gregory's study door. "Allah be praised, I never thought I would live long enough to hear you admit to your true age." He turned to Mondo. "I will go with you. You will need my help, especially since our old friend here," he gestured toward Goldstein, "has grown too feeble to assist us."

"Oh, shut your pie hole, lizard face," Goldstein muttered as he jumped from his chair and chased Mondo and Mohammed out the door. "Wait up, fellas."

"See, I told you they were pros," said Gregory, a little nervously, to Dr. Clemmins.

Dr. Clemmins wore a quizzical frown. "Whatever they are, we are committed now."

"Yes, we *should* be committed," Gregory mumbled under his breath.

CHAPTER TWENTY-SIX

Another Job Well Done

Outside the university on the busy streets of London, Mondo attempted to hail a cab. He was promptly ignored and nearly run over. Luckily, city-bred Goldstein had long ago mastered the art of scoring a taxi. He simply assumed the traditional suicidal stance in front of an oncoming cab, offering the driver the obvious choice between manslaughter and stopping. Goldstein found that the strategy worked as well here in London as it did in Brooklyn, and soon they were on their way to the airport hotel.

As Goldstein squirmed anxiously in the front seat next to the driver, Mondo and Mohammed were counting out the fifty thousand in cash in the back seat, separating it into three equal stacks between them.

"I gotta look at it," Goldstein said as he fumbled with the satchel clasp. "I just gotta."

"Be careful with that, my friend," Mohammed warned.

"Yes, please," agreed Mondo. "If anything happens to that stuff, I don't think we can replace it with a stop at a pharmacy along the way."

Goldstein shrugged off Mondo and Mohammed's comments and continued to dig into the bag.

"Dammit, Goldstein," Mondo said. "There are a shitload of people around here, not to mention..." Mondo discreetly pointed to the driver.

The cab was stopping for a traffic signal at a busy intersection just as Goldstein held up the large, white plastic wrapped bundle. "My God, look at all that coke!" he said with a glazed expression. "We should swing by a party somewhere. Between this and all that cash, even Mohammed could get laid."

Mohammed, shaking two fistfuls of money at Goldstein, was about to return the insult when one of those little sticks the British Bobbies carried came crashing through the window next to Goldstein, followed quickly by a gloved hand with a gun in it.

"Switch off, cabbie!" yelled a voice outside the door. The cabbie did as he was told. It turned out that the voice belonged to a Scotland Yard detective—which explained why he had something more powerful than a nightstick in his hand. Goldstein looked around and saw that the cab was surrounded by Bobbies and what appeared to be plainclothes detectives.

"Oh, no," crooned Mondo, dropping his face into his hands.

"Oh, shit!" cried Goldstein.

"I am not at all surprised," Mohammed mumbled.

"Would you mind stepping out of the cab, Sir?" asked the Scotland Yard detective. But it wasn't really a question.

"You don't understand," protested Goldstein, who remained seated. Mondo and Mohammed were still frozen with fear in the back seat. "We're with *you* guys! We're working for Professor Gregory and the university."

"Not unless the university has entered the illegal drug distribution business, you're not," replied the detective, who had heard it all before. "We've been watching the university since the recent break-in and murder—and we noticed you chaps left there in a bit of a hurry. Now we find you on your way to…" He turned to the driver, "to where?"

"A hotel near Heathrow, and they told me to hurry," offered the driver, trying to be as helpful as possible.

"Ah, yes, the Heathrow Hilton, is it?" mused the detective. He was enjoying what he believed to be a good, clean drug bust and possibly even apprehending the culprits from that mess at the university. "So here you are, rushing away from the scene of a recent murder and drug theft, with a rather largish amount of what I'm guessing is not baking flour, and you're off to a hotel next door to an international airport…hmmm…" The detective paused for dramatic effect and stroked his chin. "And let's see now, who did they say committed the crime at the university?" he asked the plainclothes detective to his right.

"Terrorists, sir," came the quick reply. "Hmmm…terrorists, you say?" repeated the detective. "Well, let's have a looksee." He stooped to peer into the cab at Goldstein, Mohammed, and Mondo. "What have we here? An Arab, an African, and a....someone else..."

"What the hell is that supposed to mean?" asked an insulted Goldstein.

The detective ignored the remark and continued, "...along with a pile of cash on the back seat....and a pile of drugs on the front seat. Oh, I don't know— anything suspicious to you about this lot, Sergeant?" he asked a nearby policeman.

"Maybe just a few things, Sir," the Sergeant chuckled behind his mustache.

"No, no...I'm telling you, you're making a big mistake," insisted Goldstein. "Goddammit, we're not the bad guys—we're the good guys. We're on our way to track down the terrorists and..." Goldstein looked over the seat at Mondo and Mohammed, then down at the fifty thousand dollars spread out between them, and then to the huge bag of cocaine in his lap, and finally up at the detective.

"Oh, shit, never mind," he mumbled with resignation as the impossibility of his story sank in. "Look," he said, "let's just get to the station, or wherever the hell it is you're taking us so we can get this cleared up as soon as possible."

Goldstein sank back in his seat. Mohammed said, "My friend, you have done many stupid things during our long acquaintance—but this is by far stupidest. However, I am not going to get into details of how stupid this was. Instead, when we get out of this mess...I am simply going to kill you."

"And then, I'm going to kill you again!" added Mondo.

"I'm sorry, already," Goldstein shrugged. "What can I say? Fuggedaboutit."

"I change my mind," Mohammed grumbled. "I am going to kill you now!" Just as Mohammed lunged for Goldstein, the police swiftly jerked all three flailing men from the car and slapped handcuffs on their wrists.

CHAPTER TWENTY-SEVEN

Playing God

"So what's new with our friends, the Kabrini?" Carol asked jokingly as she gently pushed a fork around in her Asian salad. She was eating lunch with Jeff in his office at the corporate headquarters of Driscoll Mining Interplanetary, which was perched atop the National Dynamics Building in downtown LA. Driscoll had added "Interplanetary" to his company name after the Space Barge had successfully drawn out the astronomically long space rod, which ultimately established contact with the Kabrini. The humongous Barge was still on its sluggish year-long trip back to Earth.

"Not much," answered Driscoll, leaning back in his expensive mesh suspension chair. He hadn't even touched his sandwich, which still sat inside a white paper bag next to his computer. "I just wish they would hurry up and tell us a little more about themselves."

As he propped up his worn boots on his desk and ran his fingers through his scruffy locks, Carol marveled that after all these years, her husband still looked more like an adventurer than a CEO. She imagined that at any moment, he might leap from his chair and jet off to the desert, where he would join his old buddies Goldstein, Mondo, and Mohammed and pull off some impossible scheme. Her red lips curled into a private grin as Driscoll continued. "I mean, I get it that they have to be careful. Since they're the 'Big Brother' here, they're somewhat responsible for us—but they're taking it so damn slow."

"Taking it slow?" Carol asked as she dabbed at her mouth with a napkin. "It sounds like you're talking about a romantic courtship—not alien contact."

Offering a breathtaking view of the city, Driscoll's expansive office was certainly luxurious—but Carol would much rather meet her husband for lunch at a restaurant where he could escape from the stress of work for a while. Maybe some little place with an outside patio where they could soak up the plentiful California sun. But eating lunch in Driscoll's office had become an all-too common compromise in recent months. Of course, she understood business was business—and Carol had to admit that digging up one of Saturn's moons and laying a pipeline clear across the Solar System to establish contact with an ancient alien civilization did go somewhat beyond the call of duty for your typical CEO; so she was willing to make concessions.

"Look at it this way, Carol," Driscoll said, interrupting her daydream of carefree lunches on sun drenched patios. "I doubt that we have anything to tell them that's going to change their lifestyle much. They're such an ancient and advanced species…they've heard it all before. So since we established contact, they've spent all this time just feeling us out. They don't want to be responsible for throwing an entire planet into a cultural riot. I guess they want to be sure we're grown up enough to handle any new innovations or technologies they turn us on to." Driscoll dropped his boots to the floor and rested his elbows on the desk. "And from what I can tell, they aren't too impressed with our maturity level," he added as he rubbed his aching forehead. "Apparently, they think we're a bunch of childish, war-mongering…"

"Mr. Driscoll?" a voice interrupted. It belonged to his administrative assistant Alice, who was hailing him over the intercom. "Goddammit," Jeff said as he reached for his phone and pressed a button. "Alice, I'm eating lunch right now," he said into the speaker.

"I know, Mr. Driscoll, I'm so sorry to bother you," his secretary apologized. "But I just received a voicemail from Professor Gregory in London…I'm so sorry I missed the call, but I had stepped away for just a moment to grab some lunch. He says he needs to speak with you…and it's urgent."

Driscoll's face broke into a broad smile as he looked up at Carol. "Professor Gregory? No problem, Alice. Please call him back and put him through as soon as you get him."

"Well, bloody hell!" Carol exclaimed in her best British accent. "It's been eons since you've heard from your good ol' mate, Professor Gregory! I wonder what's so urgent?"

"God only knows," Driscoll said. "But if I know Gregory, it will be something interesting."

"Considering all the stories you've told me, I'd say interesting is an understatement," Carol replied as she stood up from the table and crossed the room.

"True," Driscoll replied with a laugh. "I wonder if he's had any luck tracking down those terrorists of his."

"Oh yeah, whatever happened with that whole fiasco?" Carol said over her shoulder. She was digging through her husband's miniature office fridge. She finally emerged with a bottle of white wine, and promptly uncorked it.

"Well, the last I heard from Gregory, they'd gotten clean away with whatever artifact his professor buddy had dug up."

"What sort of artifact?" Carol asked as she poured herself a glass of wine.

"Not sure…Gregory never told me much about it except that it could be very dangerous in the wrong hands."

Carol swirled her glass around in her hand as she sat back down at the table. "Didn't those three strange friends of yours have something to do with that? Sounds like they screwed things up, as usual."

"What do you mean, as usual? And they're not strange," Driscoll added as he tried to mask a smile. "So yeah, Gregory hired Mondo, Mohammed and Goldstein to recover the thing right after it was stolen. But you're right…they managed to botch it up."

"I knew it!" Carol said as she took a small sip of wine. "And they are strange, Jeff. Remember the time when…"

"Mr. Driscoll," Alice announced over the intercom. "I have Professor Gregory on Line One."

"Thanks, Alice," Driscoll replied before he punched the button for Line One. "Gregory!" he shouted. "How the hell are ya?"

"Why hello, Jeffrey," Gregory replied through the speaker. "I'm fine, just fine. And yourself?"

"I'm pretty good, Gregory, no complaints." "Brilliant!" Gregory responded. "And what about that ravishing redheaded wife of yours?"

Carol blushed a little as she tipped her face down into her wine glass. "Carol is great," Driscoll said with a smile. "And she's right here…I have you on speaker."

"Oh…ahem…oh, I…" Gregory stammered, obviously embarrassed.

"Hi, Gregory," Carol called toward the desk. "Hello, Carol," Gregory muttered.

"So what happened with the missing artifact, Gregory?" Driscoll asked. "Did you ever find those guys you were after, or what?"

Gregory cleared his throat and began hesitantly. "Well, ah, actually Jeffrey…that's sort of what I'm calling about."

"Well, if there's anything I can do to help…" Driscoll offered.

"Unfortunately, it's nothing as simple as that," continued Gregory. "You see, we were never able to quite catch up with the bloody bastards— oh, uh, sorry Carol. I forgot you were listening."

"Don't worry about it," said Carol. She could sense that Gregory was distraught.

"Are you kidding me, Gregory?" Driscoll laughed. "This woman cusses like a damn sailor." "It's true," Carol agreed. "But Gregory, I can tell you're upset. What's wrong?"

"Everything, I'm afraid," he answered, "and I feel responsible, in a way. And since I know you and all— since we've been friends for so long—I felt like I should be the one to break the news to you."

Carol watched as a look of concern crept over her husband's face. "Driscoll," Gregory continued, "you'll be hearing from some of your people over there rather soon I would imagine. And it's not good news, old chap, not good at all. So I thought I could maybe explain it to you a little more clearly—give you some background as to just what has led up to this unfortunate turn of events, since I've been so closely connected with it, and your project…"

"Gregory, spit it out, man," said Driscoll. "Just what the hell are you talking about?"

"I'm trying to tell you, mate, really I am," Gregory said. "You see, this thing they stole…the artifact that my colleague Professor Danbury discovered, God rest his soul," Driscoll raised his eyebrows at Carol, "it was the legendary Cat's Eye Crystal. And inside the crystal was the formula for a drug we call Athenium." As Gregory filled them in on the details of Danbury's ill-fated discovery and their research on Athenium, Carol watched her husband's face drain of color and beads of perspiration emerge on his forehead. By the time Gregory had finished his explanation, dark sweat rings had formed on the underarms of Driscoll's light blue shirt. He could sense something was terribly wrong, but he couldn't quite put his finger on it.

"And so, you never found them…or it?" Driscoll finally stuttered.

"Oh, we certainly tried, your friends and I. But as you know our efforts were, well…unsuccessful. Eventually we had to call in the appropriate government agencies—Interpol, Homeland Security, ICE, the FBI—everybody."

"And nothing?" Carol asked.

"Well, we thought we'd found them once in New York," Gregory said. "The DEA had gotten reports of a new drug on the streets there that was killing a lot of its users in a very short amount of time. It was Athenium, alright. And people were risking and losing their lives on that fourth-time gamble—just like I knew they would. But when we got hold of some of the blokes trafficking the stuff, they turned out to be just your run of the mill street junkies and drug dealers—the Athenium they were using turned out to be a crude synthetic of the original, not good enough to have the intelligence heightening effect of the real thing…but still, just as deadly."

"Why the hell did they bother to do that?" Carol asked, wrinkling her freckled forehead. "Why would they make a fake version of the drug and hand it out to New Yorkers?"

"To throw us off their track, of course," Gregory replied, "and it worked rather well. We wasted months following that lead. And while the government agencies were spinning their wheels in New York, their little terrorist scientific researchers were holed up half way across the globe, brewing up some real Athenium and experimenting with the stuff. These bloody nutters were brainstorming with it, getting smarter…"

"How do you know?" Driscoll asked, quickly losing patience. He still couldn't figure out what all this had to do with him.

"Well…ah…" Gregory's voice wavered, "once they launched a rocket from their laboratory in Libya—"

"A rocket! A goddamned rocket?"

"So you have found them!" Carol interjected. "Well...no," Gregory admitted. "By the time the authorities reached the laboratory, it was deserted. They found graves nearby for nearly a dozen people, mostly scientists and engineers...they must have recruited folks from various terrorist groups in nearby countries. It looks like they pushed real hard on this little project of theirs...too hard for some of them. It was a bloody suicide mission. But they achieved spectacular results, thanks to the Athenium. These blokes built a rocket with a speed and guidance system far beyond anything scientists and engineers believed possible. And then they launched it from a small island in the Mediterranean, just off the Libyan coast. That's how we found their lab. We just followed the bloody vapor trail! They left enough notes and hardware behind to make sure our experts would be convinced of the rocket's capabilities....And they are convinced. This missile has a small, yet highly powerful nuclear engine that doubles as the warhead when it reaches its target. It's truly an ingenious—albeit terrifying—piece of work."

"Good Lord!" cried Driscoll. "They're trying to start a war!"

"Sounds like they've already started it," added Carol in a quivering voice.

"So where did the goddamned missile strike?" asked Driscoll.

"Ahh..." Gregory stuttered, "well, nowhere...yet."

"What do you mean, nowhere?" Driscoll asked, so exasperated he leapt out of his seat. "I thought you said this thing was fast. When the hell did they launch it?"

"The day before yesterday," Gregory answered, "and it is fast, Jeffrey, faster than anything we've got, or have any idea how to make."

"Then why hasn't the goddamned thing hit anything yet?" Driscoll said, pacing the floor now, his hair and shirt drenched in sweat. He could sense what Gregory was getting at...and he felt sick to his stomach.

"Because the missile's target is much more than a stone's throw away, Jeffrey...in fact, it's more like light years away." Driscoll stopped pacing and stared at the phone. Gregory paused and cleared his throat. "You see, mate," the professor finally continued, "these terrorist nations that fired the missile are not included in the United Nations agreement governing the information obtained from the, uh…the Kabrini contacts. And they figure if they can't have access to that information—well, then, no one can."

There was a long silence.

"I don't like the sound of that, Gregory," Carol said slowly.

Driscoll, who now stood gripping the side of his desk to keep his balance, started to speak but made only a slight choking sound. He swallowed and tried again. "G-Gregory, what…what exactly are you trying to tell us?"

Gregory's voice finally came through the speaker, very quiet and slow.

"Jeffrey," he began in a soothing tone, "I wish I didn't have to tell you this, mate. But the rocket's target is the terminal connection point at the Kabrini Network, four billion miles away. Your terminal, Jeffrey." Driscoll crumpled into his chair, where he sat motionless, not even breathing. "I'm afraid they're going to blow it up, old boy…and there's no way to stop them. The bloody thing is just too damn fast…"

Driscoll couldn't believe what he was hearing. As Gregory continued to speak, his voice became a faint echo and Driscoll felt as if he were spinning into a deep, dark abyss, falling farther and farther away from this horrific reality…

"There's no way we can catch up to it," Gregory's voice grew fainter by the moment, "and it had almost a two-day head start before your people could launch an interceptor…"

Suddenly, the mention of an intercepting rocket brought Driscoll back. It was a shred of hope, something he could dig his fingernails into and hang onto for just a while longer.

"So we launched?" Driscoll interrupted Gregory. "We did launch… then, there's a chance…" he trailed off hopefully.

"Yes," Gregory said, "but Jeffrey, I wouldn't hold out too much hope. It's really very doubtful. I mean, there's always a chance, but…"

Gregory was cut off by Alice's voice over the intercom. "I'm very sorry to bother you again, Mr. Driscoll," she said, "but there's a General Hodge on Line Two, and he practically ordered me to put him through to you at once. He said…"

"Never mind, Alice," barked Driscoll, attempting to get his emotions under control. "I'll take it. Gregory, I'll call you back."

"Okay, mate, sounds like you've-"

Driscoll hung up before he could finish and switched to Line Two. "General Hodge, what the hell…"

"So you've heard," said the general in his gruff, serious voice.

"It's true, then," said Driscoll.

"I'm afraid so, Mr. Driscoll," the General replied. "But you launched an interceptor," pushed Driscoll.

"A token effort, sir," the General said. "But the speed of that rocket it's chasing is nothing short of incredible. The only possible way our interceptor can catch up with it is if the rocket fails and stops dead in space. And soon. Otherwise…there's no way in hell."

Carol watched as Driscoll opened his mouth to speak and then closed it again. Although his eyes were focused intently on the phone speaker, she knew his mind was somewhere far, far away.

Finally, he asked his next question. "And what, do you estimate, are the chances of the Libyan's rocket failing?"

"If you want the truth, sir, there's a far greater chance that our rocket will malfunction than theirs," Hodge answered matter-of-factly.

Driscoll began to realize that what they were doing with the interceptor was similar to throwing a rock at a speeding bus that has just driven by and splashed mud on you. Even though the bus is already a block away by the time you pick up a rock, you throw it anyway because it makes you feel better than doing nothing at all. But you know you're not going to hit it. And Driscoll knew they were not going to hit this damn rocket, either.

The room fell silent once again.

"I thank you for your candor, General Hodge," Driscoll finally said soberly.

"I'm very sorry, Mr. Driscoll," Hodge replied. "If anything turns up, I'll notify you at once, of course."

"Thank you, General." Driscoll gingerly pressed the button to hang up the phone and turned to Carol, whose glass of wine sat untouched on the table in front of her. She had tears streaming down her cheeks…a sight Jeff rarely saw. But Carol could no longer hold back her emotions. She had just sat and listened helplessly as she discovered that everything her husband had hoped and dreamed of his entire life, everything he had worked for since she had known him—not to mention one of mankind's greatest accomplishments in history—were about to be destroyed by pure hatefulness.

"Jeff!" she said, choking on a sob. "Oh my God, Jeff…" She stood up, walked to the desk and stooped behind her husband, grabbing his shoulders and placing her head against his. "How can this be happening?" she said.

"It's happening," Driscoll said gravely. "It's happening…"

"But there's gotta be something we can do," implored Carol. "Something…"

"You heard the General," Driscoll replied quietly. "We just can't catch up with it."

Carol's face went blank as she crouched down in front of her husband and rested her head in his lap, tears dripping off her face and onto his khaki pants. Jeff placed one hand delicately in her auburn hair, and they sat frozen that way through what felt like the longest, deadest silence either of them had ever endured.

Carol finally broke the unbearable stillness as she stood up, pulled a chair close to her husband, and sat down. She took his hands in hers and looked up at him—and she was shocked at what she saw. Instead of the dead look of despair and defeat she expected, his penetrating blue eyes were wide open beneath his furrowed brow. Carol felt a tiny sprig of hope unfurl deep in her stomach. She knew the look—it was unmistakable. He was deep in thought, having some sort of subconscious struggle or internal debate. He was scheming and computing, drumming up new ideas. *"But what?"* she wondered as she gazed upon her husband's face.

If the situation was actually as hopeless as it seemed, what was there to think about except what to do after his life's work went up in smoke. *Was* there smoke in space when something blew up? Probably not. It would all just go up in a quick, silent flash of light, probably not even visible from Earth. She continued to stare at her husband, who was still working something over in his mind.

"Jeff?" she said softly. No answer.

"Jeff," she repeated, now a little concerned. "Are you okay?"

But Driscoll was not there in that office—his mind was racing far ahead of the General's rocket. About three billion miles ahead.

"What?" he finally answered. "Oh…sorry."

"Are you back?" Carol asked.

"Yes," Driscoll said leaning back in his chair again. "I was thinking about what Gregory said about this missile using its nuclear engine as a warhead...very interesting." He stroked the short whiskers on his cheek.

"Interesting?!" Carol exclaimed. "What do you want to do, Jeff? Give these guys a medal for making such an awesome rocket?"

Driscoll shot an enraged glance her way, though the anger was not directed at her. "I'd like to give them something, alright," he said. "And maybe I can!"

He pushed away his forgotten lunch and started searching for files on his computer.

"I knew you were thinking of something," Carol said. "What are you going to do?"

"Well, I need some information from our people first...and from Pete Teegan's people, too. They're the ones who built the engines," Driscoll muttered mostly to himself. His mind was spiraling far away again.

"Jeff..." Carol began.

"Maybe General Hodge can't intercept that damn thing, but I'll bet I can!" Driscoll said directly to his wife this time. "Just one of the pair of nuclear engines driving the Barge is bigger than their whole damn rocket!"

As Jeff furiously typed something on his computer, Carol stared at him in disbelief. She was worried her husband had gone completely mad. "The Barge?" she asked. "Jeff, what the hell are you talking about? There are more than three hundred people on that Barge!"

"And it's right between the rocket and the Network..." Driscoll was murmuring to himself again, "or close enough, at least. It could maneuver close enough...but not too close—not close enough so that the rocket would avoid it. But just close enough to vaporize that damn Libyan rocket in the biggest explosion that part of space has ever seen!" Driscoll actually chuckled, and Carol thought his chiseled face looked strangely ominous in the blue glow of his computer screen. "We can just park it there, and wait for it to come...like an ambush."

"An ambush?!" Carol cried, feeling like she herself might explode. "Jeff, have you lost your mind? This is not a western...or, or...a goddamn war movie! This is real life! And what about the three hundred people on the Barge? What about them? They've been out there for three years, and they're only a few months from home!"

Driscoll looked away from his computer screen and into his wife's hysterical eyes. "They're not on the Barge, Carol. Don't you see? They're in the City—the Crystal City. Well, I guess some of them might be working in the Barge at any given time, but they don't have to be. That's only for maintenance, especially on the return trip. We'll just tell them to all move to the City and stay put. The whole enormous thing is all controlled from within the City."

"But the City is on the front of the Barge!" maintained Carol. "If you blow up the Barge, you'll blow up the City!"

"No, no…" Driscoll answered. "It's detachable! The City can be detached from the Barge. It's completely self-contained, and they manufacture most of everything they need and eat right in the Crystal City. They could be self-sustaining indefinitely! We'll just have them detach the City and remotely pilot the Barge into position, far away from the City, to wait for the oncoming rocket."

Carol was still staring at him like he was some kind of maniac. "And what happens to the people in the Crystal City?" she asked, stiffly.

Driscoll paused. "Well…they float," he said. "They float?" Carol shrieked as she pushed back her chair and stood. "What do you mean they float? Float where? And for how long?"

"Until we can get something out there to pick them up, of course!" Driscoll said abruptly.

"But it will take years to build a ship like that," protested Carol, "and what…another two or three to reach them? And then another year to return back to Earth. They could be out there for the next ten years!"

"More like eight," Driscoll said quietly, knowing it didn't help much.

"Eight years!" Carol repeated. Her face and neck had broken out into angry red splotches, and she was clutching onto the front of her husband's desk.

"Look," Driscoll soothed. "I don't like it either, but it will work—and we have no other choice."

Carol just glared at him, her white knuckles still clutching the edge of his desk.

"We have to do it...to save the Legacy project," he insisted. "The Network is our only contact with the Kabrini. So what are we supposed to do? Just sit back and watch as it's blown to bits? Or do we just tell the Kabrini to hurry and decide if they think the human race is responsible enough to handle the information they can give us...but please hurry the hell up because some of our own people here on Earth are trying to destroy our communications link with them on purpose. Oh yeah, that would be fan-fucking-tastic I'm sure the Kabrini would jump right in and rescue us from our own self-destructive ways!"

Driscoll paused and looked up at his wife, who was trembling with rage in front of his desk.

"I am so sorry," she said through clenched teeth. "I guess I just don't like the idea of my husband making one hasty decision that involves the lives of so many other people...all so he can save his beloved project. It's like you're playing God, Jeffrey. And I don't like it."

Driscoll sat in silence and just stared at his wife. Carol finally turned her back on him and walked silently to the window, where she gazed at the smoggy hills in the distance.

Driscoll finally looked away from her rigid back and pressed the intercom button on his phone. "Alice," he said, "please get me Pete Teegan...quickly."

"I believe he's gone for the day, Mr. Driscoll," she responded.

"Well, call him on his cell!" Driscoll shouted. "But sir, he never answers when-"

"I'm serious, Alice, track him down," Driscoll seethed. "I don't care if you have to get a goddamned detective, just find him please! I need to talk to him right now!"

"Yes, sir," came the terse response.

"Well, I guess you're going to be a little busy," Carol said, turning away from the window without expression. "I'll see you at home."

She walked to his office door and reached for the knob. Suddenly she turned and added, "I love you, Jeff."

Driscoll walked out from behind his desk, crossed the room and kissed her gently on the cheek. "It'll be alright," he said. "I promise."

After Carol left, he turned from the door and scowled at his desk. He'd rather be anywhere else right now. Anywhere. Even three billion miles away. He looked out the window, his eyes scanning far above the mountainous horizon—as if he could see the huge Barge, the Crystal City and its inhabitants if he stared into the sky long enough.

"And what am I going to tell them?" he wondered aloud. "What the hell am I going to say?"

The blue sky was slowly darkening into a deep purple, and Driscoll watched as the first star emerged. He was still staring out the window at the bruising sky when his cell phone vibrated in his pocket. Driscoll grabbed it and looked at the screen: Pete Teegan.

"Pete, it's about damn time!" he answered.

"Hi Jeff," Pete said. "Sorry for the delay—I was trying to squeeze in a quick round of golf, but my assistant tracked me down on the course. What's up?"

Driscoll looked away from the twinkling point of light in the night sky and walked to his desk.

"Jesus, Pete," he said. "You have no idea, do you? You'd better sit down."

"I am sitting down," Pete replied.

"Then get up and pour yourself a stiff drink," Driscoll said. "'Cause we've got trouble."

CHAPTER TWENTY-EIGHT

Space Life: "The Real World"

The Crystal City sprawled across the front of the enormous space barge like a vast Plexiglas beehive. From the outside, the City's slow, multi-faceted dome revealed the hive-like activity of the more than three hundred people who lived and worked there; and from the inside, the workers enjoyed a breathtaking view of the uttermost blackness of deep space and its showpieces of dazzling light, in pinpoint designs—a profoundly beautiful vision no man on Earth has ever seen. Only here, in the ultimate void, in the unending emptiness, can a human see Creation through God's eyes and begin to appreciate the awesome nature of Infinity.

This was not a view for Earthman. This was a view for Spaceman. And it was such a view that spaceman Mark Ranier beheld from within the Crystal City as he lay awake watching the familiar group of stars drift slowly past the bedroom's view portal. It was the same view he had pondered a few months ago in the rear of the Barge after he had missed his shuttle back to the City—except since then, one bright star had changed its position slightly with respect to the others. The Sun, he knew. And soon they would be within sight of Earth.

A lot had happened since then, Ranier considered, mostly between himself and Marla. The view out the portal wasn't the only beauty he currently beheld. Marla slept peacefully next to him, stretched delicately across the bed, with one of her small legs slung over his.

They had moved in together—well, he had moved in with Marla at her insistence since she kept her apartment immaculate and Mark's looked like a crew of frat boys had invaded the place. After Mark vacated his messy living quarters, he joked about posting an Apartment for Rent ad on the outside of the Barge. A month later, a hydraulics repair crew reported seeing the ad painted in huge white letters near the rear of the Barge while they were outside on maintenance duty. But with Earth being the closest source of other possible occupants, and that being almost three billion miles away, Mark had yet to receive a response.

While Marla got a good laugh out of her boyfriend's impressive prank, Mark received a stiff glance from his superiors, though they hadn't officially scolded him. Although they weren't thrilled about the ad, no one seemed to mind that Mark was shacking up with his girlfriend. After all, many of the ship's residents had moved around the City during the long trip—it relieved the monotony of living in a small, closed society and helped restore the sense of normal life in a completely abnormal situation. And Marla and Mark were certainly not the first couple to decide to share accommodations since their departure from Earth nearly three years ago, so there were, in fact, several vacant apartments throughout the City.

As Mark watched the stars, Marla began to stir. She let out a little sigh, sat halfway up in the bed and squinted at Mark. "How long have you been awake?" she mumbled.

"Oh, I don't know," Mark replied, "an hour or so, I guess."

Marla sat up all the way and rubbed her eyes. As she reached for her glasses, she threw her tousled black tresses behind her, which got Mark's full attention. He loved her hair. He was the one who had talked her into growing it out a little bit longer than regulations allowed, but no one had complained. Since they had begun their homeward journey, their superiors had relaxed a little and no longer enforced some of the more stringent ship rules. After all, when the barge connected the extrusion rod to the Kabrini Network Terminal Point, the Legacy mission was deemed an overwhelming success—and the commanders decided their people had earned a few personal liberties.

"What have you been doing?" Marla asked as she yawned and shook out her hair.

"Thinking," Mark said in a serious tone. "I've been thinking, and I've come to a decision."

"Oh, have you?" Marla said. She hoped this wasn't too important because she didn't feel quite awake enough yet to deal with any heavy news. "A decision about what?"

Mark turned toward her and looked into her drowsy blue eyes. "Marla," he said dramatically, "I want you to change your name."

Now Marla was wide-awake. "What?" she said, furrowing her tiny forehead. "You mean…get married? Mark, I thought we were on the same page about this. You know, maybe when we get back, but not out here. So are you telling me you've changed your mind? You're telling me this now?" she straightened her glasses and glanced at the clock on the nightstand. "At four o'clock in the morning?"

"Who said anything about marriage?" Mark said blankly, innocently blinking his bright brown eyes at her. "I'm talking about your first name. Don't you realize how ridiculous we sound when our friends talk about us? Mark and Marla this; Marla and Mark that. No matter which way you say it, we sound like a damn dance team, or, or…a cheesy pop duo. Shit, Marla, some of our friends have even threatened to call us M&M! It's humiliating. So as you can see, this is a crisis situation. And I can't change my name because you know I'm up for a promotion, and that would cause a gigantic foul-up in red tape and delay everything for God knows how long and—"

A pillow flew from Marla's side of the bed and smacked him right in the face, causing him to tumble backwards onto the floor. As he struggled to climb back up on the mattress, he reached for Marla's foot, but she managed to wriggle away from him.

"You are insane!" she shouted as she leapt from the bed and scurried to the bathroom, giggling the whole way. She switched on the bathroom light and slammed the door. Mark heard her start the shower. That was the only disadvantage to sharing an apartment, he thought—only one bathroom.

"So what name did you have in mind?" she called out over the running water.

"I was thinking…Marty," he responded with a grin as Marla let out a hearty laugh in the bathroom. "What's so funny? You look like a Marty!"

Mark sat up on the bed and gave the stars one last glance through the portal before he reached over and switched on the lamp next to the bed. The compartment flooded with light and the universe was promptly extinguished. He gazed at the portal, which had displayed the splendor of the stars only a moment ago, but now revealed only a reflection of his face with the tiny room behind him. Convenient. He switched the light back off and peered out at the stars. A choice of space life, or the real world. He switched the light back on and his reflection re-emerged. All with the flick of a switch, available twenty-four hours a day…whatever that means out there.

He turned the light back off and chuckled to himself. After three years of pretending there was still a day and a night, the routine was beginning to get a little stale. But he continued the custom, like everyone else, to align his days with a twenty-four hour clock. It was necessary, unless they wanted to return to their planet with the worst case of jet lag in history. And there was something else, something more personal—a reason that struck closer to the heart and kept everyone from abandoning the senseless day and night ritual. You didn't want to forget who you were, or where you came from, or where you would eventually return: Earth. Home.

And when they finally made it home, Mark planned to take Marla sailing. He'd been obsessing over it for months now. He longed to glide out in the ocean, or a lake, or a river or any large body of water—something absolutely nonexistent here in space. Mark chuckled again. He didn't even like sailing.

He turned the light back on and strolled toward the bathroom, where Marla was singing a sultry tune in the shower. The real world. He smiled as he pushed open the door.

CHAPTER TWENTY-NINE

Calculated Desperation

By the time Driscoll got home, a crescent moon was hanging high in the midnight sky. As he stepped out of the limo onto his circular driveway, he thanked the driver for staying late and then climbed the few steps to the massive wooden front doors of his gigantic home. Although he generally preferred to drive himself home on these late work nights, he was glad Carol had made him promise to take the limo. She had figured by the end of the night, he would probably be somewhere between dead tired and deservedly drunk, and certainly in no condition to drive. And as usual, she had been right. Driscoll was fairly tipsy and absolutely exhausted, but he brightened visibly at the sight of his wife.

"Thank God," Carol said as she swung open the door, a lovely auburn-haired silhouette bathed in golden light from the chandelier that hung behind her. "You're finally home. I was getting worried about you."

She threw her arms around his neck and kissed his stubbly cheek. "So how did it go?" she said as she meandered toward the family room, where she had been waiting curled up on the couch with a cashmere blanket.

"I've had better days," he said with as much of a smile as he could muster. "Shit, I'm glad to be home." He collapsed into his favorite recliner and kicked off his boots. Edward, their British butler, promptly entered the room.

"Good evening, sir," he greeted. "Can I get you anything?"

"Right on cue, Edward, as always," Driscoll answered. "And yes you can. A large scotch and soda, please...with ice. In fact, make it two."

"Oh, I'm good, Jeff," Carol said. "I'll just have some coffee please, Edward."

"I didn't mean for you," Driscoll said as he rubbed his eyes. He shot a wry grin at his wife. "I meant for me. I don't think one drink is gonna do it tonight."

"Very well, then, that's two scotch and sodas and one coffee, coming right up," Edward repeated as he whisked down the long hallway toward the kitchen.

"Did you ever get a hold of Pete?" Carol asked. "Yes, I did," Driscoll said. "I sure ruined his night, I can tell you that!"

"I haven't seen anything on the news yet," Carol said, pulling the dark purple blanket up to her neck.

"Thank God…but it will probably leak out any minute now as more and more people get involved."

"Involved in what?" Carol prodded.

Driscoll reclined in his chair and stared up at their vaulted ceiling with his icy blue eyes. "Tomorrow should be a real show. Pete and I decided to start by transmitting the whole story to the Barge so they can work out the computations simultaneously with us back here on Earth. We figured that would save a lot of time in the long run because of the communications time delay between Earth and the Barge." He ran his fingers through his messy hair and chuckled. "You know, it's crazy. We can communicate with the Kabrini in another star system faster than we can with the Barge that is fairly close by comparison."

Just then, the butler entered with a tray full of drinks.

"Here you are, sir," Edward said as he set the two full highball glasses on the side table next to Driscoll, who immediately scooped one up and took a long gulp. "Damn, that's good," he said with a sigh. "Thanks, Edward. You mix one hell of a drink."

"You're very welcome, sir. Will there be anything else?" he asked.

"No thanks, and if there is I'll get it myself. Feel free to go to bed if you'd like."

"Thank you, sir," Edward said with a stiff bow before he turned to leave the room.

"Night, Edward," Carol called after him.

"So anyway," Driscoll said, glancing over at his wife's droopy eyes, "with the folks on the Barge doing their own computations, they'll have the answers as soon as we do."

"What kind of computations?" she asked. "Well, when I told you that we could detach the City from the Barge, I was simplifying it a bit." He quickly drained his first drink, set it down on the table with a *clink*, and grabbed the second one. "The Barge and the Crystal City were built separately in orbit around the Earth. After they were built, the engineers welded the two ships together at a huge coupling point. What we need to know now is how big of an explosion it will take to break the coupling, without damaging the City...which is covered in Plexiglas."

"This just gets better and better," said Carol who was still uneasy about the whole plan. "And how are you going to tell the people on the Crystal City about this little side trip they're going to take?" she asked. "And I don't even want to think about this explosion!"

Driscoll stared down into his drink. "I know, I know...an explosion is definitely risky. But hell, they just don't have anything out there that's big enough to cut through that damn coupling." He set down his drink and looked at his wife. She wilted under the blanket, absolutely weary with worry. "I don't know how the hell to tell them, Carol. There's just no way to sugarcoat it. But that crew on the Barge, they're good people—damn good. The best we have. So I'll have to tell them, and I know they'll do it. That's the bottom line. There's just no other way. And after everything they've done to accomplish this mission, I think they'll agree."

"Do they have a choice?" Carol glared at her husband.

"Of course they have a choice!" he shot back. "I mean, what could we possibly do if they refused? Tell them they can't land on Earth when they get back? Hell no! But look at everything they've been through already. Even if they come straight back, that would mean they've invested three years of their life for absolutely nothing! What would you do in their shoes?"

Carol gazed out the window at the night sky and reflected quietly for a few moments. "Yeah, you're probably right," she finally answered. "They'll probably do it. But still...I don't like the idea. Not at all."

"Well, I never said I liked it either, Carol. And I feel guilty as hell sitting safely down here on Earth in my cozy home while I'm asking them to risk their lives for the project. But…well…" he trailed off. He took the last swig of his second drink, stood up and stretched. "Oh, hell…let's go to bed. I can't even think straight anymore. Tomorrow is going to be a long day."

As she switched off the living room light and climbed the marble stairs behind her husband, Carol couldn't stop thinking about those poor people in the Crystal City, billions of miles away. She imagined that today, they were still basking in the light of success and the admiration of the world—but tomorrow, they would be thinking how quickly things can change.

CHAPTER THIRTY

Plan B

Freshly showered and shaved, Mark raced through the Crystal City, running late, as usual. With only moments to spare, he hopped on the outside shuttle just before the doors swished shut. He slumped into the nearest empty seat, strapped himself in, and gazed out into the inky depths of space as the shuttle soared toward the engineering terminal. He was headed to the extrusion station for his routine bi-weekly inspection.

About the same time, Marla and her friend Barbara were leaving the Crystal City Java Hut, steaming cups of cappuccinos in hand, heading "downtown" to the labs, as usual.

But up in Control, something highly unusual was taking place, and one of the ship's two Pilots instructed his second in command to go wake up the co-pilot. "Tell Lou to get his arse up here pronto," Tony said.

"What the hell? W-w-why?" stammered Commander Allen Braintree in his unmistakable Alabama twang.

"Because we just received a bloody special communication, that's why," Tony responded. "And when Earth sends one of these messages, both pilots have to be present when we read it. I wonder what the bloody hell is going on…"

"Aw hell, Tony, you know how Lou is when he's off duty," Allen whined. "He's gonna wring my damn neck when I try to wake him up. Can't I just buzz him from up here?"

"No way, mate!" Tony practically bellowed. "He'll just switch off the intercom and go back to sleep. This is the first time we've ever gotten one of these communications where they want us both here at the same time. I don't want to screw it up. Besides, whatever it is, it must be bloody important!"

"Well then, why don't you go get him? You two are best buddies and all. I mean, don't y'all go way back? He'll probably be less violent with you."

"Because I'm Number One and you're Number Two," Tony answered. "So stop fannying around and go get him!"

"Look, Tony," Allen tried again. "If you want to go by the book, you're only half."

"What? Whose bloomin' book is that?"

"Just think about it," Allen persisted. "The Pilot's position is shared jointly by both you and Lou, right?"

"Correct," agreed Tony.

"And the Pilot's position is Number One, right?" "I can see where you're going with this, Allen, and I don't—"

"Well, you can't both be a Number One," Allen broke in. "That would make you together a Number Two. I mean, one and one is two, and you already said I'm Number Two. So individually, you must each be only a half, and I'm a full Two all by myself, so—"

"You're going to be all by yourself, alright," Tony interrupted, "painting over that bloody For Rent sign your buddy Ranier painted on the side of the Barge."

Allen cocked his head to one side and wrinkled his brow like a confused puppy.

"Oh now, don't look at me like you don't know what I'm talking about—we all know bloody well who did that!" Tony struggled to suppress a smile. He, like everyone else, thought that little stunt was hilarious.

"Stop dilly dallying around and go wake up Lou, dammit. They want him here in thirty minutes so we'll both be present for this next transmission, so bugger off! Really do hate to pull rank on you, mate, but what good is it if you can't pull it when you need it?"

Allen strolled off mumbling something that sounded like, "Oh yeah, well I got something you can pull…goddamn British, no sense of humor…"

"I heard that!" Tony shouted as Allen exited Control for the main corridor. "And I know you got that rubbish-talk from Lou!"

Ten minutes later, Allen Braintree returned to Control with a bleary-eyed Captain Louis Tortona.

J. R. Egles

"Here's the other half," Allen said with a grin.

"What the hell is going on?" Lou complained as he groggily stumbled through the entrance. "I'm only half awake."

"Well, according to this cheeky monkey, you're only half, period!" Allen laughed.

"What?" Lou squinted and rubbed his eyes. "If this is some kind of joke, I'm gonna be pissed when I actually wake up."

"I don't know what it is, mate," Tony answered seriously, "but it's no bloody joke. We received a special communication a while ago saying they needed us both here for the next transmission. Both of us! So it's obviously some serious shite."

At that news, Lou appeared to snap out of his dream state. "Both of us?" he repeated slowly. "Is there some kind of emergency going on that I slept through?"

"Not that I bloody well know of," Tony replied.

"Maybe they're gonna give us all a medal or a parade or somethin', and they just can't wait until we get back," Allen naïvely suggested.

Ignoring Allen's ludicrous remark, Tony swiveled around in his chair to face Lou. "You know, I don't think we've both been present in Control at the same time since last New Year's Day. Remember that morning? I showed up to relieve Allen and found you curled up asleep, right here under the communications console."

"I don't know what the hell you're talking about!" Lou protested loudly. "I have absolutely no recollection of that."

"Well, I'm not surprised," Tony replied. "I heard about that wild New Year's Eve party. You not only had no recollection of how you got all the way from there to here, but when we finally did manage to wake you up, it took us the rest of the day to convince you that you were in a spaceship almost four billion miles from Earth!"

"Oh, yeah." Lou suddenly remembered. "That was a bit of a shock."

"I hate to interrupt these fond memories," Allen said, "but if Captain Lou is fully conscious now and if Captain Tony is done pulling his rank..."

"His rank what?" asked Lou with a smirk. "Oh, shut your gob!" quipped Tony.

"This cute little red light here," Allen continued, pointing at a tiny but bright, indicator flashing on the communications console, "is telling us that we'll have our answer in sixty seconds."

All three men stared at the console as a full minute dragged by. Suddenly, a jumble of nonsensical words began to stream across the communications computer screen. "What the bloody hell does that say?" Tony said, squinting his eyes at the incomprehensible series of letters.

"The message is encrypted," Allen said as he reached for the keyboard to type in a password. "Here, this should unlock it."

When Allen hit "Enter," the legible message appeared on the screen:

ATTN: CAPTS. L. TORTONA AND A. CREIGHTON FROM: J. DRISCOLL, DRISCOLL HQ

"From The Man, himself," Lou said. "Well, that's something different."

"I still say it's a medal or parade or something," Allen persisted. "Or maybe we've all been promoted!" he added optimistically.

"Brilliant!" Tony exclaimed. "Maybe I'll be a whole now."

"A hole?" inquired Lou with a furrowed brow. Allen turned away from the screen and looked at Lou. "Yeah, a whole, all by himself. You'll be a whole too, Lou, but of course, that'll make me a three. You two will never catch up."

Lou looked over at Tony, who was watching the screen as the message continued to slowly download. "What the hell have you been talking about since I got up here?" he said, sounding annoyed. "At first I thought I was just tired, but I swear, I still don't have the slightest clue what…"

"Can it, mate," interrupted Tony with no trace of his usual light-hearted tone in his voice. "Looks like there is something going on alright… and I don't think I like the way it's shaping up."

Noticing Tony's sudden serious attitude, Lou and Allen returned their full attention the screen. Words were still flashing across the monitor, and Tony was trying to read the message as it downloaded. It took a full ten minutes for the full message to transmit—one of the longest communications they had ever received in one continuous run. Once the full message had downloaded, the final line displayed on the screen:

IT'S UP TO YOU, NOW. ALL OF YOU. GOOD LUCK. MAY GOD
BE WITH YOU.
- JEFFREY DRISCOLL
REPLY MANDATORY ASAP ***DRISCOLL
HQ***END.

Lou, Tony, and Allen stood staring at the screen in disbelief.

Lou finally broke the silence. "You woke me up for this? I'm going back to bed."

"I appreciate your lack of panic, Lou," Allen said. "Myself, I don't know what to do first—scream or throw up."

Tony typed a few keys on the main communications computer to send the message to his handheld tablet. "Hell, why don't you just scream, we've already got one bloody hell of a mess! And we're going to need to distribute this lovely little note. Nobody will ever believe us if they don't read it for themselves." Tony paused and tapped at the screen of his tablet, which now displayed the full message from Driscoll Headquarters. "And speaking of that," he said, "perhaps we should give some thought as to exactly how to break this to everybody. I suppose we shouldn't just send it out in a bloody mass email. Lou, you could make one of your Captainly announcements about keeping to schedules and how this mission isn't over yet, and after you finish your usual stuff, just sort of slip in an, 'Oh, and by the way...' Or you could just go hang around the Lounge and wait for some poor bloke to ask you what's new."

Lou looked up at Tony's boyishly innocent face.

"Me? You mean we. We're going to do this together, dammit!" He turned to Allen. "Go ahead and gather up the people we need to work out these computations. These calculations are going to take a while, and we'll have to check and re-check the numbers. We can't afford even the smallest error. There is nothing programmed into the computer for a situation like this, so we'll have to start from scratch. Hopefully, the computer can come up with a few different plans."

"I still think I'd rather throw up," Allen said grimly. He turned his ashen face toward his computer and began to pull up the directories of the ship's technical departments. The screen displayed the names of various men and women—many of whom Allen knew personally.

A name near the top of the list was Mark Ranier, who at that very moment was just beginning his extrusion station inspection—placing him about as far away from Control as you could possibly get on the Barge.

Not long after his name popped up on Allen's computer, Mark's two-way mobile beeped. He reached down and unclipped it from his belt.

"Ranier," he said into it as he continued to examine a meter on the extrusion station wall.

"Chief Rainier, you're wanted up front, sir," a woman's voice announced.

"Up front? Where?" he asked. "In Control, sir."

Mark turned away from the panel of lights and meters. He didn't like the sound of this at all. Being called up to Control reminded him of being called up to the principal's office—which hadn't been an uncommon occurrence for him in high school.

"Well, okay," he said into his phone, "but I'm all the way back here at the extrusion station. I'll have to wait for the shuttle at the end of my shift. Even if I hopped on the inside tram right now, I wouldn't get back any sooner."

"Yes, I know, Chief Ranier," the voice announced from the tiny speaker. "A special shuttle has been sent for you. It should be there momentarily."

"Wait…what?" he cried before he could stop himself. "I mean…okay," he said, collecting himself. "I'll be waiting. Thank you." He snapped his phone shut and replaced it on his belt. Holy shit, what did he do now? It couldn't possibly be about the For Rent sign he painted on the side of the Barge. That had been a while ago, and everyone seemed to think it was harmlessly funny. His mind raced to figure out what this could be about. Just a couple of weeks ago, he couldn't even get the regular shuttle to wait for him…and now he got a special shuttle? What the hell?

Whatever it was, Mark knew it couldn't be good news. He quickly finished checking the damper controls on the exhaust housing of the extruder, typed in the appropriate notation on his tablet, and headed for the shuttle bay.

After what seemed like an excruciatingly long shuttle trip, Mark finally arrived at the front of the ship. When he emerged through the door to Control, he was greeted by Captains Creighton and Tortona as well as their second in command, Allen Braintree. Mark was relieved to see his good friend Allen since he didn't know either of the Captains very well.

But Allen's presence was dramatically offset by that of Tony and Lou. If he was meeting with the ship's captains, Mark knew something must be terribly wrong.

Allen sensed Mark's nervousness and tried to lighten the mood. "Look, Mark," he said in a serious tone as he pushed down a laugh, "we hate to have to do this, but it's regulation."

Now Mark knew he was in trouble. "Do what?" he asked in monotone.

"We just discovered that Marla is pregnant...and this is a shotgun wedding," Allen said unsmiling.

Mark's face went blank. "What?"

At that, Tony and Lou burst out laughing. Allen grinned ear to ear as he slapped Mark on the shoulder. "We're just messin' with ya, buddy."

When the laughter trailed off, Lou said, "Man, it feels good to laugh...I wasn't sure if I'd ever laugh again after the news we just got."

Mark stood red-faced, still looking a little confused, but he was glad that whatever was wrong didn't appear to be his fault.

"What news?" he finally asked.

"Mark," Lou continued, taking on a more business-like tone, "you're among sixteen people we need to talk to right away. The other fifteen are sitting in the briefing room next door, but since we had to bring you all the way from the back of the ship, I'm afraid you missed most of that. They should be finishing up soon."

"Oh shit," Mark said, realizing that he just cussed in front of his superiors but not really caring. "It's the Rod, isn't it?"

"Well, not yet," Allen said.

"Here, read this...very carefully," Tony said, handing Mark a computer tablet with the message from Driscoll Headquarters displayed on its screen. He pulled out a chair for Mark as Lou rushed out the door and back to the briefing room. "You're going to want to take a seat, mate. It's a lot to take in."

As Allen worked diligently at his computer, Tony sat across the table from Mark and watched as his widening eyes scanned the tablet screen. Every few seconds, Mark would scroll to the next page with quivering hands. By the time he had finished reading the entire message, all of the color had drained from his face. About then, Lou reentered Control, took one look at Mark and said, "Looks like you're finished in here. I just left fifteen other people with that same look on their faces."

"Just about to wrap it up, mate," Tony said. He turned back to Mark, who was anxiously drumming his fingers on the table in front of him. "The reason you're here, Mark, is because, according to our files, you supervised the welding crew in space during the assembly of all the heavy equipment...such as the extrusion apparatus and the main coupling."

"That's right," replied Mark, though it seemed to him that he was answering through a thick fog. Everything he had just read was still swirling around in his head, and he had to fight to concentrate on Tony's immediate questions—something about an alternate plan. "I'm sorry," Mark said, "I missed that last part...I...what?"

"No worries, mate," Tony said, "It's a bloody lot to think about all at once. But what we need you to focus on right now is your part in all this. It's an Alternate Plan Bessie suggested."

"Bessie?" said Mark, looking from Tony to Lou. "Who's Bessie?"

"Bessie is the computer," Lou said. "Captain Creighton here gave it that name. I swear, I have no idea where this zany Brit comes up with this stuff." "I told you, mate...Bessie was my beloved childhood nanny!" Tony said defensively.

Lou rolled his eyes and looked back to Mark. "What Tony is trying to say is that the computer came up with an alternate plan to blowing ourselves to bits right here and never getting the Barge off anywhere." He scratched his stubbly cheek. He hadn't had a chance to shave that morning since he had been awakened so abruptly. "I'm telling you, Tony, I really don't think much of that first plan. You know, the whole blowing up the coupling strategy? I mean, I think we should do everything we can...but let's not get stupid. In the first place, I don't think even the figures will support the explosion idea—and even if they do, it's just too risky."

"And in the second place?" Tony asked, knowing there was more.

"In the second place, Plan A just plain sucks!" Lou retorted.

"Relax, mate, I'm with you," Tony agreed. "I favor the alternate plan, as well. But we don't know if that will work either."

"Well, Bessie...I mean, the goddamned computer says it will work. And everything we need is right there."

"Yes, but Bessie says the explosion would work, too," Tony reminded.

Lou turned to Mark. "Anyway, back to why you're here. The alternate plan is to dismantle the extrusion and smelting machinery and use the parts to build a torch big enough to cut through the ship's main coupling."

"Yes, that's what we need to know from you and your people, Mark," Tony added. "Do you think this is possible? And if so, how long will it take?"

"How long will it take?" Mark sputtered, slightly stunned by the idea. "Where, out here? I mean...out there?" he pointed toward Control's massive viewport. "Forever!"

"But the computer says it's possible," argued Allen who quickly spun around in his desk chair to face Mark. "She even gave us a step-by-step procedure."

"Then maybe the computer...or Bessie...or whatever the hell its name is, should try to build it!" Mark answered abruptly, surprising even himself. Then, suddenly remembering the high-powered company he was in, he decided he should be a little more flexible. "I mean...I'm not saying it's not possible; but you have to remember when we built this stuff, we had the help of a few thousand folks who aren't here with us now."

"We don't need them, Mark," said Tony. "We'll only be using a few of the parts of the smelting and extruding machinery."

"Primarily just the power source and ignition system from the smelting machinery, and the blast nozzle expulsion system of the extruder," Lou added. "And according to the computer, the flame should be hot enough to cut through the crucial points of the main coupling. Based, that is, on the performance statistics of both systems during their full time operation on the way out."

Mark seemed to cheer a little at that information. "Well, if your figures are based on the way that baby ran on the way out here, you've got one hell of a safety margin built in there. That entire system was running so far under the red line, it didn't even know it was on! I mean, it was just coasting. For a one time use, if we pull out all the stops, the jet that comes out of that blast nozzle will be way beyond a flame—it'll be pure hellfire!"

"Then you agree that it is possible," Tony said as he glared directly into Mark's face.

"Well, ah, I'll have to run a bunch of tests through the extrusion station computer...and, uh, brainstorm this out with a few key people in my department…" Mark was stalling for time while he quickly ran it through in his head, searching for any major obstacles. He wanted to give them a tentative answer right now, but on the other hand, he didn't like being put on the hot seat—he would rather share some of the heat with a few other people.

"Okay," he finally said after a long pause. "I agree it's possible, but I can make no commitment as to how long it will take. Not yet. Give me eight hours. I'll have a clear answer for you in eight hours."

"Make it four," said Lou.

"I'll try," Mark said as he stood up and shook Lou and Tony's hands.

A minute later, Mark found himself ambling down the passageway outside Control, wondering exactly what to do first, where to begin. As he glanced down at his computer tablet which now held the official version of the communication, he thought of Marla. Suddenly, he knew exactly what he should do first. When the Captains made the announcement to the rest of the City in about half an hour, he knew he wouldn't be able to be with her. He'd already be half way back to the rear of the Barge by then. And God only knew when he'd make it back. He decided he would go down to her lab and give her the news himself before he got back on the shuttle.

Just as Mark spun around in the passageway to head for the labs, he nearly ran smack into a door. An older man in a white lab coat, who appeared to be in quite a daze, emerged slowly from the room. The man was followed by a handful of other people with the same stricken look, slowly wandering out of the briefing room one at a time. And then Mark saw her. Marla. Her long black curls were tied back in a low ponytail, and her cobalt eyes were wider than he'd ever seen them. She already knew.

Their eyes met and they made their way toward each other in the crowded corridor. When Marla finally managed to push her way through all the meandering people, she collapsed in Mark's arms.

"Oh my God," she said softly in his ear.

"I know," Mark said, trying to sound soothing—but his voice sounded flat in the muted passageway. "I have to get to work," he said. "And seeing as you were just in there," he gestured back at the briefing room, "I'm guessing we're both going to be a little busy for a while."

"Yep," she said curtly. She pulled away from Mark so she could look at him. He noticed that Marla's eyes were brimming with tears, but he could tell she was struggling to push down her emotions.

"I'll be back as soon as I can," he assured her, reaching out to tuck a stray curl behind her ear.

He gave her another hug and a discreet kiss on the cheek, and they walked in opposite directions, each to their appointed tasks—tasks that would insure they would ultimately have plenty of time together. All the time in *their* world.

CHAPTER THIRTY-ONE

Two Parties

Marla stared at the glass on the table in front of her, watching intently as a drop of water slid down its side.

"I love the sound of rain," she said, as if in a dream.

Mark looked over at her. She wasn't wearing her glasses tonight, and her long black lashes fluttered against her flushed cheeks as she gazed at a highball glass filled with melting ice and whiskey. It had been a week since they learned they would be stuck on the Legacy project for at least eight more years, and Mark suspected his girlfriend was far more disappointed than she let on.

"The sound of rain?" he asked as he reached over and grabbed her delicate hand. "What do you mean?" "I love the way it sounds…pattering on a roof, or against a window…" She drifted off momentarily, then quickly tore her eyes away from the beads of condensation and looked up at Mark, Barbara, and Allen. She looked a little embarrassed, as if she hadn't realized she had been voicing her thoughts out loud.

"Oh, nothing," she said. "I was just rememberin' some things I haven't let myself think about for some time. Like the sound of rain on my family's tin roof at the mountain house," she reflected, floating back into her memories again. Mark marveled at how Marla's southern accent was slowly creeping back into her voice as she talked about her childhood.

"You know," she went on, her North Carolina drawl becoming more noticeable with every word, "when I was little, I always thought it was beautiful when the sun shone through the rain. And whenever that happened, whenever the sun came out in the middle of a rainstorm, my Grandma would say, 'Look, Marla. The devil is beatin' his wife!'"

"The devil is *beating* his wife?" Barbara mused. "What the heck does that mean?"

"It's just an old Southern saying. You know, somethin' you say when the sun comes out while it's still raining. But I told my Daddy I didn't like it. I thought it sounded god-awful. So he told me, 'Well, honey, then we should come up with our own way to describe that wonder.' And we did."

"So what did you decide to call it?" Barbara asked as she clumsily sipped from her wine glass.

"From then on, whenever the sun came shinin' through the rain, my Daddy and I would say, 'Hey, look! The angels are laughin' through their tears.'"

"Oh, that's nice," Barbara slurred as she patted Allen's arm. "Baby, isn't that so much nicer than the devil one?" Allen nodded in agreement as he polished off a glass of beer.

"Anyway," Marla said, snapping back to the here and now, "I haven't let myself think about this stuff for a long time…I guess because I thought I'd be back on Earth soon and didn't want to tease myself with thoughts of rain, the mountains, my family. I mean, I figured I could hold off for another few months, but now…now it's so far away. I'm afraid if I don't remember it now, I may forget it forever."

"It's not forever," Mark said, lacing his fingers in hers. "It's just a continuation of…well…a different part of our lives. Or something." It didn't come out right, and he knew it was probably no consolation to Marla. He hated how every time he tried to be sensitive, it just came across as awkward.

Allen held up his glass at the passing bartender. "Y'all up for another round?" he asked. Since no one answered, he just ordered another beer for himself. "Personally," he said, "I like to look at it as kind of a sabbatical from reality. I mean, here we are, having voted unanimously to sit out here, wherever here is, for the better part of the next decade…with nuthin' to do 'cept stay alive. And I figure we can spend most of that time right here in Crystal City's super cool, not to mention *only*, nightclub."

"And it's just your luck," added Barbara as she gave her shoulder length blonde hair an exuberant flip, "that out here, it's always night!"

"Oh yeah, that's a nice fringe benefit." Allen took a gulp of beer and slammed his glass noisily on the table. "Shit, I'd say we're entitled to fringe benefits. After all, it doesn't get more out on the fringe than this! Now y'all sure you don't want another drink? I mean come on y'all, there's no better brain eradicator than whiskey, wine, and beer!"

Mark was privately wishing that he could fall asleep right there at the table. "No thanks," he murmured. "I think I've eradicated about as much of my brain as I can afford. Anyway, I've got to be back out there early in the morning." He rubbed his weary face. "But this was fun. I can't believe we were all off at the same time for once."

"Yep," Allen said. "Well, after this rush, things oughta slow down a bit. Then we'll have plenty of time for drinkin' here at the Crystal Club."

"That's right," Marla said with a sad nod. "All the time in the universe…"

"Ahem, excuse me," a bartender interrupted. "Chief Ranier?"

"Yeah?" Mark answered as he looked up with bloodshot eyes.

"You have an urgent call from Captain Tortona."

Mark knew immediately that something must have happened out at the coupling. The crew was still out there testing the arc, the device that operated the torch, for the second time. He nervously patted at his pants pockets. "Oh shit, I left my mobile back in the apartment…"

"I have him on the line here," the bartender said as he handed a small two-way mobile to Mark.

"Captain Tortona, what is it?" he said into the speaker.

"Ranier," Lou's voice shouted from the other end. "You've got to get out here right away…something's going wrong. The torch is breaking up!"

"I'm on my way," he said before tossing the mobile back to the bartender.

"What's wrong?" Marla said, her blue eyes flashing with panic.

"I'm not sure, but I gotta get going," he said as he gave Marla a quick kiss goodbye. He couldn't help wondering what the hell a ship's captain was doing out on a work crew detail. He had a sinking feeling in his stomach, and as he raced out of the room he suddenly felt wide-awake.

As Mark Ranier left his friends in the club, Jeff and Carol Driscoll waited for their friends in a similar club billions of miles away. The group in the first party had just received some bad news. The people in the second party were about to.

Driscoll stood up as Pete Teegan, the head of National Dynamics, and his fiancée Janice Blake approached the table. "How's it going, Pete?" Driscoll said, extending a hand to his colleague.

"Hi, Janice," Carol said to Janice, a stick-thin brunette in a fuchsia wrap dress. "Love your dress…that's a great color on you!"

Janice leaned into Carol and gave her an air kiss on each cheek. "Thanks," she said. "You look beautiful, as always."

They all sat down at the table, ordered cocktails, and proceeded to chitchat about the terrible LA traffic and the unusually cool weather. But Driscoll didn't utter a word. He was too preoccupied with what was going on four billion miles away.

Finally, he looked over at Pete and said, "So everything is slightly ahead of schedule on the Barge. They should have just finished the second of three tests on the arc. I'm guessing they'll be able to separate in two days."

"So far, so good," Teegan said as the waitress placed a martini in front of him. "That's great news, Jeff. This really relieves a lot of the tension surrounding this mess."

"No kidding," Carol interjected. "Thank God they went with Plan B to build the torch instead of Plan A."

"What was Plan A?" Janice asked.

"Basically, to blow things up," Carol said matter-of-factly. Janice raised a dark eyebrow at that, and Carol took a delicate sip of her red wine. She glanced over at her husband with sparkling eyes. "Jeffrey, I really do wish you would outgrow that childish compulsion of yours to blow up things that are a source of irritation for you."

"Dammit, I've told you a hundred times, that wasn't my fault!" Driscoll said, digging up his old defense as he tried to suppress a grin. "Mohammad swore they were concussion grenades…or gas bombs, as he called them. How was I supposed to know they were real grenades?"

Janice perked up and peered over the rim of her martini glass, which was filled with bright green Appletini. "Gas bombs," she said, her brown eyes widening. "What gas bombs? What on Earth are you talking about?" Unlike Pete, she had never heard about the Moombato Bay fiasco.

"It's a long story, Janice," Pete replied. "I'll tell you later, although you probably won't believe it anyway."

Janice looked to Carol, who just shrugged and took another sip of wine.

"So Driscoll, what's going on with the Kabrini communications?" Pete prodded. "Anything new?"

"Well," Driscoll said, leaning back in his seat, "so far, we've been able to avoid telling them anything about our, uh, little situation here. And if all goes as planned, we won't have to tell them."

"What if they ask about our people on the Barge?" Pete asked before popping an olive in his mouth. "I mean damn, Driscoll," he said as he chewed, "they're going to be out there for another eight years."

"Well, if the Kabrini want to know whatever happened to our people out there…" he gestured toward the nearest window, which was blinking with a neon beer sign.

"Our people on the freeway?" Carol joked.

Driscoll ignored her remark. "If they ask if our people in space ever made it back safely, we'll just say there was some sort of malfunction out there, but we've sent a rescue ship to bring them home. That they'll be delayed somewhat."

"Yes, *somewhat*," Carol added, her voice oozing with sarcasm. "Just eight years. Are you sure that lying to those folks is the smartest thing to do? I mean, I have a feeling they're pretty damn smart. And if they catch us in a lie, they won't think very much of us."

"They already don't think much of us because we told them the truth about the way we live," Driscoll said as he gazed down into his drink. "Shit, I'm beginning to think we should've lied to them from the very beginning. I think the basic problem is that they just don't like us."

"Snobs!" Carol said with a smirk.

"What do you mean, they don't like us?" Pete asked. "What did we ever do to them?"

"Nothing," Driscoll answered. "It's what we do to ourselves and to our own people that they don't like."

"Okay," Carol said as she swirled her wine glass, "then I suppose 'malfunction' is a truthful and accurate description of the problem. Only, it's a malfunction of the human race, not the Barge."

"Yep, that's my point," Driscoll added. "The Kabrini just don't understand our social and economic problems. They don't get how we could be so technologically advanced yet still so socially primitive… without having obliterated our own species ages ago."

Pete Teegan scratched at the bald spot on top of his head and shifted in his seat. "And they don't want to feel responsible for helping us do it now. Is that it?"

"Pretty much," Driscoll agreed. "They believe we already know more than is good for us. I think they see us as some kind of high-tech savages. It's not that they don't want to communicate…"

"They just don't know what to say," Carol finished for him.

"Exactly," Driscoll said, looking over at his wife. "So they've pretty much stopped talking to us. And they said they won't communicate with us again until we can prove that we're attempting to improve our situation here."

"I see," said Pete. "So we have to find some way to convince them that we're responsible…a good risk."

"Yes, I think so," said Driscoll, "and according to them, the only way to do that is if we make some social changes they've recommended and improve our general situation as a race."

"I don't understand," Janice said, leaning so far forward, the tips of her long brown hair dipped into her drink. "How could they possibly know if we're keeping our end of the bargain?"

"I can't really answer that yet," Driscoll said, "But they stressed that they would know. They were very serious about that, and it certainly made an impression on the United Nations council."

"Well, that's just ridiculous," said Carol. "Seriously, they live, what, thousands of light years away from us? How could they possibly know? Or are they just trying to use the old Santa Claus threat: 'He knows if you've been bad or good, so be good for goodness sake!'" she sang in a mockingly cheerful voice. "That trick doesn't even work on children!"

"And that's apparently how they see us," Janice added, "as children."

"Yes," Driscoll agreed, "children with guns. I guess they don't know whether they should try to get the child to put down the gun or teach him how to use it safely."

"Come on, Driscoll," Pete said with a grimace,

"that analogy is insulting. We're not all just a bunch of violent children on this planet."

"I'm beginning to wonder about that," Driscoll said as he lifted his glass to his lips. Just as he was about to take a sip, his smartphone jingled in his pocket. He pulled it out and looked at the screen: "Driscoll Headquarters."

"Gotta take this," Driscoll said rising from the table. "It's probably an update about the torch."

"Good news, I hope," Pete said as he raised his glass to Carol and Janice.

It was not.

CHAPTER THIRTY-TWO

Hitting the Fan

Ranier suited up and was transported outside the Barge in record time. As the shuttle approached the coupling, the point where the City met the Barge, he could easily see why the torch was no longer holding together. Mark wiped the faceplate of his suit and squinted as he took in the situation, attempting to wrap his brain around what had happened. From what he could tell, a support stanchion at the base of the rotating Crystal City had caught the arm of the torch, breaking it at a joint. The broken segment had pushed backwards and into the torch, smashing its hastily rigged control panel. The torch must have ignited as it rammed into the coupling, and it had already cut halfway through it by the time Mark arrived. The shuttle docked with the Barge, and Mark exited through the hatch into the Barge's main control room. He was immediately met by Lou and the Crew Chief.

"Mark," Lou said. His face was strained. So was his voice. "We can't shut it down! A lot has happened since you left, and it happened fast." Lou's description of the events matched up exactly with Mark's theory about what had happened, except for one minor detail. Mark had not made the jump to the only logical conclusion of their current situation— there was no stopping the torch. As Mark began suggesting a repair strategy, Lou abruptly interrupted him. "We have to separate, Mark," he said. "We have to separate now."

Mark stared open-mouthed at the Captain. "But...but, we can't!" he finally managed. "We're not ready, dammit. The Barge flight plan hasn't even been programmed in yet...and the final separation has to be piloted."

Mark's mind was racing about all the details that had to fall in place in order for the separation to work. They had walked through it hundreds of times. At the final moment, when the torch cut through the last of the coupling, the Barge and the City would jackknife slightly toward each other because of the rotation of the Crystal City. Tony, who would be piloting the City, and Lou, who would be piloting the Barge, would have to make the necessary adjustments to avoid a collision. But the City's response would be slow since there were only a few jets mounted around the ship's perimeter. So Lou would have to use the Barge's powerful engines to push away from the City and toward its final suicidal rendezvous with the terrorist rocket.

At that point, the only people remaining on the Barge—Lou, Mark, the Crew Chief and two of his mechanics—would transfer as quickly as possible to the shuttle and launch themselves back toward the City as the Barge thundered silently away from them. It would be the last time anyone would lay eyes on the Barge. Once Lou started the Barge's forceful engines, the ship would continue through its program to the final destruct sequence. Due to the slowly building overload, this sequence could not be stopped or interrupted. The engines would ultimately annihilate themselves and everything around them— including the terrorist rocket. It would happen neatly, efficiently and precisely on schedule.

Mark snapped back to the present when Lou grabbed him by the shoulders. "We have to be ready, Mark," Lou said, his eyes wide and serious. "And we can do it. Things were going so smoothly out here with the torch, we went ahead and programmed the Barge today. We were planning to rehearse the maneuver tomorrow."

Mark turned and looked out the viewport at the blazing torch and began to slowly accept the situation. "So much for a dress rehearsal," he mumbled. "Then, we're really going to do it?"

"We're really going to do it," Lou said. "At this point, we don't really have a choice."

Mark was startled when he heard Tony's voice crack from the two-way on Lou's belt. "Are you blokes ready out there, or what?"

Lou grabbed the mobile off his belt and said into the speaker, "Yep, we're ready. You just make sure you're ready with those extra shuttles… just in case."

That comment didn't do much to relax Mark, who was nervously looking back to the Barge's shuttle bay. The ironic thing was that the only reason he had to be here at all was to supervise the operation of the torch. But since the torch now seemed to be on automatic, he didn't really have anything to do. "Guess I'm just along for the ride," he said.

"Don't worry, mate," Tony's voice cracked over Lou's radio again. "We've got one shuttle floating and one crewed up and waiting. And Chief Ranier, let me be the first to congratulate you. That's one bloody hell of a torch you built there!"

"Yeah, it works just goddamned great," Mark muttered under his breath. "Too bad it's completely out of control."

"Hey Lou," Tony called, "to hasten your departure, why don't you have Ranier hop into the shuttle and give that squirrel a proper thrashing. You know, get it good and revved up for your get-away."

"Why don't you go beat your own damn squirrel!" Lou barked back. "I want Ranier right here watching this runaway torch! It's almost cut completely through…"

"Looks like about another minute," Mark answered, narrowing his golden eyes, which reflected the orange torch flame. While he kind of liked the idea of going back to the shuttle, he did want to see the final separation. Anyway, he'd rather do his job than just sit back and wait helplessly like a nervous passenger. "Less than a minute now, I think," he said. He watched intently through the control room viewport as the two suited up crew mechanics handled the cables, which guided the blindingly bright jet of flame through the last section of the coupling. Once the torch finally cut through, the crew workers would drop the cables and let the torch trail behind the Barge as they made their way back to the shuttle bay to meet Lou, Mark, and the Crew Chief.

Mark kept watching as the intense flame blasted through the metal, with only a few feet remaining. "Right about now," he said.

Lou jabbed the button on his two-way. "Here we go, Tony!"

"Rightio," Tony's voice answered. "Good luck, mate!"

Mark stared unblinking as the torch cut through the final sliver of metal. The next thing happened so fast, none of them saw it coming. When the torch cut through, the rotating Crystal City and Barge jackknifed so violently toward each other, it caused the Barge to lurch, nearly throwing

Lou out of the navigator's seat. Mark crashed into a wall, and the Crew Chief found himself clinging to the ceiling. When Mark got his bearings he raced to the viewport to see that the two mechanics outside had been flung into space, still clutching the cable as they dangled above the vast blackness.

"Lou! Lou!" Tony's voice squawked from the intercom. "Are you chaps alright?"

"We're good, Tony," Lou replied as he hastily pressed buttons on the control panel to start the engine program.

"Well, how about getting the hell out of there!" Tony responded. "That wasn't exactly a smooth separation now, was it? Come on, mate you don't have any time to spare. I've sent a shuttle to rescue those two poor bastards swinging on the space rope toward Andromeda."

Lou kicked in the main thrusters, and the Barge soared effortlessly away from the City. "Everything's going as planned here, Tony," he said. "We're about to jump on our shuttle and get the hell outta here."

"Ah, Lou," Tony's suddenly grave voice crackled. "Lou, I think you'd better have Ranier check out your shuttle now. Looks like we have a bit of a problem, mate."

Lou was still busy punching buttons on the Barge's flight control panel. "What the hell are you babbling about, Tony?" he asked.

"Do you know where the remains of the bloody torch are?" Tony inquired.

"Trailing behind us?" Lou replied, hopefully. "Try sticking out of the middle of your bloody shuttle," Tony said without a trace of humor.

Mark stumbled back from the shuttle bay looking pale. "Good thing I didn't get on the shuttle earlier," he said. "The damn thing is destroyed."

Lou looked at Mark in disbelief and then leapt up and ran to the shuttle bay hatch. He peered inside and saw nothing but a few charred remains. "Oh, shit!"

"The City shuttle is lifting off right now, mate," Tony shouted over the two-way.

Lou walked away from the shuttle bay and collapsed back into the navigator's seat. "Forget it," he said calmly into the two-way. "It's too late. If we were going to leave, we'd have to leave now. The first shuttle is still chasing those two mechanics," he thumbed at the viewport. "If the other

is just now lifting off, they'll probably never catch us, and if they did....
they would never get back. They'd just be stuck here with us. And let me
assure you—we are fucking stuck!"

Mark peered out the viewport and could see one shuttle moving away
from the Barge in pursuit of two tiny figures that seemed to be involved in
some strange, slow motion tug of war as they swung around each other at
the end of the cable. Far beyond that, he saw the second shuttle just leaving
the City bay. As the distance between the Barge and the City steadily grew,
a shudder raced through Mark's body. Lou was right. They were stuck.
There was no way back. Not to the City. Not to Marla. Not to anywhere
other than the Barge's pre-programmed course to oblivion in the darkest
depths of space.

CHAPTER THIRTY-THREE

The Truth, The Whole Truth…

The stunned members of the United Nations Emergency Council sat spellbound as Driscoll wrapped up his explanation. Although he had spoken eloquently and passionately, Driscoll could not hide the fatigue he suffered after two sleepless nights. He wore dark purple circles under his bloodshot eyes, his clothes were wrinkled, and he sported a five o'clock shadow—even though it was nine in the morning. In the past forty-eight hours, he had been on the phone with Pete Teegan and General Hodge practically non-stop, hastily flown from LA to Vienna in a private jet (he still wasn't sure whose it was) and accumulated as much relevant data as possible so he could convince the UN Council to agree to his one-shot rescue effort.

"Dammit, they just *have* to understand the urgency of the situation and the need for immediate action," he had told General Hodge earlier that morning. "And this course of action is the only thing that will work."

Hodge had nodded knowingly, recalling his days on the battlefield.

"I know the UN loves to talk things to death…but there's just no goddamned time for a lengthy discussion or a detailed study of this issue. If we waste another moment, those men on that Barge out there will certainly die."

"You've already lost one of your men, correct?" Hodge said, glaring at Driscoll with his penetrating stare.

"Yes…God bless the poor bastard's soul," Driscoll said somberly. When the rescue shuttle finally caught up with the two mechanics dangling in space, they hauled both spacesuits aboard. One held a mechanic who was miraculously still alive, although paralyzed with shock. The other spacesuit had a small gash in it, and it contained all the ingredients for a human being, but in puree form.

Driscoll had no intention of adding to that casualty list. They had lost all contact with the Barge, so he had no idea whether the three people stranded on that ship planned to courageously ride out the sequence and allow themselves to be blown to atoms. If suicide did not appeal to them, they may decide to take matters into their own hands. They still had maneuvering control over the ship, and Captain Tortona could make a slow wide turn and set a course that would bring them close enough to the City for them to disembark and be retrieved by a shuttle from the City. But if they wanted to save themselves, they would have to do it as soon as possible. After their departure, the Barge would need to continue past the Crystal City for at least a few million miles before it detonated; otherwise the massive explosion would annihilate the City. Of course, if the men aboard the Barge did change course and head back to the City, the terrorist missile would continue its journey unchallenged—and ultimately destroy Earth's only connection with the Kabrini.

Nevertheless, Driscoll had a plan. It was the only humane thing to do, and he wanted to be the one to initiate it so he could maintain as much control over the situation as possible. The first part of his plan was to tell the Kabrini the truth, the whole truth and nothing but the truth about their current predicament. Driscoll hoped and prayed the Kabrini could give them some advice about how to save the men hurtling toward their doom in the Barge.

But Driscoll's plan was a two-way gamble. First, he was betting that if the Kabrini were convinced of the impending destruction of Earth's link with them, they might relent and use the short time remaining to enlighten the human race with as much knowledge as possible. Of course, whatever the Kabrini decided to share would be completely at their discretion—but at this point, Driscoll felt any information they could get was better than nothing. He knew the human species had much to learn from this ancient, highly advanced civilization—if only they could convince the Kabrini to share.

But he had another bet, and he didn't tell the UN about this one. It was still a nebulous idea even in his own mind, but he had discussed it with Carol the night before in their hotel suite.

Driscoll had been sitting at the desk, bathed in the blue glow of his computer, and Carol was sprawled across the bed, staring out the vast wall-length window, admiring the twinkling stars in the cold Vienna sky. She couldn't stop thinking about those poor people up there, four billion miles away from home, uncertain whether or not they'd ever make it back.

"Something keeps bothering me…" Driscoll's voice cut into the tense silence. "Something about the Kabrini's promise that they would know if we don't keep up our end of the bargain." He leaned back in his chair and propped his bare feet on the desk. "They said they would know, and even though I don't understand how that's physically possible…I believe them."

Carol rolled from her side to her back to get a better view of her husband. He was still painfully handsome…but in recent months, she had noticed streaks of gray had quickly crept throughout his entire head of hair, and tributaries of lines had spread across his forehead and around his eyes. A pang of sadness stabbed at her heart as she realized their dreams of having a baby were probably out of reach at this point. Somewhere along the way, she and Jeff had gotten old. Her husband had been so preoccupied with the Kabrini and this Legacy project for the past few years, they hadn't discussed children in ages. Tears stung at her eyes, but she quickly wiped them away.

"First of all," he continued, "I can't come up with a single reason why they would lie." He ran his fingers through his perpetually messy hair. "And secondly, the Kabrini didn't have anything to gain from talking to humans in the first place, except for maybe their own amusement. So they must be telling the truth, right? They must somehow know."

"It's not impossible," Carol mumbled as she rolled back on her side to face the window. "I mean, if they're so technologically advanced…maybe they have some kind of high-tech, super-spy gadgets or something."

"Or maybe I'm just clutching at straws," he said, switching off the computer. Driscoll curled up in the bed next to his wife, but he never fell asleep. He simply stared at the pinpricks of light in the night sky for an hour or two as he listened to Carol's breaths grow deeper.

Well, of course he was clutching at straws.

Driscoll stepped down from the podium at the front of the UN Council conference room. He returned to the empty seat next to Carol, clutching his notes (and straws) tightly, and prayed that he had made his point.

He had. The vote was immediate and unanimous. The UN Council would back Driscoll in his one-shot effort. They would tell the Kabrini the truth and wait for the ancient civilization to offer a solution…and hopefully open mankind's eyes to a wealth of knowledge.

CHAPTER THIRTY-FOUR

From There to Here

As Mark Ranier watched the Crystal City along with everything he cared about drift steadily away, he felt as if his life were floating off without him. He thought about Marla and wondered how she was handling the news, only dimly aware of the conversation between Tony and Lou in the background.

"We'll wait, I said," Lou barked at Tony through his two-way. "Until we hear from Earth, we'll wait!"

"Look, mate," Tony replied, trying to sound as warm and understanding as he could, but the effect was lost in the two-way's tiny speaker. "We've already put it to a vote here…and the outcome was that nobody on the City would blame you blokes for turning that bloody truck around while you still can."

"That's pretty goddamned democratic of you, Tony, especially for an Englishman. But I'm in command of this God forsaken ship, and I say we're waiting until we hear from Driscoll!" Lou paused, then added much more quietly, "Anyway, we already took a vote here, too. And we all decided to stay on course."

Mark couldn't believe what he was hearing. He knew he could never explain to himself, or to Marla, what had inspired him to vote for staying on course. Whether it was an incredible act of heroism or downright stupidity, it had just felt right at the moment. Whatever it was, he was immediately certain he would regret it.

While Ranier mulled this over, wondering if he'd ever have a chance to explain it all to Marla, back on Earth Driscoll and the UN Council finished transmitting the last of the long, but truthful story to the Kabrini. They confessed, shamefully, that members of their own species had launched a missile that would destroy Earth's communication link with the Kabrini network. They explained that they had attempted to stop the missile themselves, but things had gone terribly wrong…and now three more of their men were going to die if they couldn't figure out a way to save them immediately. They admitted that they also had made a hasty decision that would leave hundreds more of their people stranded on the Crystal City for at least another eight years. They offered up every disgraceful, excruciating detail in hopes that the Kabrini could help.

Driscoll, General Hodge and the other UN Council members crowded around the blank computer screen and waited on bated breath for a response. Driscoll's hands trembled uncontrollably, and he shoved them quickly in his pockets in an attempt to hide his apprehension. After what felt like an eternity, a message suddenly materialized on the floating screen: *"ON THE LONG ROAD TO GREATNESS, THE FIRST STEP BEGINS WITH THE TRUTH. AT LONG LAST, YOUR JOURNEY HAS BEGUN."*

Driscoll turned his panicked eyes to General Hodge, who was still staring at the computer screen. "What the hell does that mean?" Driscoll muttered.

Hodge looked back at him and said gravely, "I have no goddamned clue."

As the people on Earth considered the Kabrini's answer, Mark Ranier considered how he felt. He felt strange. Very strange. He was sick to his stomach—of course, he had felt that way ever since he first laid eyes on the Barge's demolished escape shuttle. But besides that queasy feeling that goes hand in hand with a general sense of doom, Mark suddenly felt even more unusual. A tingling sensation tickled at his scalp and quickly raced through his head. It traveled through his chest, radiating out to his shoulders, arms and hands before sweeping through his stomach and legs and finally settling in his feet. His entire body had gone all pins and needles. And then the prickly feeling transformed into a throb, progressing into something more intense…something more like searing, excruciating pain. Mark felt as if his body was being torn into pieces, and he was certain he must be dying. He heard a tortured groan emanate from behind him, and when he swung away from the viewport, he could not believe his eyes. Lou was doubled over in agony, staring at his own hands like he'd never seen them before, and the Crew Chief had completely collapsed and curled up into a ball on the floor. As Mark looked at both of them, he was astonished to see that they were no longer whole. The outline of their bodies was still there—he could still tell that it was Lou and the Crew Chief—but they looked pixilated, as if they had split into millions upon millions of tiny swarming, floating points, like those bizarre dot paintings he studied in high school art class. He could actually see the Barge's control panel right through their bodies. Fighting the urge to scream out in horror, Mark decided he did not want to spend his last living moment in fear. He turned his gaze back to the viewport and tried to look through the space separating himself from Marla, but his vision seemed to be failing; everything around him was fading away. He closed his eyes and thought of Marla's angelic face, her long sable ringlets drifting in a mountain breeze. He imagined diving into her wide-open eyes, swimming deeper and deeper into the comforting blue depths until he curled up at the sandy bottom, content to rest there for all eternity. And then he felt movement, a tugging feeling, as if he were being swept up in a current. When he forced open his eyes, he discovered he was enveloped in blackness…and just as quickly as it had arrived, the pain was gone. Only the prickly feeling remained. The tingling sensation swept back up through his body, this time from the bottom of his feet through his legs, chest, arms and neck, before exiting through the top of his head. His vision slowly cleared, and once his sight returned and he gathered his wits, he realized that he was not dead, after all. He, Lou and the Crew Chief were standing side-by-side, all completely whole again…and they were staring nose to nose with the Crystal City's main shuttle bay. The Barge was dead and motionless, so close to the City that they could almost jump across.

"It's gone!" Tony's voice shouted through the mobile.

"No, Tony," Lou yelled back, just as perplexed as Mark. "We're here… the Barge is right here!"

"I know, mate," Tony replied. "And I can't tell you how goddamned thrilled I am that you're back. We just saw the ship suddenly appear…it's a bloomin' miracle. But I was talking about the missile. It's gone! It just disappeared off our long-range scanners. It bloody vanished!"

Less than two hours later, Mark was reclining in a bed in the City's hospital with Marla curled up next to him. He was trying as best as he could to explain to her what had just happened. Marla gazed at him from behind her glasses and stroked his face gently...as if she were trying to convince herself that he was actually there with her. "I'll never understand what the hell just happened," she said. "But I'm just so glad you're back!" Her voice cracked as she hugged Mark tightly and nuzzled her small face into his neck.

Barbara suddenly dashed through the doorway and threw her arms around both of them. "Oh, Marla!" she said, "Thank God he's okay!"

"Neat trick, Mark," Allen said as he strolled in behind Barbara, "but would you mind telling us just what the hell is going on?"

"I was just trying to explain it to Marla," Mark answered, still holding Marla close. "I was on the Barge thinking it was...well, all over for us... when all of a sudden I started to feel...strange. I don't know exactly how to describe it. At first I felt all tingly..." Mark squinted at Allen for a moment and then looked down at Marla, who was still nestled close to him. "Oh my God...it's happening again! Do you feel it, Marla? Can you feel it?" He squeezed Marla closer and looked up at Barbara and Allen. They didn't utter a word, but he could tell they could feel something.

"Mark, I'm scared," Marla whispered as she looked up at him with a pale face. "What's happening? I feel all...prickly. What is it?"

"It's okay, Marla, I promise," he reassured her, stroking her fading black curls. "I don't know what it is, but we're going to be okay. Whatever it is, it saved me."

Allen looked over at Barbara, who was paralyzed with fear. He took her hand and said, "It's gonna be alright, baby. It's all gonna be just fine..."

At that very moment, back on Earth, a small jet took off from Vienna and pointed its nose towards Los Angeles. It was the same jet that had flown Driscoll and Carol to Vienna, but this time Pete Teegan and his fiancée Janice were with them. It turned out that Pete was the one who had arranged the private charter that had so hastily flown Driscoll to Vienna. He and Janice had hopped on a commercial flight the next day and met Driscoll in Vienna.

"They're going to help!" Driscoll insisted. Carol had been peering out the tiny airplane window at the pink sun-streaked clouds, but now she turned to look at Jeff's profile. "I just know they're going to help us. You'll see. I don't know how…not yet…" Driscoll's bright blue eyes shone with anticipation and his knee shook rhythmically as he bounced his foot up and down on the floor. Carol took his hand in hers, hoping it would calm his nerves.

"I think there's a lot more to the Kabrini than they've let on about. But I feel like they've been hinting at it," he said, rubbing his bristly face with his free hand. "I think they planned to tell us eventually, but these recent events will force them to spill it. They've been holding back something big, I just know it. They didn't want to tell us because they knew we were lying to them…but now that we're in a tough spot, they'll let it all out. They'll have to!"

"But they're so far away," said Janice, as she placed a glass of sparkling champagne on the table in front of her. She and Allen were facing Jeff and Carol, kicked back in the private plane's comfortable, oversized leather seats. "What can they possibly do from way out there?"

As if in response to Janice's question, a flight attendant walked up and said, "Excuse me, sir, but your headquarters are on the phone." She motioned to the armrest of his seat, and Driscoll flipped open the top and pulled out a phone.

"Jeffrey Driscoll here," he said, barely able to contain his anticipation. Carol watched her husband intently as he listened quietly for a few moments. Suddenly his face went pale. "That's impossible!" he said quietly. "Wait, are you absolutely positive? This has been confirmed?" He listened again, frozen solid in his seat. "Okay, thank you," he finally muttered through a clenched throat. He tried to put the phone back in his seat's arm, but he missed, and it clattered to the floor.

"Jeff?" Carol asked softly, taking his hand again.

"Holy shit," was all Driscoll could manage. "Jeff?" Carol repeated. "What is it? What happened?"

Driscoll's face had gone completely blank, and he had a wild look in his eyes. He turned slowly to face Carol.

"It's back," he whispered.

"What's back?" Pete asked, leaning forward in his seat.

"They're back," Driscoll answered. "All of them. They're all back. It's all back…in Earth's orbit. The City, the Crystal City. And the Barge. And everyone.

197

They're all just floating out there in Earth's orbit…all of it. All of them. It's all back…"

"But…how?" Carol asked, gripping Driscoll's arm, her bright red fingernails digging into his skin. "How is that possible?"

"I-I don't know…but just all of a sudden. Poof! There it was! And that's not all…"

"What?" Pete said anxiously. "What the hell else?"

"The missile…the terrorist missile," Driscoll said, still staring into his wife's emerald eyes, her freckled brow crinkled with fear and confusion. "It's there, too, Carol! The missile is just dead in space…no power emanating from it at all. Just floating in Earth's orbit with all the others."

"But…what…" Pete stammered from across the table.

"They sent it all back, that's what! The Kabrini…they sent it all right the hell back to us! I knew they were advanced, but…holy hell, I never even imagined they could do something like this. It must be some kind of highly developed telekinesis, spanning time and space…or…or…my God! It's unimaginable…" He held his head in his hands as if his brain might explode. And suddenly, he burst into laughter.

"What's so damn funny?" Pete asked, sounding annoyed. "I don't see anything funny about it!"

"Don't you see?" laughed Driscoll. "The joke is on us."

Pete, Janice, and Carol just stared open-mouthed at him, as if he'd completely lost his marbles.

"Don't you get it? They never needed it!" Driscoll explained, his blue eyes frenzied with fresh understanding. "If they are capable of…of…this, they don't really need the Network at all! I mean, maybe they used it a long time ago, but these beings have transcended space and time itself. I mean, this little trick they just pulled…it's nothing short of teleportation. Teleportation of living, breathing beings! My God, just think of what they can teach us."

"So the Network was just….what…a hobby?" Carol asked.

"Yep…like an antique radio they enjoy turning on every now and then to see what they can pick up on it. And they picked US up on it!"

"I bet by now they wish they had changed the channel," Carol remarked.

"Too late," Driscoll said, shaking his head at her.

"They're too involved to back out now. They've already shown us too much. They'll have to stay in pretty close touch with us from now on, I'd think."

"But why?" asked Pete. "What's to stop them from just saying, 'The Hell with Earth,' and pulling the plug?"

"No way," Driscoll argued. "I bet they feel obligated to maintain some sort of control over the things we learn from them. Otherwise, we'll do what we always end up doing with this kind of information—use it for profit or destruction. Damn, come to think of it…I doubt we're the first socially inept race the Kabrini have come across and had to coax along."

He drummed his fingers on the table in front of him as his mind drifted far beyond the airplane cabin. "I mean, just think how the Kabrini could enlighten us," he finally said dreamily. "With their guidance, we could make the world a better place. Mankind could take a giant evolutionary jump ahead of itself."

"Nothing wrong with a shortcut, I guess," Pete said thoughtfully.

"You're goddamned right, there's not," Driscoll fired back enthusiastically. He finally relaxed and leaned back in his seat. As he propped his scuffed boots on the table in front of him, he gave Carol a boyish wink. "Yep…I've got a feeling we ain't seen nothin' yet!"

CHAPTER THIRTY-FIVE

Eyes Wide Open

Less than a week later, Driscoll stood gazing out his massive office window at the smoggy skyline. General Hodge, dressed in full uniform, was sitting straight as an arrow at the table behind him saying, "The Kabrini resumed communications immediately after they rescued the Crystal City."

"I knew it," Driscoll said turning to face the silver haired general, whose medals glinted in the LA sunset. "They just wanted us to be honest with them…and somehow, they knew we weren't telling them the truth."

"I have to admit, Mr. Driscoll," Hodge said as he folded his hands on the table in front of him, "that was one hell of a stunt they pulled. I still can't quite wrap my brain around it. How in God's name did they neutralize that missile and send it, the Crystal City and all of those people back into Earth's orbit…within just a matter of minutes?"

"Teleportation," Driscoll said as he collapsed into the leather chair behind his desk. "It's the only explanation."

"Well, whatever the hell it was, the Department of Defense sure could use it," Hodge added as he glared at Driscoll with his penetrating stare.

"I think that's precisely the opposite of what the Kabrini wants," Driscoll said, "which is exactly why they won't share that technology with us until we can prove we're socially responsible enough to use it only for good."

Hodge started to roll his eyes at Driscoll's anti-war sentiment, but checked himself and decided to change the subject altogether. "So I heard you got all your people back on the ground safely."

"Yep, we shuttled the last group of them back to Earth yesterday," Driscoll said, a grin spreading across his face. "And let me tell you, those folks were goddamned thrilled to be back on solid ground. There was even an impromptu proposal right there on the NASA tarmac."

"A proposal?" Hodge said, raising his white eyebrows. "What kind of proposal?"

"A wedding proposal...what else?" Driscoll said with a chuckle. "Yep, as soon as they got off the ship, good ol' Chief Ranier dropped to a knee in front of his girlfriend, ah...one of the lab workers...Marla, I think is her name? Anyway, he asked her to marry him right then and there."

"Well?" Hodge said, leaning forward in his seat. "Well, what?" Driscoll answered.

"What did she say?"

"I'll be damned," Driscoll said as he slapped his knee. "Who would've guessed that the General is a romantic at heart? She said yes, of course! They're planning to get married somewhere in the North Carolina mountains in a few weeks. And Mark said something about going sailing for their honeymoon..."

Hodge cleared his throat and shifted in his seat, feeling a little embarrassed that he had been so curious about a wedding proposal. His own wife had divorced him years ago, and he still regretted that he hadn't tried harder to save the marriage. He decided to change the subject again.

"Anyway, ever since you left Vienna, the messages from the Kabrini have been pouring in," he said gruffly. "Our team keeps asking them questions, and they keep sending us answers. And these responses are much more detailed than the cryptic shit they were sending us before the rescue."

"Incredible," Driscoll said, his eyes shining. "Is there any way you could get me back into the UN office so I can read them?"

"No need," Hodge answered as he reached for a black briefcase resting against the leg of his chair. He sat the briefcase on the table in front of him and slid two silver clasps to the side. The lid instantly popped open. "All of the transcripts are right here." He reached in the case and pulled out a small flash drive.

Driscoll's chin dropped to his chest. "Wait a second, general," he finally managed. "The last time I asked to read the Kabrini transcripts,

I had to fly all the way to Vienna, got molested by UN guards at no less than ten security checkpoints and had to have my eyeball scanned by a talking computer…which I will admit, is one of the highlights of my life. And this time, you're just handing them over to me? I mean, don't I have to sell my soul to the devil or something?"

And then Hodge did something Driscoll had never seen him do… he laughed. In fact, the general laughed so hard, his sides shook, his face turned red, and tears streamed down his face. After a few minutes, Hodge wiped at his eyes, caught his breath, and finally said, "Oh…shit, Driscoll. Did anyone ever tell you you're a damn funny guy?"

Driscoll, who was now standing dumbfounded behind his desk said, "Well, hell yeah, people tell me that all the time. But I never imagined I'd hear it from you!"

Hodge chuckled again before adding, "Anyway, we plan to release all of the transcripts to the public within a week." He stood up and handed the flash drive to Driscoll. "I figure it can't hurt to give you a preview, seeing as you're the guy who initiated…and saved the Legacy project."

"Holy shit," Driscoll said, gripping the small device in his hand. "So you're actually going to reveal the Kabrini messages to the world? All of it?"

"Yes, we are. All of it—every last word. Unfortunately we have no other choice," Hodge answered curtly. "The Kabrini gave us an ultimatum: if we want to maintain communications with them, we have to share their messages with the world. Some bullshit about how this information is for all of mankind's benefit—not just a select team of 'self-important, covetous beings,' as they called us." The general mumbled this last bit under his breath as he stared down at his freshly polished shoes.

"Wait…they actually called you that?" Driscoll said, trying to hold back a laugh.

"Yes…they actually did," the general said through gritted teeth.

As soon as Hodge left his office, Driscoll inserted the flash drive into his computer and started poring over the most recent Kabrini transcripts. His eyes scanned quickly through the pages, searching for the most significant messages.

UN: *We cannot thank you enough for rescuing our people on the Crystal Ship and returning them safely to Earth's orbit. We are greatly indebted to you for this heroic feat. How can we ever repay your planet for this miraculous deed?*

Kabrini: *Your honesty is payment enough. Your species must learn to consistently live truthful lives. After all, it is the truth that will unshackle mankind's intellectual chains.*

UN: *But why did you save our people? What do you stand to gain from this action?*

Kabrini: *We are not concerned with what we stand to gain. It is merely our instinct to help any living being when they are in need. When you find a baby bird that has fallen from her nest, do you not take her in, wrap her broken wing and nurse her back to health? It is your duty to do so. When you do not care for others, you only harm yourself. After all, we are not separate beings. Everything in the universe is connected.*

UN: *What do you mean by, "Everything is connected?"*

Kabrini: *There are no boundaries between you, your loved ones, your neighbors, your country, your planet. There are no boundaries between mankind and the Kabrini and any other living being in the universe. The only boundaries that exist are those you have built with your own minds. Mankind has the ability to communicate freely with us and any other being across the universe, whenever and however you desire. You simply have not trained your feeble minds to access that faculty. This will come with evolution, growth, and guidance.*

UN: *Are you saying you can communicate freely with other beings throughout the universe? Without using the network of rods?*

Kabrini: *Yes, and you have the ability to do the same. But you must be patient, as this skill develops slowly. At the dawning of our existence, our own species was not unlike mankind. The first Kabrini were impatient, greedy, narcissistic, self-serving, war-mongering savages.*

UN: *Gee, thanks. How long ago was that? Exactly how old is your civilization?*

Kabrini: *Unlike humans, we do not measure time. In fact, time does not truly exist at all, at least as mankind understands and experiences it. It is merely an illusion. Your relationship to time will change dramatically as your species evolves—and eventually, the mirage of time will disappear altogether. Only when you release yourselves from the burden of time will your species see and understand the universe clearly.*

UN: *So you're saying that as humans evolve, time will cease to exist and we will also be able to communicate with other beings across the universe…using only our minds? Do you realize how ridiculous that sounds?*

Kabrini: *Yes, that is what we are saying. And the only thing that is ridiculous is your narrow-minded view of the universe. But this is to be expected. Your species is extremely young. Once you evolve and develop pure universal awareness, you will no longer focus on what is best for yourself. You will finally realize that there is only us. The us represents one collective soul of every living being across the universe. Your species will soon understand that when one person positively affects something in their small part of the universe, the entire universe benefits. This is when your minds will elevate to a collective consciousness in which mankind can tune into any other living being across the universe.*

UN: *You believe that all minds across the universe are somehow joined?*

Kabrini: *We do not merely "believe." We know. The horrors that face mankind—war, poverty, disease, starvation, racism—all of these struggles are the manifestation of the rifts in the collective human mind. You do not realize your minds are joined, and thus you do not know how to think as one. Once your species learns how to tap into the collective mind, these issues will quickly resolve and your species will discover ultimate peace.*

Driscoll read on for hours. When he finally finished, he pulled his bloodshot eyes away from the computer screen, rose from his chair, and walked slowly across the room. He rubbed his weary face and leaned over to fix one eye on the telescope pointed out of his office window. The sun had set while he was reading the transcripts, and the smog had cleared from the undulating horizon. Above the Los Angeles hills, the stars glimmered in a royal blue sky, extinguished briefly by passing wispy clouds before reigniting again.

"I knew you were out there," Driscoll whispered to the darkness. "But I had no idea…I never could have imagined….the magnitude of what you can teach us."

As he studied the few constellations he could see through the bright dome of city lights, Driscoll tried to digest everything he had just read. A collective mind? His thoughts were interrupted by a loud alert emanating from his computer that sounded like a droplet hitting a puddle of water. It meant he had just received an instant message.

"Dammit, Pete," he muttered as he reluctantly pulled his eye away from the telescope and made his way back to his desk. Pete Teegan had an uncanny knack for messaging Driscoll with some urgent work-related dilemma or question just as he was walking out the door.

He plopped back down into his leather desk chair and pulled up the instant message. The user name was simply, "Kabrini." The message read:

Kabrini: *Hello, Jeffrey Driscoll. This is the Kabrini.*

Driscoll just stared at the screen, his face eerily immersed in the blue glow of his computer screen. Another message popped up and the water droplet sounded again:

Kabrini: *Please respond. We know you are there.*

After a few moments with his hands frozen above the keyboard, Driscoll smiled and typed:

JDriscoll: *Very funny, Pete. How the hell did you score that user name? What do you need? I'm walking out the door.*

Kabrini: *This is not a "user name." This is not Pete. This is the Kabrini. And you are Jeffrey Driscoll. Your wife is Carol Driscoll. Your mother was Betty Driscoll. Your father was Tom Driscoll (a fine specimen, he was).*

JDriscoll: *Wait a second...that was sarcasm! The Kabrini aren't capable of sarcasm. Nice try, Pete.*

Kabrini: *Of course we are capable of sarcasm. We know that's one of your preferred means of communication, Jeffrey. We also know you just finished reading our messages to your UN people. You were looking through your telescope when we contacted you.*

The color drained from Driscoll's face, and his hands shook violently as he typed:

JDriscoll: *How the hell do you know all of that?*

Kabrini: *Because we are the Kabrini. We know. We also know you have been watching the skies for many years. You have a deep connection with the universe, Jeffrey. A much stronger connection than most of your fellow humans.*

Driscoll's heart raced as the realization hit him like a tractor trailer. He was having a one-on-one conversation with the Kabrini. He started typing again:

JDriscoll: *So it is true. You really are connected to everything and everyone in the universe.*

Kabrini: *Yes, of course it is true. We are all connected. Deep down you have always known, Jeffrey. We have reached out to you many times throughout your lifetime, and you have never failed us. If it were not for you, mankind may never have discovered our message. We want to thank you for listening... for hearing us...even when others did not or could not believe.*

Driscoll's eyes practically bulged from their sockets as he attempted to absorb this information. Uncertain how to respond, he finally forced his fingers to type again:

JDriscoll: *You're welcome. I mean, no problem. Dammit...I mean, I always knew there was something, someone out there listening, watching, looking back when I was looking up. I felt as if it were my duty to prove this. To be honest, I probably became a little too obsessed with confirming your existence. At times I was so fixated on discovering what else was out there, I neglected my own family.*

Kabrini: *You mean your wife, Carol.*

Driscoll's mind wandered back to just a few days before, when he and Carol had met in a nearby park for lunch. She brought a bag full of deli sandwiches, sodas and chips, and they sat at a picnic table in the shade of a sweet-smelling tree bursting with pink blooms. "It's a Pink Trumpet Tree," Carol pointed out. "They're so beautiful this time of year."

As Driscoll tore into his sandwich and prattled on about work, he glanced up at his wife's beautiful profile. He noticed that she had a dreamy smile on her face and tears glistening behind her bright green eyes. When he followed her gaze, he discovered Carol was watching two mothers pushing their toddlers on the playground swings. He felt that familiar pang of sadness as he reached across the picnic table for his wife's small hand. She quickly pulled it away before he had a chance to take it, briskly wiped at her eyes, and tucked a stray crimson wave behind her ear. "So you were saying?" she said abruptly. "Something about the shuttles from the Crystal City?"

Driscoll snapped back to the present and started typing again:

JDriscoll: *Yes. Carol wanted to have children. I mean, we…we wanted to have children. But she couldn't get pregnant. She tried everything, but at some point, we just gave up. And then I was so caught up in the Kabrini project…I mean the Legacy mission to communicate with your people. I just let it go, I guess. I failed her.*

Kabrini: *Jeffrey, you have taken care of the universe through your actions, and now the universe will take care of you. Yes, it is true…you have been so fixated on communicating with our civilization, you missed the messages right in front of you. Yet this is to be expected. You are only human…you have much to learn. Be alert and aware. Pay attention to the signs around you. Open your eyes, and you will find the way.*

Now Driscoll was typing furiously.

JDriscoll: *But how do you know? Where do I look? And how can you watch us from so far away? Are you psychic or something? Do we all have that power, the ability to read each other's minds? How do we tap into it? Is there a God? What happens to us when we die?*

Kabrini signed off.

"Dammit, no!" Driscoll shouted as he violently clicked at the instant messaging box hoping he could recover the connection. "Don't leave now! I have so many questions…" He ran his fingers through his now sweat-drenched hair and stared out his office window with stunned eyes. "Oh my God," he said out loud as everything started to sink in.

As the Kabrini's words tumbled inside his brain, he suddenly felt bone-tired. He reclined in his office chair and closed his throbbing eyes. He'd just rest for a minute before he went home. He had to tell Carol… And within seconds, he had fallen into a deep, dreamless sleep.

"Bing-bing!" Driscoll's email alert chimed loudly, startling him out of a dead sleep. Feeling groggy and confused, the first thing he noticed was the terrible crick in his neck…and the second thing he noticed was the morning sun streaming through his office window. "What the hell?" he said aloud, sitting upright in his office chair and rubbing his left shoulder. He wiggled his computer mouse to make the screen saver disappear and looked at the clock on the screen. "Six-thirty!" he shouted. "How damn long was I out?"

Just as he was reaching for his office phone to call Carol, the bolded new email that had just landed in his inbox caught his eye. It was from Mondo, and the subject line read, "Greetings from the Moombato Bay Orphanage!"

"What the…?" Driscoll trailed off as he clicked on the email. He hadn't heard from Mondo in years. When he opened the message, he saw an image of his tall, jet-black African friend standing in front of a red brick building. Mondo's chiseled face displayed his usual wide, child-like grin, and he was surrounded by a gaggle of dusty yet smiling African children, ranging in age from about two to twelve. There were also three women dressed in nurse uniforms, holding swaddled babies. Driscoll's eyes darted from the image to the message.

Hello, my friend Driscoll! It has been very long time. I hope you and your wife are well.

I want to let you know that I sell my house in California and move back to Moombato Bay. California did not suit me and I decide I could do better here in my hometown. My money will go much further here in this "goddammed bush city," as Goldstein like to call it. Haha! It is good to be home.

Anyway soon after I come back home, I playing soccer with some of the orphans from Moombato Bay Orphanage when I notice their building was in shambles, as are most buildings in Moombato. The children were not getting the things they need and it make my heart sad. So I donate large portion of my money to the orphanage and they use it to build new building. But the orphanage is still low on many item like baby bottles, blankets, toys, books and such and I just want to write to see if you could maybe donate some of your money. I know you have plenty, my friend. Please let me know if you can help.

Your African friend,
Mondo

Suddenly feeling wide-awake, Driscoll turned his gaze from the computer screen to his office window, where a mass of puffy gray clouds hovered above the hills on the horizon. A brilliant rainbow curved from the blue sky above and through the center of the clouds before disappearing behind the tree line. Driscoll silently took it all in, his round eyes mirroring the same stunning shade of blue as the sky.

"Well, if that isn't a damn sign, I don't know what is," he said aloud as he reached for his phone.

CHAPTER THIRTY-SIX

The Visit

Jeff and Carol were tangled up together beneath a blanket on their black leather couch, giggling like two giddy teenagers. They were both looking at a tiny Polaroid picture Carol held in her hand—an image of a beautiful ten-month-old African boy named Badru. "You don't want to change his name, do you?" Carol said as she gazed lovingly at the photo and ran a single ruby-polished fingernail down the little boy's cheek. "It means born at the full moon, you know. It has to do with the planets...you should like that!"

"Yes, I did know that's what it meant," Driscoll said with a smile as he played with her crimson locks, which were splayed out across his bare chest. "And no, I wouldn't change his name for the world. Mondo named him himself!"

It had been six months since that surreal morning after his late night conversation with the Kabrini—the morning Driscoll had received the email from Mondo. After texting Carol to let her know he'd fallen asleep at the office and would be home later that morning, he had immediately picked up the phone and dialed the Moombato Bay Orphanage. The next day, he and Carol started filling out paperwork, and now the time had arrived. In just a week, they would be flying out to Khartanga to pick up their son.

"I already feel like he's ours," Carol said dreamily, still admiring the photo. "I love him so much, it hurts..." her voice cracked, and Driscoll wrapped his arms around his wife and squeezed her tight as his heart swelled with happiness. Although he hadn't met him, Driscoll already loved his son with every ounce of his being. He planned to fill Badru's world with affection, laughter, happiness, devotion and all of the other things his own shitty father had never given him. Driscoll now realized that's why he had spent his entire childhood looking skyward, searching for love or attention wherever he could find it.

Driscoll's cell phone vibrated in his pocket, and Carol leapt up off of him. "What the hell was that?" she said with laugh. "Is that your phone buzzing on my ass, or are you just happy to see me?"

Driscoll grinned at his glowing wife as he dug into his jeans pocket to retrieve his phone. Carol had been bubbling over with joy ever since they had begun the adoption process. He hadn't seen her so peaceful and content since the day they met in Jamaica.

He glanced down at his smartphone, saw "Professor Gregory" on the screen and immediately hit speaker. "Gregory," he shouted into the phone, "how the hell are ya, mate?"

"Why hello, Driscoll! I'm just fine and dandy, and you?"

"Never been better, thanks for asking."

"And what about that saucy wife of yours? God only knows how you ended up with such a sexy minx!"

Driscoll looked over at Carol, whose face had turned beet red. Grinning from ear to ear, he waggled his eyebrows up and down at her, and she promptly burst into laughter.

"Carol is right here, Gregory, so why don't you ask her? You're on speaker phone, you know."

"Hello, Professor Gregory," Carol said teasingly. "Oh, I…well, I, um…" Gregory spluttered awkwardly on the other line. "Well, how incredibly rude of me. I just have absolutely no excuse for myself. I suppose I deserve a good tongue lashing for those demeaning comments, so go right ahead, Carol…"

"I'll pass on the tongue lashing," Carol said with a giggle, "but maybe you can repay me by sending over some of that lovely English sparkling wine we had at your flat in London. I just can't seem to find it anywhere in Los Angeles."

"Well, that won't be a problem at all, my dear," Gregory responded. "I'll just bring you a case of the British bubbly when I meet you in Moombato Bay next week!"

Driscoll sat upright on the couch. "Wait...you're going to be there?"

"Wouldn't miss it for the world, chap!" Gregory said cheerfully. "I mean, really...I must see it with my own eyes to believe it."

"See what?" Driscoll said.

"A child adopting a child!" he answered playfully.

"Oh, Gregory," Carol said with a chuckle, "you know, Jeff's grown up quite a bit since your wild adventures in Delos. Anyway, not to worry...I plan to do most of the child rearing myself." She gave her husband a wink.

"A jolly good thing, my dear!"

"Well, I'll be damned, Gregory," Driscoll said into the phone as he stood up from the couch and stretched. "It'll be good to see that pale British face of yours. Oh, and that hair. That always perfectly sculpted hair. How I've missed it."

"Oh, mine isn't the only familiar face you'll see, mate."

"You're right," Driscoll said with a grin. "Our African friend will be there, of course. You know Mondo practically runs that orphanage now..."

"Ah yes, Mondo, of course. But also his two partners in crime..."

"Mohammed and Goldstein?" Carol shrieked, practically jumping up and down with excitement.

"You've got it, missy," Gregory responded with a laugh. "The whole bloody crew will be there. Should be one helluva reunion!"

"I can't believe I'm finally going to meet the famous threesome! Mondo, Goldstein, and Mohammed!" Carol said. "Oh, and of course I'll be thrilled to see you too, Gregory."

"But of course," Gregory muttered. "Yes, maybe we can give your lovely wife the historical tour of our madcap adventures in Moombato Bay."

"Oh no...I don't think we need to relive that one, professor," Driscoll said with a chuckle. "Let's just keep it clean and simple this time around. After all, we're parents now."

"Ah, yes, very true," Gregory responded. "Alrighty then. See you two next week in the African sticks. Cheerio!"

"Goodbye, Gregory!" Carol called out.

"See ya," Driscoll answered before hanging up.

He stuffed his phone back in his pocket as Carol picked up the remote and turned on the flat screen TV. "Let's see what's new with the Kabrini, today. Ah, I see Rhonda is wearing her standard uniform," she joked.

The busty CNN anchorwoman, sporting her usual low-cut top, reported, "In the past six months, there have been accounts from around the world—people claiming they have been contacted directly by the Kabrini, via instant messaging, email, text message and even short-wave radio! These reports have not been confirmed or denied by the United Nations." Carol shot a glance at Driscoll who winked back at her. "In other news, the UN has noticed some interesting global trends since the UN released the official Kabrini transcripts a few months ago. In the past five months, crime rates have declined worldwide and charity donations are skyrocketing. To top it off, many non-profit groups report they've been so overrun with volunteers, they've actually had to turn people away. According to the UN, the latest communications from the Kabrini indicate that the ancient alien civilization is impressed with mankind's improvements, but the Kabrini say we still have a long way to go…"

Driscoll leaned down and kissed the top of Carol's head. Completely absorbed in the news, she took a sip from her glass of chardonnay as Jeff announced, "I'm headed to my office to take care of a little bit of paperwork. I want to get everything wrapped up before we fly out next week." He planned to take at least a month off from work so he could spend some quality time with Badru after they brought him home.

"Alright babe," Carol answered. "I'll probably head on up to bed soon. Love you."

"I love you, too, beautiful," he responded as he strolled out of the family room.

A couple of hours later, Driscoll was toiling away at a report in his home office. The house had fallen completely silent, and he assumed Carol was sound asleep upstairs. He turned away from the computer screen to rest his eyes and gazed out the huge arched window in his office. A crescent moon hung from the sky, and he could make out Mercury twinkling below it, just above the horizon.

And then he heard it…the unmistakable water drop alert. He had an instant message.

He swung back to his screen and his face drained of color as he saw the message:

Kabrini: *Jeffrey Driscoll. It is the Kabrini. We wish to visit your planet.*

Driscoll's hands trembled as he reached his fingers to the keyboard. He took a deep breath, trying to calm his nerves, and typed:

JDriscoll: *When?*

He waited as two, three, four seconds passed, listening to the old Grandfather clock tick loudly in the corner of the room. Finally, the next message flashed on the screen, and it took Driscoll's breath away.

Kabrini: *Now.*

His entire body quivering, Driscoll instinctively turned away from the computer and faced his office window, where the stars were twinkling silently in the velvet sky. A hot flash of white light filled the room, causing his black pupils to shrink in his bright blue eyes, and he impulsively threw both of his hands up to shield his face. The blinding light faded to a golden glow, and Driscoll lowered his hands, which were no longer shaking. Instantly, all of the fear drained from his body, and Jeffrey Driscoll felt blissfully serene, peaceful and overcome with hope.

~ AFTERWORD ~

It was late in the spring of 2011 when I was in my attic digging through a box of photos that had come from my mother's house. My mother passed away in 1994, and I must have received the box shortly after that, but I had not gone through it until this particular day. Inside the old box I came across a large manila envelope marked in my mother's handwriting: "Joe's Book." The manuscript was dated 1987.

My brother Joe passed away in 2010, but I vaguely remembered, many years earlier, hearing my mother talk about a book he had written. She was typing his handwritten manuscript for him. She and Joe had a special relationship; she believed in him and always encouraged his greatest hopes and dreams.

I don't believe I ever heard Joe speak of the book himself, and I had never heard another word about it until now. I tossed the envelope aside to take downstairs, thinking it might make for good summer reading.

Although sci-fi is not my usual genre, I found that I couldn't put the book down. I was amazed at the imagination, the twists and turns, and the intricacies. Most of all, I loved the quick wit and humor in the dialogue between the characters.

Joe was extremely intelligent, had a fabulous sense of humor and a sharp wit, so similar to that of some of the characters in his book that I could hear his voice as I read their exchanges.

I decided to see to it that *The Kabrini Message* became a published novel as a gift to both my brother and our mother who always believed in him. The gift of finding Joe's manuscript and the experience of getting it published has had more twists and turns than most novels, has taken so much longer, been so much more challenging and yet so much more rewarding than I ever could have imagined. The journey has been a fun, fascinating and educational labor of love.

Joe's wife Gwen and I sincerely hope you enjoy the timely and timeless lessons of benevolence contained in *The Kabrini Message* in the true spirit of love from which it has come forth.

Marie Egles Carhart

Author J.R. Egles and Mom, Marie Egles

~ ABOUT THE AUTHOR ~

Author J.R. Egles was born on November 23, 1949 in Elizabeth, New Jersey to Marie and Bob Egles. He was the eldest of four children. Other than a three-year period from ages nine to twelve when the family lived in Hialeah, Florida, Joe was a lifelong New Jersey resident.

From an early age, Joe developed a fascination of astronomy. Joe ground his own telescope lens from a big thick circular piece of glass about the diameter of a dinner plate. Day after day, he spent endless hours in the basement of his family's home grinding it with rouge. When it was finished, he installed the lens in a large telescope that he built himself from scratch. Joe's father set a pipe in concrete in the backyard to serve as a mount for the telescope. Joe was also an avid photographer whose favorite subjects were, of course, the stars and planets. With that telescope, Joe was able to combine his passions for astronomy and photography by capturing amazing photos of the moon, planets and constellations.

The one thing that surpassed even his obsession for astronomy, however, was his enduring love of ham radio. At a very young age, Joe joined the close-knit community of "hams" when a neighbor introduced him to this unique world of communication.

When the sky was clear, Joe would spend the entire night out in the backyard gazing upward. When it was cloudy, he would retreat inside where he'd chat with folks all over the world on his ham radio. Back then, his ham call letters were "WB2UXJ," and he could be heard calling, "This is Whiskey, Bravo, 2, Uniform, X-ray, Japan" throughout the night. Later, after receiving what is known as an Extra Class license, the call letters became K2UX (and the mantra became "King, 2, Uncle, X-Ray"). It was the pre-Internet version of online chatting.

Therefore, we should not be surprised that *The Kabrini Message* combines both of Joe's loves: outer space and communication.

Joe graduated from Governor Livingston Regional High School in Berkeley Heights, New Jersey. This was not the high school most residents of his home town of Garwood attended—Joe hand-selected the school because it offered electives in electronics. After graduating from high school, Joe attended Union County College.

Joe wrote *The Kabrini Message* in Loveladies, New Jersey in 1987 over the course of about six months. At the time, Joe was serving as a full-time, live-in caretaker of another Joe, his elderly grandfather.

Joe most recently lived in Ship Bottom, New Jersey with his wife, Gwen. He was a father of three and a grandfather of four.

In January, 2010 Joe passed away at the age of 60. Although he wrote a few short stories and did some freelance writing for a local newspaper, *The Kabrini Message* was his first and only novel. *The Kabrini Message* was an idea 25 years ahead of its time, and there is no doubt that Joe is very pleased that his novel's time has finally arrived!

Discover more about J.R. Egles here

Blog
www.kabrinimessage.blogspot.com/

Pinterest
www.pinterest.com/kabrinimessage/

Facebook
www.facebook.com/kabrini.message

Twitter
www.twitter.com/KabriniMessage

YouTube
The Kabrini Message, The Official Book Trailer, by Author J.R. Egles
www.youtube.com/watch?v=Z1O6XrcHOpg

Printed in the United States
By Bookmasters